Irrational Numbers

by

E.A.Gray

ISBN: 9781907130076
Copyright 2009

Chapter 1

If you fear loss then you'll never live.

A mind can only experience a finite amount of pain and anguish before it ceases to allow more stimuli and shuts off. Self-preservation, the strongest of all concepts. Like breathing, we have no control over it, it simply happens. Bright summer colours become muted autumns, and like turning a television down until it's a bare hum, vibrant emotions dull to that which we can cope with.

Rebecca sat in her office and balled her fists so hard her perfectly manicured nails bit into the tender flesh of her palms. She couldn't leave; appearances had to be maintained. If the corporate sharks sensed weakness they'd swim through the shallow waters and take her out in a bloody mess and she hadn't built this business from the ground up on her own by being pathetic.

She banged her fist on the rich mahogany desk. He wasn't ruining this for her, too.

Her day had been booby-trapped from the start. Nine A.M. was breakfast while going through the finer points of a real estate proposal with the Tokyo office. Ten A.M. had long standing problems with the Paris office unravelling even further. Eleven was when it crumbled. A courier delivery. An innocuous envelope. It sat unopened for half an hour, until, while on speaker phone to her assistant, Joy, she ripped it apart. It did the same back.

She pulled out her divorce papers. Her finger pressed down on the phone's conference button and Joy's voice disappeared.

She stared, feeling like a pedestrian curb side, watching the fire brigade trying to free bodies from a twisted car wreck. *Don't cut there, it'll collapse. Careful with the sparks. We'll get you out. Don't worry, ma'am, any second now...*

Those empty promises...

Except there were no saviours, just her lawyer calling to say he'd received copies and...something about claims and counter claims? She wasn't sure. Her stomach churned as the mainstay of her emotional security began to break free.

She sighed heavily. It wasn't a total surprise; he'd left the house months ago. But still, this, now? Nausea reared, and if anything other than an espresso had passed her lips for breakfast then it probably would have been coming back up.

With a deep breath she went to stand under the powerful stream from her cooler unit. Something caught her eye: a spider's web in the corner of her perfectly clean, perfectly arranged office, as though fate herself had left it there. She managed to move one foot in front of the other, in front of the other, in front of the other, ending up at that sticky snare, those thinly tangled woven strips of silk. She squinted. No venomous beast, just a terribly small fly in the very centre; a dry husk, done with struggling, done with everything. Dead, still, without life or movement. Yesterday she'd have swiped it away with a file. A lot had changed in a very short time.

"I know how you feel."

With a sigh she went back to her desk and picked those papers up, unfolding them slowly.

Precise folds speak of a person, her grandfather always used to say.

"Sharp corners and precise folds haven't helped me keep my husband," she muttered sadly.

Martin's secretary was probably an origami champion - and a few other things, she bet. Again a nauseous wave hit because this was it. There was no reconciling, no time apart to sort things out, just the end. Her fingers skimmed the papers, as if trying to read a hidden message with the sensitive tips. But there was no code, no secret. It was what it was: closure.

She slumped into the chair, leaning heavily, splaying hands down on her desk. She took the pen he'd given her for their tenth wedding anniversary and signed excessive amount of copies carefully, trying to keep her signature normal, as if the overhang of an R or the incline on the H would give her plight away.

And so she sat and waited for the day to end. The phone rang off the hook, her mobile, too, and even her pager never ceased. She ignored them all.

The day dimmed and gave way to encroaching darkness.

A light rapping and Joy poked her head around the door. Her mouth opened and shut quickly. Joy spoke to someone behind her.

"She's not in. She's probably on-site."

Her assistant closed the door behind her.

"Is everything okay? I have a stack of messages for you."

Rebecca didn't even look up.

"I don't want to speak to anyone."

Joy was sharp. Even in her initial interview over four years ago, Rebecca had been impressed with that acumen.

"You don't have to," Joy said as she walked over to the unusually messy desk. With a hand on the middle of the paper in front of her boss, it was twisted to get a better look. "You signed them."

"Preliminary ones."

"You still signed them."

Rebecca nodded slowly.

"I'd have to eventually."

Joy took that silver pen, put the lid back on it, and lay her warm hand on Rebecca's.

Sometimes it's the small gestures that crack defences so meticulously constructed. Sometimes you don't need streams of condolences from streams of people. Rebecca looked at their hands. Sometimes small things mean the most and tell you you're not alone.

"It'll be okay. I'll be outside if you need me."

Sepia skies turned monochrome as slate clouds welcomed the storm. It was the only sign that time had come and gone.

Rebecca's muscles ached with inaction as she closed the office door. Joy put her book down and gathered her things. The clock ticked twenty after eight. Yes, it's the small gestures that matter. A warm hand to say you're not alone or staying late to make sure a friend is okay.

Joy didn't say a thing while switching off the lights. Rebecca was grateful for the silence.

The wind was vicious as it clawed at her eyes, her lips, her cheeks. Tree branches swayed at peculiar angles. Cars moved slower; skated sideways as their tyres lost purchase on the tarmac. Pedestrians held onto their hats, their coats, themselves.

Joy put her into a black cab and squeezed her hand once more.

"It'll get easier."

Rebecca took a deep shuddering breath.

"I hope so."

Joy's grip tightened, "It will," before letting go.

The sound of crunching gravel ripped Rebecca right out of her mental shutdown. She massaged her temples, trying to still the throbbing that had started hours ago. She longed to fall into bed, shut her eyes and sleep today away.

The cab smoothly took the last curve and brought her sprawling house into focus. Throughout her childhood here she'd gotten used to the lack of neighbours - it always seemed so lively with her parents and grandparents but as it whittled down to just Martin and her, the quiet became overwhelming. However, she'd been content. Now, as the cab slowed to a halt, she saw a frightening future: a sprawling mansion for one. She frowned deeply.

After two attempts she entered an alarm code that hadn't changed in ten years. She kicked her heels off in the hall, scooped them up by the backs, and padded into the library.

Tapping the answer machine on as she went, Rebecca poured herself a generous measure of gin and then, exhausted, flopped into her favourite chair by the lifeless blackened fire. Her heels slipped from her grasp, gently plopping onto the thick burgundy carpet.

Five messages regarding work issues sounded crisply over the speaker. She half listened, rolling the heavy crystal glass over her forehead. The next message made her take a little more notice. It was Sophia.

"Darling. I ran into that scoundrel Martin, today. You should see his car. Most ridiculous. When will they learn that a receding hairline can not be solved with a bright yellow Lamborghini?"

Despite herself, Rebecca laughed. One thing Sophia always did was to bring some sanity to a situation.

The message continued.

"Anyway, I'm calling to make sure my best friend is alive and well and hasn't been kidnapped by corporate pirates; you know I'd pay the ransom." A booming announcement in the background, 'Sophia Green, please contact reception'. *"See what happens when I don't answer my calls for ten seconds? They hound me. Call whatever time you get back. I worry when you don't pick up for a whole day."*

The gin burned a thin trail, replacing the pain in her chest with a very real one in her throat. She squeezed her eyes shut; she hated the spirit, but today did call for a large measure.

Leaning over she picked the phone up, hitting speed dial one, knowing she'd better do this now before the alcohol took hold and maudlin set in.

The deep pulsing ring was like a calming lullaby. Her eyes closed, only to flick back open at pick up.

"I was about to call the mounted police!"

Sophia did have her peculiarities.

"We've moved to Canada?"

"You always quash my fantasies. Where have you been?"

Rebecca considered a lie but dismissed the thought almost instantly.

"I got the first round of divorce papers today."

A harsh expulsion of air crackled the line.

"I knew I should've taken the opportunity to back my car into the side of that idiotic monstrosity he bought."

Rebecca simply sighed, tipped her head back and drained the glass. Sophia continued, turning her comments as serious as the subject matter.

"We need to see this as a positive thing."

"Finding my husband screwing his secretary in my own bed is positive?"

"Actually, yes. You found out. It could have carried on for years."

It didn't feel positive.

"Always a silver lining."

"You've been in limbo for months over this. You've been completely miserable. This is rock bottom and the only way out is up."

Rebecca mulled over those words. She gently lay the heavy glass down and nodded, getting to her feet and putting the bottle of gin back into the cabinet. She clicked the doors shut and turned, taking a deep cleansing breath.

Finally she replied, determined to try to mean the words.

"You're right. I didn't get where I am by letting anyone take me down."

"Good on you. Take a long bath and I'll be around in the morning."

They said their goodbyes.

Her brow descended into a deep scowl as she remembered what Martin had when he came into the relationship. Nothing. And now he was driving around in a sports car and probably swanking about in a new flat somewhere?

Her revelation fell out.

"All on the back of my hard work, but more importantly, my money."

Turbulent emotions swept through her. She glanced at the clock. It was late but with the size of her portfolio she doubted calling her personal accountant would matter.

"Finally a benefit of coming from such a well to do family," she declared to the empty room.

She'd hated it growing up, always being classed as a one dimensional rich kid, but, she had to say, she was glad of the power it weighed at this very moment.

He picked up on the fourth ring. She bet he was sitting there in his pyjamas and thought caller I.D. was a godsend.

"Stephen. I need you to shut down all of my accounts including my cards. Open up new ones. Swap all of my direct debits over. Oh, and make sure I am not used as a financial reference for Martin."

Not even the hint of a pause. She liked Stephen. He never questioned her, never made her explain.

"Of course. We'll emboss a new card and have it delivered in the morning. The others will be a few days. Your accounts..." She could hear the clacking of keyboard keys. *"...have been shut down and new ones opened."* More clacking and she wondered if he slept with his laptop permanently connected. *"All passwords to your accounts are changed. You have an e-mail*

- now - with new log in details. Anything else, Mrs Boyd?"

She sighed. That was another thing.

"It's Miss Cavendish now."

That did get a pause.

"I'll have it amended. Anything else, Miss Cavendish?"

"No. Thank you."

She slipped the phone back into its cradle.

The house was deathly silent, and, it seemed, likely to remain that way for the foreseeable future.

She picked her empty glass up, weighing the heavy lead crystal in her palm. Her grip tightened, and with an expulsion of frustrated anger at this, at losing her husband to some slutty twenty year old, but most importantly, losing, full stop, it ended up hitting the far wall and snowing to the ground like ice chips.

Rebecca sat down and cried.

Chapter 2

Strength is an illusion. It is one of the few possessions that can be flaunted without physically having it. It's all a matter of perception. The trick is to get your enemy to perceive what is required. Like a magician, placement is vital. It's about positioning your targets at just the right angle so that the hidden trapdoors cannot be seen.

Today Rebecca had to be a mistress of illusion. She had to be the magician and assistant; the trapdoor and sliding chute.

It was one thing doing it in the business world, but this was personal. This was her life, not a building to buy and sell, not a slab of land to cut up and hand out to the highest bidder. Martin had woven himself into her being and he had ripped himself out. And it hurt.

The mixture of anguish and anger fought a well matched battle inside of her and at this point she didn't care which won. She wanted to get through today, and maybe, if life would give her a break, she wanted her dignity back.

She waited outside the building. Glancing at the clock, time slipped subtly by until her plan ticked into place.

Twenty minutes late she moved from the car to the lobby, to the lift, to the floor where the big cats were. Taking a deep breath she walked slower than usual. There was no rush. She needed to gain focus, to condense her very spirit into a sharp pinhead of intensity because this was the meeting that mattered.

It had been a paper war so far, a terribly tragic tango; a sensual sinner's dance. Martin's people sent one demand; her lawyers sent a blocking motion. The play switched; different angles, same agenda. All the time she wondered what he was telling himself in that obviously deranged mind of his. He was punishing her? Lunacy!

She'd been wronged and never saw it coming. Like a sideways collision, it had ploughed her into the central reservation of her own life and now she was a wreck waiting to be towed away - if only he would let her go.

She took hold of her emotions at the same time she grasped the door handles of the meeting room. She opened them, peeling the layers away, revealing the den of lawyers, and her soon to be ex-husband.

She'd practiced this moment over and over. She needed it to be faultless. Framed by the smooth grain of the oak door all heads turned. Their eyelashes fluttered. It was good to see six weeks of personal training had paid off. Already toned, there wasn't that much to do, but she had a plan, wanted to be perfect as much outside as in.

The dress was a one-off. She'd smiled and thought of it as almost prophetic after seeing the display at her favourite store. It didn't scream Siren or Harlot, but rather cruelly whispered the wearer was here to get her own way by whatever means necessary. She'd not looked at the price tag. She wasn't interested.

Thin silken straps criss-crossed subtly across her alabaster shoulders. She brushed a glossy strand of dark hair back. Her heels clicked on the expensive granite floor, replacing the silence.

She knew where she should sit. She also knew where she was going to: head of the table. Despite himself, her husband's lawyer pulled the chair out. She smiled politely and sat.

She glanced down the long oak table. The sheen was as oily as the lawyers.

Hers were conspicuously absent. Her grandfather once told her, *You're the strongest weapon you can ever use, and no one can jail you for doing so. Beat your opponents with skill and grace - and do it with no mercy.*

Wise words from a wise man. She wished he was here now to advise her, tell her one pearl of wisdom that would condense the madness back to sanity. Still, she had her plan.

She drummed manicured nails on the arm rest, sending a random patter through the room.

Always keep your opponents on edge from the get go. He'd told her that on the side-lines of the netball pitch when she was eleven. They'd thrashed the opposing team.

It'd taken countless sleepless nights pacing, days spent mentally absent from her own life, a loss of appetite that almost worried Sophia to the point of intervention, until finally, all the strings pulled together at just the right time. Rebecca felt in control, charged, like a rolling storm holding its power close, ready to unleash it in a fraction of a fractional second.

Martin's lawyer smiled politely.

"Should we wait for your team or...?"

Her nails paused, head turned and tilted, eyes grabbed hold of his gaze and shook it like a dog with a toy.

"Do you think I need a team?"

He smarmed his answer.

"Professionally speaking, I'd have to advise you not to try to deal with this alone."

Rebecca flicked open the brass clasp of her handbag and pulled out one sheet of paper. Perfect folds; precise.

Taking her time it was opened carefully, like a fragile treasure map. Her eyes glinted as she looked up through long eyelashes. Martin looked back, fiddling with the Lalique cufflinks she'd bought him last Christmas.

She slid the piece of paper across.

"Please sign our agreement, Martin. You can keep what you have."

This operation was designed to cauterise the wound, stop the bleed. Martin took the paper, moving closer to it, blinking.

"What's this?"

"The loan for your father's business."

Martin frowned and looked up.

"What has this got to do with today?"

"I bought the loan from the bank. Sign the agreement and we can both move on."

Martin's worst trait was his impossibly stubborn streak. It had caused more arguments than anything else during their marriage. Fights over holiday destinations, paint colours, restaurants, even clothes worn to events she accompanied him to.

Rebecca had mostly let him have his own way. She'd been of the opinion that one should save all energy for the important fights. This was the rainy day her stash had been piled for.

"You can't blackmail me, 'becca."

The nickname was like a dropped piece of cutlery at an important dinner. It made her teeth grind.

She took her phone out of her bag, lips curling into a relaxed smile she'd spent an hour practising last night. She pressed speed dial seven.

"Stephen. Call in the loan. Throw everyone out of the building. Rent it to the local church at one tenth of the market value." She covered the mouthpiece, momentarily, addressing Martin. "I have to top up my karma because I am not going to be nice to you." She resumed the call. "Contact me when it's done."

She placed the closed shell down on the desk. Martin's cheeks flushed and he started whispering to his lawyer, gesturing wildly.

"Mrs Boyd..." The lawyer started before Rebecca interjected sharply.

"Miss Cavendish."

He nodded an apology.

"Miss Cavendish. Is this really necessary? My client only wants what's rightfully his. The beach house, that's all. We don't want to be malicious."

She felt like pointing out that this whole battle was malicious and dictated by his client, just because he had been caught in the wrong and his ego was suffering, but she didn't. It wouldn't win her any ground.

The truth was normally an idle missile so Rebecca primed and fired it.

"Let me tell you something about don't wants. I don't want to have walked into my own bedroom in my own house and found my husband screwing his secretary in our bed." She leant elbows on the table, her chin on the back of a hand. "I don't want to have seen that." She sucked in a breath. "Martin keeps what he took when he left, and it's more than he deserves."

Everything apart from my dignity. That I'm taking back right now, she thought.

The legal team conferred heatedly. She didn't expect an agreement. She wanted the sting of the fight, the claws, the tearing, the pain, the satisfaction of getting something despite the struggle. And she wanted him to hurt, too.

But not this day, it seemed. It was an anti-climax. An agreement on her part to let his father's business remain; Martin was to sign away claims - not that he had much of a chance of winning in court - to any of her fortune.

Rebecca stood outside the building on the granite steps, looking out over the heads of people going to and fro; over cars speeding by; over endless concrete; over tops of trees and city bushes that were cropped to perfection.

She sighed, closing her eyes and tilting her head upward into the streaming rays of the sun. It suffused her skin, warming her very core, forcing out the negativity of the meeting, of the last few months.

The city beckoned. She walked into the crowd.

Chapter 3

Inertia: the tendency to preserve a state of rest or uniform motion when acted upon by an external force.

Rebecca unbuttoned the neck of her shirt. She paced the length of her office, trying to solve her latest problem. She stopped, spun around and regarded the map pinned to her wall. The blocks of land she needed to purchase were marked off in red. The ones she'd acquired were in blue. She'd gotten all of them apart from three. That red outlined interruption to her plans was all she needed.

She hunted around in her bag, grabbing a pack of antacids. Popping one, she crunched fiercely, shifting as her stress became corporeal.

Over the last months as her private life had finally fallen apart, she'd welded her world of work into a solid mass. While - despite the signed agreements - Martin still played little games with requests, papers and lawyers, she became untouchably fierce in business circles. Rebecca sculpted her damaged self into something more manageable. It wasn't perfect but it was functional.

Work now offered a safe place to hide from the strain of the divorce, from the fact she seemed stuck fast in an emotional quagmire. Like a sprinter losing footing, the will to move on was there but no matter how much she tried she couldn't manage it.

Only once had Joy broached the sudden change in routine.

"Let me know if you're going to stay late."

Rebecca hadn't even looked up from the contracts she was scanning for loopholes.

"I always tell security."

She hadn't meant it to sound harsh but lately concentrating on social skills was more and more difficult.

Fingertips removed her focus from the papers. Joy gently lowered to eye level with the woman who'd been her employer and friend for over four years. Rebecca's eyelashes fluttered, taken aback. Joy's professional demeanour melted.

"I don't care who locks up our floor. I do care about you working fourteen hours a day for six days a week. If you tell me, I'll make sure you have a sandwich and some soup for dinner."

Rebecca's shoulders slumped as if all the weight she was carrying descended in that very moment. A cavernous pause carved its way into the space between them.

She took a deep breath before she dared to speak.

"You don't have to worry."

Joy smiled and squeezed her arm.

"It's an occupational hazard of liking you." *Joy raised an eyebrow, the silent question hovering between them before it was given form.* "So, soup and a sandwich later?"

Rebecca nodded, barely managing to keep her voice from cracking.

"Thank you."

She crunched another antacid and slapped the three blocks of land she wanted hard. She growled.

"I'll be damned if this falls through due to some old man wanting to keep the land because his dog had puppies in the back garden."

Her mind tamped down on the part that understood and even admired that resolve.

She wrapped her scarf tighter, slipped her heavy woollen coat on, and decided to sort this out once and for all. She needed to come up with a plan and that meant some fresh air and calm.

"I'm going out."

"Elliot called again about a meeting."

Rebecca sighed.

"I'll speak to him later."

Joy didn't have a chance to say anything more before the outer doors swung shut behind that fast moving dark shadow.

Rebecca loved this time of year. The weather was getting eclectic. Colours were turning from greens to burnt oranges and browns. Summer was a frenetic mass of activity with tourists inhabiting every inch of the city streets. But now the boil of life had been turned to a gentle simmer; it was a cello compared to a trumpet; a soft meringue dessert instead of a slice of grapefruit.

She inhaled the cool crisp air and walked through the tall gates of possibly the only significant piece of park land left in the city. A few years ago a sheikh had approached her to set up a deal so he could build a house in the middle and fence the rest off as his grounds. She politely declined but made sure the local environmentalists and television stations knew. The furore was enough to secure the land's use as a public park for the next twenty years. She'd declined all publicity and happily settled for a small brass plaque on a bench in her favourite section.

She followed the gently winding path, crunching through occasional leaves, the sound making her smile. Finally she found her way to her bench overlooking the lake. She patted the weathered wood.

"You have to help me find a plan."

Rebecca gazed out over the flat expanse of calm water. She willed just a fraction of stress to leave.

Suddenly her serenity snapped like a dry twig. A dark figure sat far too close for comfort. Rebecca glanced about discreetly, not specifically interested in the slim brunette who now took up space on *her* bench, but more in the fact that all of the others were empty. She clenched her jaw, grinding her teeth.

"It's such a beautiful evening," came the smooth lilting voice.

Her attention was snagged - and it annoyed her.

She quirked an eyebrow and leant back, hooking arms over the bench. Her reply was short and verging on terse.

"It is."

The woman pulled a card from a thin tanned-leather holder and put it in the dead space between them.

"My card, Rebecca."

The muscles in her arms tensed as she kept staring ahead. She'd had enough shocks in her business career to know that you did not rise to any bait unless you wanted to be dangling from a hook.

"Should I be impressed you know who I am?"

The laugh was low but seemed genuine.

"Anyone who reads the F.T. knows who you are."

Slowly Rebecca turned, finally taking in her mystery companion. She was instantly reminded of one of the lifestyle posters in her gym that promised you too could look like this. Rich chestnut hair spilled over her shoulders, and strong features were taken over by the lenses of dark sunglasses despite the fading light. Rebecca stared back at her own reflection.

However, it was her business to notice more, to look deeper: the woman was young, maybe mid-twenties; didn't spend a lot of time in the sun but wasn't overly pale. Delicate diamond stud earrings showed taste and a modicum of class.

Next was the suit. Rebecca knew it was shockingly expensive. She knew because she'd toyed with buying it but given way to sense after realising she could go on holiday with the same money. She'd wandered out of the store, smirking at how thrilled her grandfather would have been that it had only taken thirty six years to learn to manage her wealth.

The woman tapped a manicured nail down on the card sitting temptingly between them.

"It doesn't bite."

"My mother told me never to take gifts from strangers."

She got up but her way was barred by the sudden rise of her mystery companion. Tall and slim, the woman wore that suit like it'd been fitted to every curve. Slender fingers removed the barrier of sunglasses and set free two light green eyes that Rebecca found utterly captivating. She stared deeper, a vague afterthought permeating her consciousness.

What a doozy of a trick to pull on first meeting someone.

Before she realised she'd slipped, it was out.

"Coloured contact lenses?"

The younger woman frowned then caught on.

"Oh. No. It's the sunlight. They look greener. They're normally dull."

How unexpectedly honest. It took Rebecca by surprise.

"So you didn't polish them especially for me?"

The woman laughed.

"Would you have been impressed?"

"Very."

It took a moment before Rebecca resumed her work persona. She frowned as the card was offered again.

The woman smiled easily, a gentle waft of charisma carrying through the crisp autumn air.

"Would you take it if I said please?"

"Do you know how many people offer me their cards?"

The woman's easy smile widened.

"Lots?"

"And what makes you any different?"

"Do they all sneak up on you and potentially polish their irises?"

That deserved a loud laugh - and got one. However, she wasn't going to let this be a complete walk over.

"Certainly not."

Rebecca took it, slipped it in her pocket, and began to walk away without looking around - despite the fact she really wanted to.

The woman's voice carried, "Nice to meet you."

Rebecca chuckled.

It wasn't until she was in her office, behind closed doors that she took it back out. It was thick, almost calico in texture, and the type was a heavy matte. A strong font. As cards went she approved of the design.

Her mystery companion remained that way. She didn't know the name: Annah Stevens? The company was vaguely recognisable: head-hunters.

Her chair groaned as she flopped into it. What did a headhunter want? She owned the company so... Rebecca sat back up. Unless they were here to try and buy her out and take over?

Being actively pursued by a head-hunter trying to make her name by catching a big fish was not her favourite thing.

Rebecca scowled upwards, addressing the God of...bad luck, misfortune, or whoever else had decided she was the target for all this awfulness.

"Should I sacrifice a goat to appease you?"

Her question remained unanswered.

Her brain, as always, worked through this new occurrence quickly. The revelation made her hit the intercom firmly with a single finger.

"Joy. Can you come in for a minute?"

Her assistant walked in, notepad at the ready. Rebecca held out that card.

"I need an in-depth background check on Annah Stevens. I want to know everything: where she shops, every job she's held, what she had for breakfast." No use investigating the company just yet. Rebecca didn't want those rumours in the wind, not if they were trying for a take-over. She tapped a nail on the arm of her chair, "I want a dossier that'll put M.I.5 to shame."

Joy turned the card over and over in her fingers.

"No problem. When do you want it by?"

Rebecca grinned.

"Tomorrow morning."

Joy stared at her for a moment. Her only reaction was a soft snort of displeasure.

"I'll have it on your desk for nine o'clock."

"I know you will, and that's what scares me the most."

Rebecca thought of something else.

"And make sure they find out what colour eyes she has."

Joy paused and stared at her.

"Eyes?"

Rebecca pointed at her own.

"Yes. These things."

Joy blew a breath out and pointed to an ear.

"I thought you meant this. Lucky you clarified."

Rebecca smiled and waved her away. Joy quirked an eyebrow, pivoted sharply on her heels and, like a boulder gathering momentum, picked up the pace for her task ahead.

She'd had a sleepless night and ended up in her sanctuary, the library, doing what had become the norm - falling asleep, book in hand. She rubbed her stiff neck muscles and walked by Joy's desk. It wasn't doing any favours for her body. Her assistant sprung up like a cobra, arms laden with files.

Joy opened the door for her and followed after.

"I'll wait 'til you get your coat off."

Rebecca paused, one arm in, one arm out. Joy flicked through a manila file.

"Leaving it on won't make me go away."

"Because that would be too fortunate."

Rebecca hung up her raincoat and sat down. She sighed and wiggled her toes. Damn new shoes were torture devices.

Opening the top folder she realised what this was. A picture of a smiling brunette with jade eyes greeted her on page one. Without warning she found her smile matching that of the subject. She quickly turned the page. Rebecca glanced up at the clock. Eight fifteen.

She scanned the papers.

"Where's eye colour?"

"Page two. It's green."

So she was telling the truth.

"Joy, your efficiency is frightening."

Joy went back to reception, looking discreetly pleased with herself.

Rebecca found another picture. This wasn't a business one. Totally different, it was of Annah Stevens in a pair of well-worn jeans and a thick knit black jumper, getting into a car. Nevertheless it was just as enchanting. Rebecca squinted at a billboard in the background. She knew that one. It was on her way to work. They changed it every six weeks, too. She flicked the paperclip away, freeing the snap. It'd obviously been taken last night. She knew her people were good but clearly they all needed a pay rise.

Rebecca stared. The girl held a real wholesome charm, and yet, there was something else. She scrutinised the other picture, comparing the two for a moment.

"You are a woman of many faces, Miss Stevens."

And so the rest of the pile was digested. There was a lot of information. She licked a finger, turning another page, scanning for pertinent facts: normal university; very good education; some travel around Europe; not married; lived alone; family and two sisters; no pets. Work experience; bank, fraud section; finance; headhunted by headhunters. Nothing stood out.

She fluttered through the pages until she came to more personal details. Rebecca quirked an eyebrow as she read about the young woman's rock climbing exploits.

"Adrenaline junkie, huh? Explains the bold faced meeting on *my* bench."

She unhooked the business card from the front of the dossier and flipped it over and over hypnotically.

"Your move, Annah."

Chapter 4

The only journey is the one within. Rilke

Emotional pain can be overwhelming. Sometimes a moment is so damaging that the mind files the incident away, unable to deal with it until it has become stronger, until it has reinforced its weaker parts. Some call it delaying the inevitable but others, clever others, they know it's the most fundamental principle of existence. Survival.

Rebecca sighed, staring out of the window as rain slashed and clawed it. Dense sheets were thrown down by coal dark clouds. Her fingers moved smoothly in the sheen of condensation on the glass. The sky seemed ripped apart at the seams.

Taking a sip of hot chocolate, she felt the house tremble at the roar of thunder. Just as her grandfather had taught her when she was little, she concentrated, counting six seconds until the explosion of lightning.

Each second is God giving you one mile's grace to get yourself home, he used to tell her.

She smiled at the memory.

Padding over to the softly crackling fire, she relaxed back into her favourite chair, wiggling her toes in the warmth.

The real fireplace was one of the only things she'd insisted on restoring, despite Martin. He'd argued about the mess, about the smell. She'd shrugged him off and had the original rebuilt. The heavy marble surround ruled the room and she loved it; the curves and angles were bold, commanding and beautiful.

They'd fought for months after, even years when he was being particularly childish. She'd always found it curious he'd never questioned her motives. To him it was a silly whim. She'd found it more curious she'd never wanted to explain about her family's winter house or how she'd hold her mother's hand tightly as they walked through the deep crunching snow. Or the nights they'd sit in front of the fire to warm up and her mother would read stories of far off places.

Now she was glad she'd kept that little part secret. Glad, even after all those years, she'd kept some things just for herself.

She took another sip of hot chocolate. The logs on the fire sang a soothing lullaby in the silence of the house.

A shrill ring cauterised her mood. Her heart rate jumped. She grabbed the phone.

"Yes?"

"What a way to greet me, darling."

She rolled her eyes, leaning back in her comfy chair, hooking her legs over the arm.

"I should've guessed you'd be the one to shatter my peace."

"Is that what they call becoming a hermit these days?"

Rebecca readied herself for this subject again.

"I am not a hermit. We're in the middle of a hurricane..."

"It's a drop of rain."

Rebecca's brow furrowed as she pushed the phone closer to her ear, trying to hear. A crack of thunder hit in surround sound.

"Sophia, is that thunder where you are, too?" Rebecca paused as her brain did swift calculations. Sophia lived miles away. The thunder should have a delay. "Where are you?"

The doorbell rang. She unhooked her legs and trudged off to get her best friend.

"Typical," she muttered as she left her empty mug on a side table.

She opened the ornately carved heavy oak door. Sophia smirked, tilting her flame red umbrella away, shaking hundreds of water droplets free.

"Hurricane. Pft." Planting a cold kiss on both cheeks, Sophia swanned by, leaving a dripping wet coat and brolly in the hallway. "We're going out."

Rebecca baulked.

"In that?"

"Well, in that to the car and then toasty heating."

"I was relaxing."

Rebecca followed before almost ploughing into her back as Sophia whirled around, skirt swishing.

"You were moping. And we're not doing that anymore because we find it boring."

"Do we now?"

Sophia smirked.

"Yes, we do."

Rebecca's hand was grabbed and Sophia pulled them up the winding stairs holding centre stage in the hall.

Rebecca's grandmother had bought this house after seeing those stairs. She always said their quiet grandeur had spoken to her. It'd taken the family five years to restore the building and ever since then it'd not left the Cavendish name.

Rebecca stilled her friend's enthusiasm with a sliding hand up the balustrade.

They headed towards a guest room.

"Still not using the main bedroom?" asked Sophia.

"Could you?"

Rebecca's fingers got a soft squeeze.

"No, I'd never use it again. Although, if I were you, I'd have sold this place long ago."

"Yes, but..."

"I know. Memories. Growing up. Family heirloom. Blah blah blah." Sophia paused. "Which room are you using?"

"The one you hate."

"I'll just have to guess then."

Rebecca steadied the side table as they made a whirlwind through the long hall.

"I'm trying the one you refused to stay in last year."

"Oh, yes." Sophia grimaced. "It was a horrid shade of peach. My clothes would have killed themselves if they'd had to lounge a whole night."

Sophia winked and pushed open the door. Rebecca was deposited in her new room. Sophia glanced around.

"When did you decorate?"

Rebecca sighed as she remembered Martin picking the shade. She wasn't keen but she left him to it. It was only a guest room after all.

"It's butterscotch."

"It's nicotine beige." Sophia's wide eyes darted around. "It's like a whole troop of smoking monkeys took up residence."

"Why monkeys?"

"Because they're inconsiderate."

"Of course."

Sophia nudged her and they both laughed.

There was no use fighting against the tide that was Sophia. Not that she wanted to. Not at all. She loved being carried headfirst into her enthusiasm. It was why they got on so well, even from the initial meeting. Rebecca was calm and considered; Sophia was impulsive and wild. Rebecca loved wine and a good book; Sophia, margaritas and salsa. Like strawberries and cream they brought out the best in each other.

"Here's my concession as your best friend. I'm not dragging you dancing tonight. How do a few hours at the spa tomorrow sound?"

The last month had ripped through Rebecca like a tornado, sweeping up the entire infrastructure that kept her functioning until she was a shell, a hub around which things worked.

"Sounds perfect. I can't take too much." She snorted a laugh. "Some days I feel like my old self, like I can do anything I put my mind to. And others I feel...fractured, as if some integral part of me can't take the load anymore."

Sophia gave her a warm hug. "It'll feel like that for a long time but we'll solve it with baby steps." Rebecca hugged her back.

Chapter 5

Success is a lousy teacher. It seduces smart people into thinking they can't lose. Bill Gates.

Joy tightly clasped the microphone of the headset, whispering as the travel company read out details in the earpiece.

"I can get you on tomorrow's flight."

Joy raised an eyebrow, waiting. Rebecca remained po-faced and crossed her arms, an internal argument shouting a storm. Joy leant back, used to it.

Rebecca frowned. The last thing she wanted was to go all the way to Las Vegas just to hold Elliot's hand because he wasn't sure where to build his casino. She hated babysitting duties. To her Las Vegas was simple. Find a space and build on it. It was all prime real estate. Rebecca sighed. But then the commission was good and the work easy.

"At least get me a business class seat this time. I'm not doing sardines again."

Joy scribbled on a post-it note and held it up while reciting details to the flight operator.

I'm putting you in economy, near the toilets.

Rebecca snickered and padded back into her office.

She spent the next few hours synchronising her laptop with the files she'd need. Like every other piece of technology she owned, it'd taken a long time finding something perfect. In the end she'd sat with the boys down in

I.T. and poured over catalogues both off and online. It'd taken a while to convince them she was genuine and it wasn't some obscure trap to downsize the department; no-one in her building was unaware of Rebecca's reputation especially lately. She was the deal maker, the ball breaker; the woman who it was rumoured had made a senior manager of Sony cry. When Joy mentioned that gossip, Rebecca answered with a loud laugh and the explanation, "I'd cry, too, if someone spilt hot coffee on my lap. Anyway, he got a good price on that building as an apology."

The rest of the time went quickly. She was busy. Just the way she liked it. She poured over agreements and found beneficial loopholes, gave advice to regional offices and generally sorted out that which eluded all others. It was how she'd earned her nickname, The Magician; she didn't make elephants disappear but wealth and success reappear.

As she emptied her bag of the usual clutter accumulated in life - receipts; small change that weighed more than it was worth; various packets of gum she came across that small calico card again. She paused, running her thumb over the raised type. Ever since that meeting a week ago, she'd expected...something of the brunette. There'd been zero, zilch, nada, nothing. No calls, e-mails, visits. She turned the card over and over, chewing her lip as her mind flitted through what the plan could be.

"I'll have to be patient with you, I think, Miss Stevens."

She deposited the card back in her bag, leaving the office before it was pitch black outside to get ready for her flight in the morning.

Joy followed her out of reception, pulling a small trolley case, utilising every moment until the cab arrived for the airport.

Rebecca neatly folded her itinerary. Joy went through it by memory.

"You're in the Hilton. There's a jeep waiting in the airport car park."

Rebecca popped a chocolate covered peanut into her mouth as she shifted, her laptop bag strap already cutting into her shoulder.

"Did you remind them to put some kind of fuel in it this time or is that a quirk us English have?"

Joy smiled and moved the heavy files into her other arm then pressed for the lift.

"You could always use that strange thing they have now called a petrol gauge."

Rebecca chuckled.

"The clerk told me it was filled up, Smarty."

"As soon as they had your name in the computer, I'm sure it flashed up a warning after your last visit."

Rebecca popped another sweet.

"It's a desert. They deserved to be shouted at."

They got in the lift, each woman watching the bright neon numbers descend.

"After you arrive you have a couple of hours to freshen up and then you'll be meeting with..." Joy handed over a thin dossier. "...his people."

Rebecca flicked through it as Joy took out a slim plastic oblong and waved it in the air.

"Mobile phone, please."

Rebecca didn't look up as she scrutinised the photos and initial breakdown, trying to get a feeling for all involved. She handed her assistant the phone.

"So, just Elliot and his closest advisor? Intimate."

Joy deftly swapped the battery.

"Slim line. Optimised version. New and fully charged."

Rebecca flicked through the last of the thin pages.

"What would I do without you?"

"Get another assistant."

There was a deep pause, and finally Rebecca looked up, frowning at that answer. Even in the abstract the thought was horrible. After a beat Joy quirked a single arched eyebrow and finished off.

"And she wouldn't be half as efficient."

Rebecca swatted her gently with the file, smiling widely.

"No-one else would have you. You've got too much of a smart mouth."

With a ding the doors shh'd open. They walked through the cavernous lobby, both sets of heels tapping an impressive rhythm louder than the wheels of the case. Security nodded respectfully; various people from various departments said polite hellos as the women cut through the building's entrance hall.

The wind was biting. Rebecca shivered and tugged her coat tighter. The doorman opened the cab door and she slipped into the back.

Her assistant leant in through the open window. Rebecca knew the drill and pre-empted her for once.

"Call you when I land. Call you if I have problems. Call you if they forget to put those miniature bars of soap in my bathroom." Rebecca patted her arm. "I've got to leave home some time."

Joy tutted, barely managing to keep a straight face.

"Safe trip, Miss Cavendish."

Rebecca plastered a totally fake grin on her lips and settled back in the seat, crossing her long legs and smoothing out her skirt.

"I love babysitting billionaires."

The taxi rolled away.

Chapter 6

You cannot find peace by avoiding life. Virginia Woolf.

Rebecca leant her head against the cool window of the cab. As they sped along, impressive structures were reduced to flashes of bland colour, the concrete buildings elongating like stretched putty.

She flexed slender arms. With all the hours she'd been putting in lately, gym time was getting harder to come by. Since passing the marker of thirty, she'd realised the days of coasting and expecting your body to do the same were gone. But time...it was a rare commodity. It was just work and a restless sleep.

Tired hazel eyes went back to watching the speeding city. In the quiet of the cab there were no ringing phones, no faxes or piles of folders to go through. It was just the silence.

Unwanted memories whined until, like an animation flicker book, images, snapshots, freeze frames, slipped through her mental blockade and blossoming brightness exploded behind her irises. The intensity was crushing as she remembered the day she'd gone home early, catching Martin and that blonde whore in the bedroom. At times, honest times, she couldn't tell if she'd do it all again or take ignorance, oblivion, over the agony of her life falling through her fingers like grains of sand.

She brushed invisible lint from her skirt, fidgeting, trying anything to stop that pain gaining purchase. But not everything could be controlled so easily, especially memories. Once again they resurfaced, howling through the darkness like a behemoth.

She grabbed a dossier, determined not to be a victim again. Her phone pierced the moment.

"Thank you for distractions."

She glanced at the screen. It was Martin. The inside of the cab filled with a happy ringtone as her mind filled with something less ecstatic. Her fingers lay paused and it rang off. A ding announced a new answer machine message.

She returned to watching the buildings stretch.

Check in was a blur. Lights, noise, movement and form, all linked together to provide a totally forgettable experience. It wasn't until boarding that she was woken from her trance by a smiling stewardess dressed head to foot in a pressed to perfection uniform.

"Madame, business class is this way."

Rebecca blinked and mentally slapped herself awake.

"Thank you."

She divested her aching shoulder of the heavy laptop case, as the stewardess reached forward to help her slide it into the overhead locker. She slipped into her seat, not taking her suit jacket off, not fiddling about with files or using the phone up until the last moment like usual. Rebecca rubbed her temples gently, trying to massage the throbbing away.

Vaguely sensing a tall figure standing by the next seat, her attention snapped back. In a slight daze she looked over to her potential travelling companion.

Annah Stevens smiled and stared back.

Chapter 7

Reality is different from person to person. Like the ebb and flow of the tides, it depends where you are as to what you see.

Annah waved a small square ticket, emerald eyes shining out like a warning.

"I think this is me."

Rebecca blinked incredulously at the brunette inhabiting her field of vision. Wasn't this the icing on the cake. Materialising this displeasure would freeze everything in a ten foot radius into ice blocks.

Annah didn't seem fazed as she took off her suit jacket and put a small sturdy looking case, minus one thick paperback, in the overhead locker. Parting the seatbelt ends she sat down and did them up right away, patting the cool metal of the secured belt.

"Always be prepared," Annah added.

Rebecca didn't utter a response because at this point tempting fate to make her day worse might make the wings of the plane fall off. So instead she surreptitiously watched as Annah concentrated on that paperback. After five minutes, Rebecca's brain ground the clutch and crunched into gear.

Rebecca divested her of the book. Paused, Annah's hands remained stuck in that pose. Rebecca turned it over, nodding at the cover.

"You like Dostoyevsky?"

The younger woman held a slight pause.

"I got it from the airport."

Rebecca placed it back as if it had never left.

"Hint. When pretending to read a book, always remember to turn at least one page every two minutes."

Annah tilted the book sideways, highlighting the sheer girth of the thing.

"Even Dostoyevsky?"

"Maybe every three minutes with him."

Annah looked down, a smile tugging her lips, "Busted," and slammed the paperback closed, jamming it down the side of the seat.

It could've been the way the young woman projected charisma or maybe it was the relaxed smile that reached all the way to those eyes, but whatever, Rebecca couldn't help but be slightly more amused than volcanically angry.

"You were, rather."

But despite that temporary respite of amusement, her stress level was uncompromisingly high. She waited patiently through take-off, and as soon as the seatbelt sign dulled, it was time for one drink to help the bitter medicine of today go down. She got up and shifted by.

"Excuse me."

Annah smiled and gracefully moved.

One of the benefits of a hundred thousand miles on her frequent flyer card with the airline was occasionally recognising a stewardess - and when that happened, goodies ensued; high mileage customers were prized and treated like family members by cabin crew.

The impeccably suited blonde airline employee smiled and beckoned Rebecca through to first class where she was treated to a fine malt whisky. They chatted as she finished it, and then the stewardess, with a mischievous wink, organised a ten minute slot with the onboard masseur.

In a specially designed chair, as those talented hands worked their magic, Rebecca had time to think about this insane new occurrence in her insane new day. She shifted as the masseur's hands dug in deeply. It was now obvious why Annah hadn't contacted her before, not if this was her plan.

Rebecca muttered under her breath, "A ten hour flight."

She chuckled and closed her eyes.

She felt like stretchy chewing gum as she walked back to her seat. Annah moved her legs in as she passed.

Like removing a plaster Rebecca wasted no time in working through that which was bothersome.

"Annah, you have two minutes to explain what you're doing in the seat next to me."

Annah opened her mouth but seemed to think better of whatever wanted to come out right away. Instead, with a sip of drink, there was a momentary pause before a reply was given.

"This is the only way I'd get to talk to you."

"And why do you think I'd want to talk to you?"

Green eyes turned on her. Annah shrugged lightly.

"Curiosity?"

There was little charitability left in Rebecca's day. If she were at home, she would slam a door, perhaps find a vase she hated and take great pleasure in tipping it from whence it stood. But she was a little short of options here.

"Are you asking me or telling me?"

"Are you saying you're not a little curious?" Annah parried. "Not even a little?"

Rebecca wasn't ready to show her hand yet. She kept her face straight. "I think you must be a little insane and that has me a little curious."

Annah didn't seem offended at all. In fact her lips curved upwards.

"Not the impression I wanted, but it's not the worst it could get."

"True. I could ask you to be seated elsewhere."

Annah's fingers tapped a light rhythm out on the padded armrest.

"I know. I hope you won't."

Rebecca looked at Annah, at the arch of her eyebrow, the way her hair lay across her shoulders, at how she was comfortably lounged in that seat just like the first time they'd met on her bench in her park. Annah looked back. It was solid and unwavering; it was intense; it was like two big cats sizing up the competition.

Annah was the first to look away.

"Use your time wisely," Rebecca advised.

After a long beat, Annah drained the last of her drink, placing the cup down gently, carefully, taking her time. Rebecca knew the tactic. She'd used it herself. Something interesting was coming.

"I know how much your company is worth. I'd say we'd double it, but if you needed the money you'd already have sold up."

And it was interesting.

"So what are you offering me?"

Then it came, the thunderous revelation. It was as if it had been saved for the perfect moment when Rebecca's weak points were undefended.

"I'm offering you a new start."

Rebecca blinked, taken aback. It was obvious what was being referred to; she'd tried to keep the divorce out the trash magazines but Martin had wanted to be malicious. Of course, it'd backfired on him. There wasn't a team of staff working in the Cavendish camp for nothing. He never stood a chance. But still, it'd done the unthinkable and paraded her private life.

Rebecca pulled herself together enough to answer. Her words drifted through the background noise of the plane.

"Meaning?"

"No details without a yes."

"I'll think about it."

"It's all I ask."

Such a small request. Such a huge impact.

"But now I need a drink."

Rebecca got up and slowly walked away.

Chapter 8

Attitude is a little thing that makes a big difference. Winston Churchill

Rebecca took delivery of two drinks from the glowingly chirpy stewardess. She knew she shouldn't, because her food intake had been minimal through the day, but this new development to her abysmal week had made that choice for her. Hers was a double.

It'd been a long time since she'd been hunted. Sure, there had been one or two approaches every few years, but she'd put the word out that she was not selling; she liked ruling her kingdom how she saw fit and breaking in another place and another set of employees - or worse still, having a boss dictating - didn't inspire her like it would have done ten years ago. Match that with trademark harsh refusals and the sharks had been scared away.

She glanced down the aisle. That damn girl was up and about. A tumultuous mixture of emotions pumped through her veins. On one hand she was mad as Hell to be ambushed like this, especially since this was such a disgusting day. But a niggling part was impressed at such a bold move. Still, the timing stank. Rebecca picked an ice-cube out and destroyed it in a single bite. She wondered how bad her global karma was to have this and Martin, all in a handful of hours.

"What did I do in my previous life?"

The stewardess smiled.

"Excuse me?"

Rebecca managed a grimace. There was no way she could roll out a smile.

"Ignore me."

She trudged back to her seat.

Encountering the tall brunette's back, she waited, leaning on an empty seat as her 'guest' obliviously sorted through her bag. She gave Annah a thorough once over: perfectly layered chestnut hair; gentle copper highlights; no visible split-ends; knee length, dark grey skirt; thick material so as not to crease in-flight; woven cotton shirt for the same reason; two inch heels for comfort, and, Rebecca just knew, so as not to tower over her mark. That last point made her smile.

Suddenly her lazy view of the back of Annah Stevens was replaced with a very sharply focused front. This close, her most striking feature shone. Simmering verdigris eyes were arresting. Flecked with shards of azure they held her attention for a heavy moment.

The thought drifted like waves retreating off a shore.

Regaining some composure, she handed the drink over. The self-assured young woman slipped it away politely.

All smiles and promises are a dangerous thing, her mind lulled. She didn't add what her consciousness was whispering: especially in this limping state. She felt like a car running on half pistons. It'd operate, but there was a significant loss of power, a chug-chug-chug to take it from A to B.

She watched Annah sip whisky like a pro. Not a glimmer of shock, and she'd picked a particularly harsh Scotch in deliberate punishment for her unwanted flight companion. But that wasn't what made her skin tingle. No, it was the shadowy lipstick stain on the edge of the glass that cut into her attention.

A shark's business card, she thought, appraising her brazen guest.

Annah seemed like a femme fatale. A walking trap designed to get what she wanted, exactly when she wanted it.

The two women remained paused, tension creating a thick mist between them, until another passenger sliced it in two with a bare, "Excuse me." Rebecca frowned and let him pass.

Rebecca wordlessly settled back in her seat and shut her eyes, her mind on emotional overload. Beaten and bruised, she longed for peace somewhere. God, the thought of getting to the hotel room and standing under the steaming stream of the shower until it peeled the last day away, was nirvana. And yet reality was an hour stopover to change clothes and then an entire evening spent with Elliot Peters, who, despite all of his money, had not been able to buy a brain. Her fingers tightened around the glass.

Exhaustion was overwhelming. Like quicksand, it dragged her under in a matter of seconds.

It was a soft caress that woke her. The warm skin of another removed the cold chill from her own. Eyelashes fluttering open, she was greeted by sea green pools. It took a moment, a slight shake of her head to get her bearings: a blanket she didn't remember; her empty glass gone; the table folded up; blind down; tanned fingers on her own for a moment, waking her gently. She resisted the urge to rub her eyes, having enough sense to remember she had mascara on.

Annah looked down the aisle.

"You've only just missed the meal."

Gentle words almost lulled her back to dozing. A month of sleepless nights had left her irritable, jumpy, and less than her usual welcoming self. But even after such a short nap, she did feel a smidge more human.

She cleared her throat, watching the stewardess walk away.

"I doubt my stomach is sorry."

"There was a nice salad."

It sounded almost like genuine concern.

"I'll catch up when we land."

Annah held out a cereal bar. It was the same type Rebecca had Joy keep stocked by the box load at work.

"I salvaged this."

She divested the brunette of the slim bar and turned it over in her palm. Yup, not only her favourite brand but her favourite flavour, too. Annah seemed to be on a roll.

"There was a choice of two but this has a yogurt coating and slithers of Brazil nut underneath so it's a real find." Green eyes narrowed. Annah presented the true prize. "Which is why I got three."

Any aggravation at the shock of seeing this woman was deftly replaced by something much more positive. Who could fail to be amused by such a resourceful companion?

Rebecca wiggled her bar.

"I should thank you, then."

A smile worthy of a beauty pageant contestant dazzled back.

"Share the fun. It's my motto."

Rebecca tugged the blanket off, glancing over to her companion who shrugged sheepishly.

"That was me. I wasn't sure how to explain a frozen body next to me."

As usual, the harsh breeze pumping from air circulation units had lowered the cabin temperature. Rebecca clenched her icy hands to try and warm them as she regarded this woman with curiosity. Just like earlier, Annah didn't look away.

Rebecca was confused, a little disoriented from waking, and with everything going on, displaced from her usual calm and collected self. She couldn't help her question; like watching a head-on collision, you know what will happen but can't stop it. Some part of her that found Annah Stevens curious, did manage to soften the edges.

"What do you want of me?"

Honest and unguarded eyes gleamed.

"I want you to keep an open mind."

She squeezed the bridge of her nose, trying to ease the tension building. Martin had said the same thing when he'd attempted to

reconcile his actions, 'I need you to hear me out and have an open mind.'
She'd slapped him so hard he'd stumbled backward. Now that phrase was
like a nail bomb, innocuous looking but ready to shred anything within
two hundred meters.

The animal anger inside reared. She knew her expression was dreadful.
She knew because Annah sat back in her seat, as if that loss of ground
would keep her safe.

Some part of her shouted over the ruckus of her temper.

Don't take it out on her. At least she's been honest from the outset.

Rebecca ran a hand through her hair, the smooth auburn sections
falling back into place effortlessly. She wished her façade would do the
same.

"Fine."

They stayed silent for a long time.

The seatbelt sign flashed on. Rebecca complied, snapping the ends
together harshly. She glanced over, sure her neighbour was already
strapped in. She was right. It was reminiscent of Sophia's nieces when
they were happily ensconced in the back of the car. It was verging on
sweet, the way Annah's fingers tapped out a rhythm on the metal buckle.

The captain's voice filled the cabin, his English accent calm and
professional as it announced turbulence.

She settled back, wondering what else could go wrong. It was as if fate
heard her plea. Out of the corner of her eye she noticed slim fingers
gripping the arm rest. She watched the shark floundering in shallow
waters; Annah glanced around the cabin and shifted in her seat. Viridian
green disappeared in a long blink as the plane bumped along.

Something tugged inside of Rebecca as she saw discomfort growing in
the pristinely turned out woman. She knew it was only the timing of
Annah that had momentarily annoyed her. Without the torment of the
last few months, the attention would have been flattering.

Cut the girl some slack, she sighed.

"I didn't realise you had a problem flying."

'tho, not that much slack.

"I don't. I have a problem crashing."

"We're going over the mountains. It always happens."

Annah nodded swiftly.

"Sounds reassuring. You know, having something large and immovable
for the plane to plough headlong into."

She couldn't help but laugh.

"At least it'll be quick if we..."

A warm palm lay over her hand, pressing down, forcing her words to stop.

"I understand you want revenge for me sitting here, but maybe later?"

They hit a juddering pocket of air that shook the plane. That hand squeezed instinctively for a moment before slipping away. It settled on its owner's lap.

"Sorry."

"Don't apologise." Rebecca smirked even though she felt a little guilty for finding this all very amusing. "It's just karma."

She couldn't make out the mumbled words of her companion, but she could imagine it wasn't language for public consumption.

Annah rested a warm hand near Rebecca's for a moment.

"I feel as if the wings are going to shear off. Share a drink with me? I'll feel less guilty if you do."

Annah's calm was gone now and her face was a visual plea.

"Of course."

The words were out before she knew she was going to say them.

Annah organised two double Scotches with a passing attendant.

The younger woman seemed happier to crunch a liquored ice-cube than drink the malt. Rebecca swirled the amber liquid, inhaled that heady peaty fragrance and took a long sip. She was not a seasoned drinker but it made her terrible day just a little bit easier.

As quickly as the turbulence started, the air ahead evened out and the bumps and jarring lessened to nothing. The seatbelt sign stayed on but from experience Rebecca knew it was because they were near the airport.

Annah expelled an audible breath.

"Bring back the days of cruise liners."

Rebecca couldn't help it.

"Like the Titanic?"

"I'm never travelling with you again."

Rebecca playfully clapped her hands like a kid.

"Goody."

Annah just laughed.

With a bounce of wheels on tarmac, the plane landed, took a few minutes to taxi, and then began to unload its living cargo. Both women remained seated.

Annah unbuckled her seatbelt and volunteered some reasoning.

"I always wait for everyone to get off first. I don't like being in the throng. Squeeze by if you want."

Rebecca wondered if Annah really did the same thing as her, or if this was just excessively thorough research. With a shake of her head she went back to staring out of the window, mentally preparing for her meeting.

"I'm fine waiting for the hordes to leave, too."

What she couldn't figure out was why this woman wasn't trying push any points or try to force a Vegas meeting, or talking incessantly about her company. Rebecca snuck a glance. She was at a loss and that was not the norm. Her talent was figuring people out - at least enough to get the upper hand in business. She glanced across. Annah, eyes closed, patiently waiting, sat, happily confusing the Hell out of her.

Rebecca went back to watching the airport crew scurrying about the tarmac.

They didn't disembark together but eventually they were walking next to each other. As usual, Las Vegas airport was a hub of frenetic activity. Rebecca glanced at the foolish desperates playing the airport slot machines. She rolled her eyes, knowing the low payout odds.

"Idiots," she mumbled to herself.

Annah's lips curled into a soft smile.

"Don't approve of gambling?"

"I don't approve of losing."

It was an unguarded reply. Annah didn't seem like the other vicious adrenaline fuelled, caffeine addicted head-hunters she'd brushed off. Rebecca felt relaxed here - which was odd.

Her companion's chuckle made her smile.

"Who does?"

Passport control was never pleasant. Rebecca found the rudeness unnecessary, but, as she always said, "If you're one step away from a job where, 'do you want fries with that, sir?' is a phrase you'd use a lot then you're going to have a bad attitude."

The reasoning escaped her but they even ended up at the same car rental desk. They chatted happily, Annah making amusingly wry observations and just joking around as paperwork was filled in, boxes signed, and copies printed.

And then the clerk handed Rebecca the keys. She turned around and regarded the intriguing woman who'd dared to hijack her flight.

"If I didn't know better, I'd say you were following me, Annah."

A brilliant smile lit up everything within a ten foot radius. It was uplifting.

"Actually, not even I'm that good. This is a coincidence." Annah's smile faded around the edges. "And I suppose goodbye?"

Rebecca was sure the entire airport hadn't emptied out at that second, but it certainly felt like it. A hush fell heavily as she stared into the lively face of such a curious woman. Annah had none of the sharpness or ferocity of a shark, and the femme fatale judgment didn't hold water now. Rebecca was at a loss until it came to her.

Less of a shark and more like a dolphin; all brains and impressive tricks.
At least it was a compliment.

Rebecca's hand slid forward of its own accord and was accepted in a warm embrace. Neither said a word. Eventually Rebecca forced herself to let go, fingers finally slipping away.

"No other corporate,..." vulture, "...finder has ever let me go so easily."
Her happy companion chuckled easily.

"I'm not here to pressure you. I'm just here to show you another path. You have my card. You can call me any time."
Rebecca nodded.

"I'll think about it."
She meant it. The younger woman shifted under her gaze.

"Good. I won't force anything."
Those words were delivered with anything but discomfort. It was an honest offer. Rebecca just knew it.

"Maybe that's why you actually stand a chance."
Rebecca pivoted and walked away, some part of her wishing she could turn back, catch the look on Annah's face as the words hit. She knew it'd be a brilliant smile, wide and genuine, unlike the other fakes who were always sent on her trail; endless old hands at the game; jaded, stale; tired and crumpled.

At the door to the parking area Rebecca finally succumbed to the pull, her gaze bouncing back through the crowded hall. Elbow on the counter, chin in her palm, Annah was chatting and smiling with the booking clerk. Even from this distance, she could feel that surge of charisma - or that's what she thought it was.

Annah Stevens was like an autumn morning. Refreshing, crisp and calm. Rebecca sighed, glanced down at her map, and walked to the lot to find her jeep. If she'd waited one moment longer, she'd have caught the sad look from Annah who had turned to watch her go.

Chapter 9

I have noticed even people who claim everything is predestined, and that we can do nothing to change it, look before they cross the road. Stephen Hawking.

Rebecca slipped on her sunglasses. The explosive glare of the desert sun bounced off of row after row of identical 4x4's. She shifted uncomfortably, her shirt sticking to her back.

Turning the map around, she squinted at the nonsense.

"Next time I'm in a hurry I'm getting a cab."

After checking twenty or so number plates she finally found hers. She wanted to get to the hotel, wash the flight away, deal with this business, and then, finally relax, maybe take in a show, see some sights.

She opened the vehicle door. The explosion of hot air reminded her of the days spent baking with her mother. She'd always peek in on the cakes, often getting a friendly little tap because the mixture would fall into a pancake that no one would want to eat. No-one but her.

Rebecca smiled. And then something caught her eye. A small sign on the welcome literature on the far seat. Red and blue it sang out over the noise from the airport.

Do not drink and drive.

She tallied up the doubles and how recently she'd had the last. She virtually screamed up at the sky at her own stupidity.

"Did you leave your brain someplace else?" she growled, fighting the urge to kick a dent in the side of her rental. Instead she slammed the door so hard the whole vehicle rocked.

She spun around, taking a moment to reign in her temper before it popped like a chewing gum bubble.

Rolling rubber over heated asphalt stopped, taking up all of her view. She frowned at the huge silver 4x4 that looked as if it should be towing a house. A tinted window dropped and a smiling brunette leant an elbow on the sill. Annah peered out, slipping sunglasses on top of conker brown hair.

Annah's even tones wafted through the haze of heat.

"Lost?"

"No." Rebecca threw her arms up, unable to hide her frustration. "I forgot I was driving when I had those drinks on the plane."

Annah looked apologetic.

"I got you the last, sorry."

Rebecca's eyebrows sank into a frown.

"And you're okay to drive?"

Annah nodded.

"I crunched the ice in my last one."

Firing synapses calculated what they needed to. The solution churned out and fluttered into Rebecca's palm. She didn't need to be a math genius to figure out the only sensible option given the time frame and how far away the taxi rank was.

"This is a massive imposition but I need a ride to the Hilton, Annah."

Annah's smile was brilliant as the wheel got a friendly pat.

"I am your knight in a shining automatic vehicle."

Rebecca grabbed the soft straps of her bag and hefted it over a shoulder.

The traffic moved graciously along the strip. Even now, the lights and grandeur of monolithic structures held Rebecca in rapture. She relaxed back in the comfort of coursing cool air.

The designated driver took the turn as smoothly as the conversation.

"Who'd have thought putting all of this in the middle of the desert would work out?"

"I would love to have sat in on the original sales pitch." replied Rebecca.

Annah scanned the road ahead automatically.

"Can you imagine the architect's model: two square feet of empty desert and an inch and a half of buildings?" Annah paused for a beat, frowning. "Not that the mafia used models, but you know what I mean."

Rebecca nodded, watching the blazing neon lights floundering in the sun. She answered, almost in a daze.

"And now it's eating the desert."

Rebecca loved Vegas at dusk, when the sun went into hiding and allowed the city to rise from the red rock floor and ooze sin from its pores. That was Vegas to her, not this pseudo Disney-esque attraction that parents could use as an excuse to drag their kids along to.

Annah made a snorting point.

"I wish my gran had bought a plot of land before it all started. If she had, I'd be living in a castle now."

Rebecca laughed.

"Castles are just giant wine cellars."

Annah smirked.

"I obviously read too many Prince and Princess fairy stories growing up

-or maybe you've lived in too many castles?"

"Can one ever have too many?" joked Rebecca easily.

"I come from simple stock," Annah took a turn as smoothly as she did the conversation. "My gran still lives in the same house she bought sixty years ago. They upgraded the inside years ago, but she still has an outside toilet."

"I do, too."

Annah snorted.

"Do, too," Rebecca repeated.

Annah's lips twitched into a smile.

"Really?"

"It's called the gardener's cottage," Rebecca chuckled.

Annah groaned.

"Fell into that, didn't I."

"Sure did."

Road works ahead slowed them to a bouncing halt. Annah pushed the sleeves of her shirt up.

"The brakes and my heels aren't compatible."

Rebecca's pocket vibrated and she hauled out her phone, checking her message alerts. As usual her answer machine begged attention and she pressed the phone tightly against her ear. Martin proceeded to talk about the box of papers he needed from the house. She'd forgotten about him. She punched delete, stored two more, managed a smile at Sophia's request to bring her back either a millionaire or a chunk of rock from Area 51, and quickly returned Joy's call.

Her assistant answered in clipped tones.

"Rebecca Cavendish's office. How can I help?"

"I'm checking in and returning your call."

An exhalation buzzed the line.

"The meeting's been brought forward two hours." Papers rustled. *"You need to be there...five minutes ago."*

Rebecca's head banged back against the seat as she squeezed her eyes shut.

"Joy. I've just landed and haven't even got changed yet."

"I tried to reschedule but they insisted." A pause. *"I know. You don't need this."*

"I don't." She scowled deeply, remembering one niggling thing. "Martin called. He needs a box of papers in the attic. They're in a large tea chest labelled with his name. Can you organise it?"

Joy's response was soft.

"Of course."

She held the phone to her chest for some privacy. There was no choice. Damn it.

Rebecca touched a hand to her potential saviour's arm, getting a bright smile in return.

"Annah, if I give you directions can you drop me off somewhere else? My meeting's been brought forward."

"Sure. Point and I'll drive." Annah patted the wheel. "I've got a Toyota at home. This thing is like driving a spaceship."

Rebecca would have laughed at that bizarre image had this news not royally peeved her. She resumed the call.

"Tell them I'm on my way. And Joy, in your own inimitable style, please make it known that I lack a charitable attitude towards such short notice rearrangements."

"I will."

She flipped the phone shut and fought the urge to javelin it out of the window. At this point she all but expected a piano to fall from the sky and crush her in the passenger seat.

"Where to - if you don't mind me knowing the address? I can do directions if you'd prefer."

"I trust you with this." Rebecca softened her tone considerably. "If I didn't, I would've gotten a cab."

Rebecca didn't even attempt to rationalise that sentence or the fact it was true. She was beyond trying to figure it all out.

Annah's expression transformed wonderfully, and at that moment Rebecca could see something in her: a gentleness, a genuineness, an amiable way that made her glad she'd run with her gut instinct.

"When you put it like that," Annah smiled.

She repeated the address of her client's offices in the middle of nowhere. Rebecca flipped down the visor, checking her make-up. Passable. Which meant it didn't cut it.

"No bumps, please, I'm not auditioning for Cirque Du Soleil."

Annah nodded seriously, her face a mask of concentration.

"Okay, I won't use the brakes."

Eyeliner, lip liner, lipstick and clear mascara were applied. It was her barely there look. She wished she was barely here. Her usual meetings with Elliot were in the familiarity of Europe, perhaps Lyon or Roma, not half the way across the bloody globe. She looked forward to sealing this venture and moving back to pastures known.

Annah navigated a junction, her attention not leaving the road.

"You scrub up well. Definitely not Cirque Du Soleil."

Rebecca blotted her neutral lipstick, chuckling at Annah's turn of phrase.

"One thing's going right."

"At least you had an interesting companion on the flight."

Rebecca glanced across. Annah's lips pursed, trying to keep her smile in.

"Interesting, you say?"

"Probably want to thank her for saving you from the cycle of bad movies."

Rebecca laughed loudly.

"Maybe she should thank me for not using my influence to get her squashed into economy?"

Annah relaxed back and reached a hand over and lay it on Rebecca's, squeezing gently, before going back to the wheel.

"Thank you. I hate economy."

Rebecca brought her hands together, idly massaging where Annah had touched, carrying on that gentle soothing feeling.

"Me, too."

Rust red rock puffed up in a dust trail behind the huge vehicle as they made their way along the unkempt track. It'd taken a while but Rebecca had finally found some recognisable landmarks. They were now twenty minutes late.

Annah glanced around.

"Are you sure this is right?"

Rebecca nodded.

"I broke down here last time. It's not a place you forget when you had to walk a mile in heels and a hundred degree heat."

Annah did a double-take.

"I hope you're joking."

"I wish I was." And now here she was again, stressed out in the same place. Fate sure had a lot to answer for. "Sometimes life throws the unexpected at you."

Annah pressed the accelerator down and they sped up towards Elliot's offices.

Chapter 10

The dread of evil is a much more forcible principle of human actions than the prospect of good. John Locke

"It really is quite simple, Elliot. I want those papers."

Elliot sat stubbornly, body rigid, bloodied lip from the first time she'd hit him, not quivering at all. He simply pushed his grey hair back slowly, patting it back into place.

"And you think by hitting an old man that he'll just give in?"

He glanced at the two men in ski-masks guarding the door then at her. Masks were good. It meant he could be getting out of this alive.

She walked closer, blue eyes shining through the neat slits in the fine knit material.

"I went to one of the facilities, Elliot. Poppies grow there now. Legions of long stems carrying beautiful blood red faces. Quite ironic."

She leant closer.

"And you have to wonder, Elliot..." Her tanned hand lifted; elegantly long leather-gloved fingers went to her neck. And she peeled the mask away. "...if all those bodies you put there didn't help."

His movement was slight but she saw it as he shrank back in the seat just a fraction. But it was still a fraction. You give, I take. It all counts. Every victory. Every miniscule inch.

She stared deeply into his eyes. It seemed nothing would warm this man up. But then warming wasn't her task.

She turned to gaze out of the long blackened glass. The desert stretched. It was a beautiful emptiness. But even from here she knew that underneath that beauty was a ferocity that would fry your brain in a matter of hours.

"One should take care with that which can cause one harm, Elliot. Did the time with your children teach you nothing?"

She squinted. Something else. Something different. A cloud of dust. And like a whirlwind giving no time to its targets the 4x4 rolled through the gates.

She turned around, addressing the two masked guards.

"We have company, boys."

Chapter 11

At the touch of a lover, everyone becomes a poet. Plato

The vehicle slipped through lavish iron gates that stood out amongst the desolate surroundings. Annah slowed to a crawl, eyes darting about.

"Interesting design."

"Yes. I think it's horrible, too."

The sprawling, low level building was distinctly out of place. Glass was not a material favoured by sane members of the local community, just hoteliers looking for the wow effect - which only lasted as long as it took the customer to bake in their glass room.

They pulled up a few yards away from a ratty looking dark sedan. Hanging in it was a glinting decoration throwing out a mirror ball of flashing reflections. Rebecca had to squint not to get blinded. It was tacky to the extreme.

"Thank you for the lift. I can get a..."

Annah turned quickly, brows descending into a deep frown her relaxed expression tightening in an instant.

"I'm not leaving you in the middle of the desert. No can do. I'll wait. Accept the offer graciously because there are no strings attached."

It silenced Rebecca's main concern that the younger woman expected a favourable decision based on a bit of chauffeuring. However, her perversely English streak of torturous politeness made an appearance.

"I don't want to keep you."

Annah snorted a not very amused laugh.

"I don't want to read about your body being found in the desert because you had to walk back in..." Annah raised a stiff hand, motioning towards the blazing sun. "...this insane heat."

Rebecca laughed.

"If I'm going to be more than an hour I'll call you." She arched an eyebrow. "I have your card."

Annah chuckled brightly and rooted around in a soft beige bag.

"Let me check my battery."

Movement on the bare landscape caught Rebecca's attention. Not rattlesnakes or an apparition, but two men walking quickly out of the building.

Like a picture with twisted perspective, something was askew. Something was wrong. A part of this crawled into her head and cried out for her to notice. Her arms prickled. A cold chill descended and she had no idea why. And then she saw. She blinked in the shimmering haze, squinting to clarify what she thought...and clarify she did.

Why do you need to wear ski-masks in the desert?

Her mouth went dry and eyelids peeled wide open. Her nervous system got nervous.

"Annah. Put the car in reverse right now."

Annah carried on hunting around in her handbag.

"I need my phone so..."

The men started a fast paced march towards them. Dust puffed under their boots as arms pumped them into a sprint. Something metallic glinted in the shorter one's hand. Rebecca barked her command.

"Annah. Put the car in reverse and get us out of here."

Annah looked up, then around, obviously not comprehending why, but still obeying. They sped backwards and around in a perfectly executed manoeuvre that took them out of the gates in a cloud of dirty red. The wheels carved up the rocky ground as they spun and raced down the only road out of there.

"What happened? You've freaked me out."

There was a slight tremor in the young woman's voice and Rebecca bet it'd be nothing to the one in hers if she didn't take a moment to calm down. She blew a long breath out.

"Rebecca?"

"Let me think."

It was more an order than a request. She needed quiet.

Her brain popped a gear and squealed as its tyres hit the track. She turned, checking behind. Nothing but a thick dark mushroom cloud. She tried her phone. Pitiful reception, just like when she broke down here before.

"Annah, we need to drive to the nearest police station."

The brunette gripped the wheel, knuckles turning white.

"You're scaring me."

"They scared me, so all in all I'm glad we're on the same page."

Annah banged the wheel, her demeanour shuttering into seriousness.

"Explain what just happened."

"Why do you think you'd ever need to wear a ski-mask in the desert?"

Annah's eyelashes fluttered as her nails dug into the wheel.

"I don't think there are a lot of artificial ski slopes here."

"Exactly. There were two goons coming out of that building, wearing masks. And when they saw us...it looked like they didn't want us to leave."

Rebecca left out the possibility of there being a gun. "I am not becoming a crime statistic."

The 4x4 sped up dramatically.

"Me neither."

Chapter 12

I began to have an idea of my life, not as the slow shaping of achievement to fit my preconceived purposes, but as the gradual discovery and growth of a purpose which I did not know. Joanna Field

The two men came back in, clearly out of breath. The taller shook his head. She closed her eyes, clicking through possibilities of who that was and what they wanted. Blue eyes flicked open once again. Alert. Clear. Precisely focused she precisely focused them on him.

"Did you get a number plate?"

He waved his mobile.

"A partial. We're running it now."

She nodded.

"No more surprises. Recheck the building."

As they left she glanced back at Elliot. He looked her straight in the eye. This was getting messy.

"I need those papers, Elliot."

"I don't have them."

She clenched her fists, the leather crunching in the quiet. She pulled her mask back down.

"Then we're going to have to do this the hard way."

Seven minutes. An ad break; the time it took to heat soup. Seven minutes was her walk to the local underground station in the morning; the section of her favourite Mozart piece. It was also the time it took to turn Elliot from a walking, talking person into one she had to prop back up into a seated position. In seven minutes his eyes had swollen, his nose had broken and so had another stanchion to her ethics. So many years. So much along the way that even in the bright of the desert she still walked in the shade.

She went out into the hall to get some air, to take a moment to remember why she shouldn't just break a chair leg off and get this over with. She might not get the papers that way but at least there'd be closure for the few survivors of Elliot's past. And anyway, what more would that do to her already tarnished record with whatever Godly entities ruled the afterlife?

The air-con hummed. The monitors and computers, too. But it wasn't that. No, it was more subtle, more out of place. She tilted her head, trying to listen to something that made her skin prickle even more than her men not being at their posts. It was like a water cooler bubbling. She watched the serene flat calm of the only water cooler in the office.

She didn't breathe as she slipped her gun out, as she took light considered footsteps towards the receptionist's half-moon desk. She glanced over. One of her men. Liquid pooled around his neck like the red of a thousand poppies. His mouth opened like a landed fish. The gill slit across his neck did the same.

Her first had been like that. His neck slit like a peach. Cleanly, the sides falling open with that same soft duress. It'd been Berlin. Winter. Cold. And his warm blood sprayed like the Neptunbrunnen. It was grotesquely functional.

She swung back around as the door opened. Her arm pivoted up and she squeezed the trigger in an instant, before registering his slight frame, the bag of donuts he carried, the small round glasses perched on his nose, the perfectly pressed suit and crisp white shirt, and the fact this wasn't the person who'd done the damage.

She blinked once and the scene registered.

He dropped like bodies do when they cease to function, when you've ripped the soul clean out with a swiftly delivered shank of metal. A donut tumbled out of the bag just as a voice behind her whispered.

"Wrong way."

Something hit her on the head and it all went black.

Chapter 13

Be as you wish to seem. Socrates

Rebecca wasn't sure what to expect from the police but utter indifference was not it.

She paced back and forth in the claustrophobically sized room. It was hot, dark, and had a rancid smell, as if whoever had been here before had no concept of personal hygiene.

For the sake of her sanity, she tied her hair up, trying to get air to the glistening skin that wept for air conditioning. She massaged the back of her neck and glanced at Annah who had been sat stock still, staring dead ahead for the last half an hour.

Finally the door opened and a figure in a badly pressed suit walked in. Both women gave him the once over and came to a very similar thought. Voicing it, Annah whispered carefully, injecting a shot of humour into a dark situation.

"He's twelve."

Rebecca muttered back.

"And wearing his father's suit."

"My name's Agent Kent. I just wanted to let you ladies know you can leave."

His voice lacked the commanding boom of a seasoned agent. It had a sort of squeaking break like a teenager.

Rebecca blinked.

Nope, not what she expected to hear.

"You found the men?"

"We didn't find anything, ma'am." He strutted to the table and perched on the end, straightening his tie. It hung badly like cheap nylon always does. "A patrol car went to the offices. Nothing was out of the ordinary."

Annah got up, hands on hips.

"So that's it?"

He shrugged nonchalantly.

"What do you want me to do with no crime being committed and no description of the men or car?"

He might be young but he had a point, Rebecca acknowledged, annoyed she'd not taken down the number plate.

Annah stood her ground, apparently not going anywhere. Agent Kent sighed and rubbed his baby smooth chin.

"Okay. Wait here."

He exited with a click of the door.

Annah frowned deeply.

"He'd get carded in a bar and he's heading this investigation?"

"Doesn't seem to be much of an investigation, by the sound of it."

"I'm not leaving until they take us seriously." Annah declared.

The door opened. The agent and another man walked in. The stranger was imposing. Tall and solid, he looked like the archetypal bodyguard.

Rebecca looked him over, noticing the small details: expensive suit but the leg was a little too long; cheap shoes; badly knotted tie; tacky cufflinks. Then one more: a red mark on his ear in the shape of a covert radio that he obviously wore too much.

"Miss Cavendish. Miss Stevens. This is Mr Peters' personal assistant who was kind enough to come down to clear any issues."

And as a lover of small details, she also noted that Elliot's long-time assistant had changed dramatically since their last encounter three months ago. No longer a short, balding man with glasses in his late forties, he appeared to have expanded upwards and outwards.

"I've spent the last week here with Elliot, and up until about thirty minutes ago when I left to come here, he was very much alive and well."

That was a new one. Rebecca doubted from his suit, demeanour, or accent, that this man was anything more than a walking bullet stopper. She certainly doubted Elliot would have swapped his butler-esque assistant for this bucket of muscle.

She shook his hand, curious he'd not made any mention of their planned meeting. Annah smiled tightly - and then proceeded to confuse the hell out of her, too.

"We've talked and we're sure it was a mixture of the sun and too little sleep. I'm surprised we didn't see six foot bunnies." The men laughed along with Annah. "If you say everything is fine then we'll be off." Her smile fluttered over to Kent. "If that's okay with you, Agent?"

He nodded slowly.

"Glad we cleared it up, ladies."

Rebecca blinked, wondering what had prompted this?

Annah carried on and picked up her bag and jacket.

"We're sorry if we wasted anyone's time, really."

The last words purred out, the flirtatious tone not missed by Agent Kent or Rebecca. His smile twinkled as they left.

Annah set a furious pace down the halls, dodging waiting bodies, simply saying, "Wait 'til we're outside."

The pounding heat was intense as they left the building. Rebecca had to mention something important.

"I've met Elliot's assistant numerous times. That was not him."

Annah stopped, not a hint of a smile on her deathly grey face. "I don't doubt it." Annah breathed deeply. "Did you hear him say he was here all week with Elliot?" Rebecca nodded, still not understanding. So Annah clarified. "That's strange because he was five seats behind us on the plane."

They both got into the jeep in silence.

Annah just drove.

Chapter 14

Everything you can imagine is real. Pablo Picasso.

Rebecca sat in the diner booth, gripping the ceramic mug tightly. She stared into the muddy liquid. Nothing made sense. Men in ski masks with guns, lying 'assistants' on the same flight...? She grabbed her phone, leaning back on wipe clean vinyl. She dialled Joy.

"Rebecca Cavendish's offices. How can I help you?"

"It's me." No pleasantries. Straight to the un-pleasantries. "Who called you to shift the meeting forward?"

Paper rustled and keyboard clacks sounded in the background. Rebecca smiled tightly as Annah returned. The young woman's colour had not come back.

Annah whispered, "I had to get something sweet," slipped along the seat opposite and started picking at a thick, golden slice of apple pie.

Rebecca winked just as Joy returned.

"It was a call from Elliot's Vegas office. Not someone I'd dealt with before, though. I confirmed. Did they break the appointment?"

"Something like that."

She drummed her nails on the heavily scratched Formica table top, thinking. Something her grandfather used to say sprung to mind: best place to start is at the beginning.

She watched Annah jabbing the pie. She had an urge to lean over and stop her, not because it was annoying, but.... She sighed. But what? But she didn't like to see Annah so agitated and thrown because...? Because? She exhaled sharply. Another unanswerable question.

"Rebecca, are you still there?"

"Sorry. Yes. I'm thinking." The beginning: the call. "Get Elliot on the phone. I want to speak to him about this meeting I was dragged halfway across the world for."

She paused, realising something quite important. She held the phone to her chest, which she knew to be pointless with the age of the digital microphone inside these things but still, it was a gesture.

"Annah?"

The brunette stopped picking at her pie and looked up, her calm exterior clearly damaged.

"I was miles away."

"How did you know what flight I was on?"

Annah's mouth opened but slammed shut just as quickly.

At least she hasn't crossed her arms, Rebecca noted.

Annah crossed her arms. Rebecca just sighed.

"If you got the info then maybe our friend used the same source?"

Annah rubbed her temples. Rebecca chewed her lip.

Suddenly the young woman looked like her old self, business-like and very determined. Annah paused, blowing a breath out.

"If this gets even a tiny bit weirder then I'll spill, but otherwise I have to protect my source."

Singular. At least there weren't spies everywhere.

"Male or female?"

"It's not a game of Guess Who."

Annah scowled, mimicking, with an exaggeratedly over the top accent, "Do they have glasses? Is it...Steve?"

Despite herself, Rebecca laughed. Not many people told her to go to Hell anymore. It was refreshing.

"Okay. I appreciate your allegiances but you need to appreciate mine, and the fact we have some very odd things happening." She resumed the call. "There's a spy in our offices. They sold my flight info and I had some problems."

She preempted Joy's exclamations.

"I'm okay and it wasn't anything..." She watched Annah curiously. "...bad. I need you to deal with it."

She could almost hear the fracturing of her assistant's temper.

"Call me back the moment you get in touch with Elliot. Day or night."

"I will."

She hung up, eyebrows rising.

"I would not like to be your spy when she finds them."

Annah flopped back in her seat, staring out over the concrete lot, speaking as though her thoughts were far away.

"What do we do now?"

Rebecca pondered that for a moment. Her manners deftly reappeared.

"I'm sorry about all of this. You go ahead." Rebecca smiled the best she could. "And thank you for helping. I do appreciate everything."

"You want me to leave you..." Annah looked around. "...here?"

Rebecca's eyes darted around the anonymous diner. The counter stretched and stretched; the kitchen steamed via the square serving hatch; a middle-aged woman was meticulously filling a sugar shaker up without a grain being spilt.

"I'm sure they won't cook me."

Annah prodded her pie.

"Don't be too sure. I think I saw a fingernail in this."

Rebecca chuckled.

"And I was going to order a slice."

Annah raised her eyebrows with a slight smirk, pushing the plate across with a rigid index finger, "Have it. It's a lot of sugar with a tiny hint of apple."

The plate stayed in the middle of the table.

"While my own cooking skills are limited, I try to keep such wonders as pastry filled with apple flavoured sugar to a limit."

"I'll never invite you around for tea at my place for homemade cake, then. Are you a whizz in the kitchen?"

"Truly downright dangerous," Rebecca snorted a soft laugh. "I'm not even allowed in the kitchen regarding baking and sweet things. Therefore I leave that to the professionals."

Annah quirked an eyebrow, "For example not here."

"Vegas has great breakfasts but desserts - pure type two diabetes waiting to happen." Rebecca sat back, staring out of the window. "And yet I quite love it here." Rebecca turned to Annah. "Your first time to the city of sin?"

Annah seemed to pause for a moment.

"No. Been here a few times. Enough to know my way around."

"Not a fan?"

Annah looked out of the window, a thoughtful frown on her face.

"Love the weather. Hate the tourists."

Rebecca laughed.

"But we're tourists."

Annah chuckled.

"I never said I made sense."

"I think it's quite beautiful here."

Annah looked over, a soft smile eliciting the same in Rebecca.

"Beautiful, yes."

Annah sat back with that happy, relaxed look back on her face.

"Listen, at least let me take you to your hotel."

Rebecca sighed. It'd be stupid to decline.

"If you're passing, it's the Hilton near Circus Circus."

"I know it. It's on my way."

"Maybe on the journey we'll realise this is all a strange misunderstanding."

Annah snorted softly.

"Sure, because it's not just criminals who wear ski-masks in the desert."

Rebecca tried to massage the tension from her temple. It was a good point.

Chapter 15

It is always one's virtues and not one's vices that precipitate one into disaster. Rebecca West

A vicious slap brought her back to life. Pain transmitters did what they were built for; from the surface of her stinging cheek and all the way back to her damaged pride.

Her mask lay on the floor next to a large crumpled heap. Tarpaulin. She glanced back, twisting to get a better look. Clarification. Tarpaulin covered bodies. She recognised their soles sticking out of the end. Her men.

Next week would have been their year long anniversary of working together: months in the heat of Jordan, in the cold of Iceland. Weeks in the wonders of Dubai, and hours that stretched like years dodging bullets in Beirut. And now they had been reduced down to two pairs of boots.

His tanned face lowered. Eyes unblinking. Hand held in an unnatural pose as if waiting for a smart reply.

She couldn't help herself.

"Did your mummy not teach you basic...?"

His arm uncoiled and struck her again. He was strong, that was for sure. However, he'd not factored in two very important things: he was too close and she was not secured yet.

In a fluid arc controlled by lats sculpted by hours of Tai-Chi, she struck the underneath of his chin and followed through as if he had not been there. The break was audible but before he had even hit the floor she was off the chair and aiding his body in a silent and graceful fall to the ground. She stayed crouched, scanning for approaching danger. Elliot and his assistant were in another tarpaulin, filled with coagulating burgundy threatening to slip over the plastic sides, like a horrific paddling pool.

This was no longer getting messy, it was a cluster fuck gone bad. It was the example they give while training operatives what to do when every ounce of shit within a five mile radius hits the fan and blows in your direction.

She lifted the shroud off of her men just a little, keeping sounds to a minimum.

She rooted around in the pocket of the nearest fallen colleague for his phone and keys. He was warm; his aftershave was clean and fresh; it didn't make it worse. She understood death. She'd been the bringer and avoider for a long time. So much so that sometimes, when she rested in whatever safe house she didn't think was safe, she wondered when it would come for her. It had to at some point. There were scales, you see. And despite believing in what she was doing, in her goal, she knew her way had become muddied over the years. It all added up. One bad deed to save ten more from happening didn't let you off the hook. Your actions were recorded like a permanent record from school. Nothing went unpunished. You learnt about higher powers, doing this job. You learnt that there had to be something bigger than you, than us, in play. She stared into his eyes. There had to be.

She lay the tarp back quietly. There was no time for goodbyes or whispered apologies. Now she had to get out of here in one piece, and get to a safe house. She felt her warm cheek from that slap.

She took off her shoes and padded quietly and quickly across the thick carpet to an open doorway. Voices stopped her and there she remained, flat against the wall while they spoke.

"Did he have the documents?"

"We think she has them."

"Have we dealt with the police?"

"Of course."

Thick Israeli accents. And that meant only one thing. She needed to get out of here - and now, before they gutted her.

Slipping the stylus out from the side of the phone she carefully called up the floor plans of the building. The bikes were parked close. The window on the opposite wall would take her to them. Except in her path was an open doorway with at least two Israeli operatives on one side. She glanced down at the plans. Oh, and one more thing. That was not a window that opened.

These things sent to test us....

In initial training her mentor used to repeat: one does not panic. One ascertains all dangers and calculates the safest options.

Yes, well, you're not stuck in a bloody building-shaped coffin, she thought to herself.

She frowned. There was only one choice. She padded back to the man who'd slapped her out of, and almost back into, unconsciousness. She pulled out his gun, aimed it at the window and started running - by the open doorway - speeding up at the exclaimed shouts - her hand bouncing at each step, and when ten away, she pulled the trigger twice. The glass fragmented, her arm folded down to shield her face as she plummeted through, crashing out into the desert heat, the steaming air, and crackling sun. She hit the ground running in a zigzag pattern as projectiles whistled close.

She got on the bike, jammed the keys in and skidded out of the line of sight and into the empty desert.

Chapter 16

What will be, will be. The sensible amongst us go with what fate has chosen, and do not try to hijack our own destiny.

The air was heavy with heat, slowing things physically and mentally. Not that either of the women needed help. After the flight, pseudo meeting, and teenage law enforcement officer, neither had much energy left. It was like watching a wind-up toy, wind down.

Rebecca cut through the warmth bouncing up from the cracked concrete parking lot. She regarded the silver 4x4 again.

"What sort of person builds something this big for urban use? This should be in a monster truck event."

Annah tenderly patted the scorching bonnet and walked around to the driver's side.

"She's great, isn't she?"

Rebecca climbed into the cab.

"Not sure about great. I'm sticking with, huge."

Annah's lips curled into a cheeky smirk.

"I'd feel guilty owning her back home, but she's okay for a few days here."

Rebecca sat back in the soft leather seat as Annah gracefully slid in. She watched Annah move for a moment, watched her find the keys, slip them in and then throw a perfectly relaxed smile she couldn't help returning.

The safety and silence of the vehicle locked everything far away. As if all that existed was them and this moment. Annah's smile reached all the way up to eyes that caught the sunlight fighting through the darkened windows. Annah didn't turn away like you were meant to. Neither did Rebecca. Everything paused.

Dancing sunshine and dappled shadows created a confusing picture. It was then that a subtle shift in their interaction became apparent. Rebecca couldn't say why her consciousness picked that very moment only that it did. It was like Chinese whispers - faint, holding back for a different time to step out into the open. Rebecca could feel them tingling her skin. Her gaze slipped away and she took a deft evasion from those thoughts. "You keep saying she."

Annah's expression was quite unreadable for a moment before the brunette frowned, seemingly shaking it off to smile tightly.

"Too pretty to be male."

The engine pumped to life. Like the deep throbbing bass of a cello, you could feel it in your bones.

Annah clicked the seatbelt on but did nothing other than drum fingernails on the wheel. Rebecca watched. Annah was clearly processing something complex as eyes narrowed, brow creased in concentration. No, Rebecca didn't interrupt that kind of focus. It was where great ideas came from.

Annah's head snapped around.

"We need to go back to that weird glass office."

Rebecca chewed on that thought, twisting it here and there, checking the validity. Maybe she could figure out what the Hell was going on and what was happening with this meeting? Maybe there was a plausible explanation to the goons? Jet lag, mirage…? Rebecca rolled her eyes at her own doubts. She waved a hand to the open road.

"Let's go."

"That easy?"

Given another few minutes to think this through, she was sure she'd have come to the same conclusion.

"Yes, that easy."

Annah slipped her sunglasses down and took the monster off the leash.

The 4x4 devoured the road hungrily until they were on that one path that led to one place. Rebecca could taste the tension, the mix of apprehension, fear and determination. It was like the rolling clouds of a heavy storm.

They slowed to a crawl as they passed through wrought iron gates. Rebecca scanned the vista, checking for danger. There was nothing. No car, no goons, just the glass building stretching out, reflecting the desert like an elongated piece of modern art.

They bounced to a stop, clearly Annah's trademark.

Silence expanded as both women sat still. It was Rebecca who popped it.

"Time to look around."

Annah held her forearm for a moment, her grip firm and gentle.

"Don't you think it's odd there's no security?"

Rebecca paused, remembering back to her very first visit last year and the fact the gates were manned and her I.D. checked.

I must be getting old not to have noticed.

Annah carried on.

"I mean, I kind of wondered the first time. This place doesn't look cheap. The gates alone probably cost more than my flat, and yet there's no-one here."

Rebecca looked around. Apart from the building there wasn't a single living thing, or item derived from one, in sight. Just endless lazy heat reaching up from the ground, hazing the air like a blanket of petrol fumes.

"Is it strange enough for you to tell me who sold my flight info?"

Annah swept glossy hair back with her sunglasses and grinned. The light caught gleaming gems and Rebecca returned the expression, suddenly not caring that much about her question.

Annah relaxed into the seat.

"Nope."

Neither broke that odd moment, the magnetic spell, the...look.

"I don't give up easily on what I want, Annah."

It was an evanescent smile that accompanied a soft response.

"Good."

The silence drifted on and on, happily entrapping Rebecca. Her worry vanished, creating a bubble, a respite in this horrific day. And so it was just Annah and that soft, gentle expression that seemed to come to the younger woman so easily as if it was confirming it was her natural state.

Rebecca had enough experience to feel the genuineness in her core and try as she could, her warning bells weren't sounding. Not a hint. Happy silence.

Wind buffeted the high side of the 4x4 shattering the spell into a million pieces. Annah's response was a skating glance away, the start of a blush and to quickly vacate the cab in favour of a weather beaten and desolate plain. Rebecca frowned, a little confused and a little enlightened. It seemed to be the theme of today.

The wind hissed around the vehicle. She opened the door and dropped down, heels hitting the rocky ground. Annah seemed uncomfortable, staring off into the distance, hands on hips then crossed then free again. Annah delivered a tight smile.

Rebecca sighed and decided it was safer not to hang about but to put her business hat on and get investigating. She walked over to where that car had been. Nothing but bare tracks in the gritty sand. She looked around, still feeling a little edgy, but it was just them and the stretched out, low confines of that glass building.

Suddenly Annah's command broke the silence. It was succinct.

"Wait there."

Before she could say a thing, Annah was striding purposefully towards the building. Rebecca blinked.

"What are you doing?"

Annah spun around, walking backward.

"If something happens to me the keys are in the jeep, my mobile in my bag."

Annah spun back and carried on. Rebecca was incredulous. She looked between the building and Annah, and the safety of the jeep. Reality clicked her brain in gear as the threat level became apparent. Her eyes scanned everywhere and everything as best she could. For a few long minutes she lost sight of Annah who disappeared around the back of the building. That was when her muscles really tensed up. Added to the baking, unbearable heat, this wasn't going to plan. Then Annah reappeared, walked back and shrugged.

"I checked the door. No one answered. The lock isn't forced, though. At least we know Elliot's not in there."

Rebecca's stress popped and a chastising sentence rushed out.

"Please don't go walking off like that again."

Annah slipped her sunglasses on top of her head, having enough sense, it seemed, to look a little contrite.

"I didn't want to stand here and have a building full of heavies come running out to surprise us."

Rebecca swallowed an edgy sentence about sense and a hundred reasons why it was a stupid thing to do.

"Valid point." However. "But still, do not do that again."

Annah seemed to bite back a comment then just sighed, nodded and ran hands through her hair.

"Okay. I won't."

"I'm jumpy. Sorry." Rebecca sucked a hot breath in. Adrenaline pumped via every artery. "Where is Elliot?"

Annah stood beside her, thinking out loud.

"It's like they all disappeared. Security, his assistant...his whole office."

So much for getting the revelation of a clue, Rebecca thought as her gaze skittered around. Except: two white cylinders near the tip of her shoe were not part of the desert - unless the desert smoked menthols.

Rebecca leant down, taking a closer look. She soon had a companion as Annah scooted down, too. Rebecca tried to ignore that tingling in her skin.

"Cigarette butts."

They were in a hollow in the hard earth. She tapped one gently with the tip of her shoe, revealing the brand mark: a Maltese cross.

Annah peered closer, tucking a strand of hair behind her ear.

"What brand is that?"

"I don't know yet. Don't touch them."

Annah frowned.

"Should either of us be moving them?"

"The police don't think anything happened, so this isn't evidence - at the moment."

Annah voiced the main point here.

"Who'd stand in the middle of the parking lot, out in this heat long enough to smoke two cigarettes?"

"Exactly."

Rebecca walked back to the 4x4. She flipped open her bag and pulled something out. She rejoined Annah who was now up and about, scowling, clearly on a terrible connection, mobile phone pressed to her ear.

"I can't hear you. Bad line," Annah shouted, covering her other ear with a hand. "I'll call later." The phone clicked shut with, "Work." Annah did a double-take. "Do you always carry those around?"

"I once lost my briefcase key at airport security, so now I bag it and tag it, and I'm careful." Without touching them, Rebecca slipped the butts into the clear baggie and then added with a self satisfied smirk, "Also, I watch C.S.I."

Annah snorted a laugh, slapping a hand over her mouth afterward, cheeks turning a rosy shade. Her muffled response was adorable.

"Sorry. I wasn't expecting that."

Rebecca's eyebrows slipped up.

"I wasn't expecting that, either. Anything else I should know about? Can you sneeze with your eyes open?"

Annah grabbed the baggie, walking off to the 4x4, shouting over her shoulder.

"Next time I sneeze I'll make sure I'm facing you so you can find out."

Rebecca burst out laughing as she watched her climb up into the cab.

Annah leant out of the window and called over.

"Come on, we have a mystery to solve!"

She whispered, keeping it to herself, as the brunette smiled.

"A mystery...? Yes, we do and I think there's more than one."

Chapter 17

Rigor mortis: stiffness of death.

"Do you want to stop anywhere before the hotel?" Annah enquired over the deep hum of the engine as it powered them along.

An urge for something she had in Vegas last time floated to the surface. Sometimes cravings were an odd thing. She pondered it. Well, it was based on the only English drink that was guaranteed to restore one's sanity. She smiled to herself. Made a little sense.

"Actually, yes. I could do with an iced-tea."

Annah glanced across.

"That's bizarre."

Rebecca smirked.

"You did ask."

She pointed out of the windscreen at the fast approaching diner. Annah pulled into the parking lot, stating simply with raised eyebrows, "This place has seen better days."

Rebecca hadn't noticed the previous time she was here, mainly because she'd been too focused on hydrating back from the crispy shell the sun had transformed her into. Red paint was peeling from the sun-baked wood and the glass was blurry from dust, dirt and, she bet, grease. It wouldn't be her first, second or hundredth choice to cure hunger pangs. However, they weren't here to have dinner by candlelight. She needed to think.

"Shame on you, judging a book by its cover, Annah."

Annah bounced the jeep to a stop with a rueful smile and a, "Sorry," then glanced out of the window. "You've eaten here?"

The incredulousness of her tone shone. Rebecca found it quite amusing.

"It's a long story."

Annah shifted side on.

"I think we've got time."

Rebecca mirrored her pose, happy to chat. Part of her brain questioned this chemistry, this connection, but the part that worked on instinct was tired of listening. Whatever the reason, she didn't want to tempt fate into recalling the gesture of goodwill to bring someone so interesting into her life, however temporarily.

Rebecca sank into the languid moment.

"We do?"

Annah nodded.

"We do. Long version, please, Miss Cavendish."

"You make me sound like a school mistress."

There was a pause as Annah's gaze flickered over her.

"I'd have gone to school more if you'd been mine." Annah winked and before Rebecca could even react she carried on, "Anyway, I've never known a school mistress who wears exclusive designer clothes." Annah reached across and lifted a strand of hair with one finger. "Has her hair cut every four weeks." The strand was turned over. "And if it's dyed, I'm having trouble telling." That finger dropped to Rebecca's hand. "Manicured nails. Scar-less hands." Pausing, lifting Rebecca's index finger with her own warm hand. "Except this one. Rogue nail file?"

Rebecca was transfixed.

"A chisel, actually."

Annah smiled softly. Seemed she was, too.

"That's a story I'll enjoy hearing." Annah gently put the hand back where it was found. "Anyway, I'm diverting you. The story, please."

Rebecca's skin tingled as Annah's fingers left it. For a moment Rebecca lost her words, her train of thought deftly failing to stop at the next station. She frowned and with an inhale pulled the emergency cord. Her mind clicked back on track.

"I was here quite a few months ago. I'd hired out a jeep but, for whatever reason, the tank didn't get filled up and the gauge was stuck on full. I broke down halfway between Elliot's offices and..." She tilted her head over to the ramshackle building. "...there. My phone had no reception. I was in a knee length skirt and heels that got shredded after a hundred yards. One thing in my favour, I'd just missed the midday sun." She rested her head on the seat, eyes focusing off somewhere in the distance. "It took me an hour to get here, and I've never been happier to see a half lit neon sign in my life." She smiled. "They serve the best iced-tea I've had."

"Could that be a judgement derived from being dangerously dehydrated?"

Rebecca laughed, glancing at her companion.

"Yes, it could. I'm holding back my final decision for today, so..."

A small flash like a watch-face reflection made Rebecca squint. She held her hand up, deflecting, before it fired a shot through her mind and blasted everything else into silence. Her muscles froze.

"What happened?" Annah asked.

Without shifting her tightly focused gaze, Rebecca slipped out of the 4x4.

"That flash. It's from the offices."

Annah jumped out, joining her. They marched towards a parked, beaten up sedan.

"You've lost me." Annah said, eyebrows furrowed, slipping sunglasses down to stop the penetrating rays of the sun that were happiest grilling peoples' pupils.

Rebecca's answer was more to herself.

"I didn't remember before."

Another flash and Rebecca squinted and pointed. Annah looked over, oblivious. They stared at a reflective...something, hanging from the rear view mirror inside that dark car.

Rebecca's pulse was racing and, despite the dry heat, a bead of sweat trickled down the V of her back. Rebecca carried on as they closed in.

"This is the same car that was outside Elliot's offices."

"Are you sure?"

Rebecca got her phone out and dialled.

"Rebecca Cavendish's offices. How can I help you?"

"Joy, it's me. Can you text me the number of whoever rescheduled the meeting? I'll call you later to talk through the other things."

There was a pause.

"Sent. I'm working late tonight so I'll be here if you need anything."

Rebecca ended the call. Finally her phone beeped as an envelope flashed received. She opened it, hitting dial, not holding it to her ear. A dull ring-tone sounded from somewhere close. They both turned to the only somewhere close: that dark car.

They stood in front of the rusting bonnet. The windscreen had a thin layer of dust, making it hard to see in clearly. Rebecca moved to the side window, swiping away a gritty streak with her palm and looked in. What she saw made her snap upright.

She flipped her phone shut and the ring-tone died.

"Annah, go into the diner and call the police."

Rebecca felt her blood drain; her chest heaved as she gulped fire hot air.

Annah walked closer, glancing around, eyes scanning alertly.

"Explain."

Rebecca tried to spin her back around. Annah took her hand gently, twisting it and freeing herself with expert grace.

"I'm not moving. What's in there?"

Rebecca looked deeply into her eyes. This was a time for compartmentalising the bad stuff. She held Annah's face in her hands.

"Trust me and go to the diner. Call the police from a landline so they have the address."

Annah frowned for a moment but finally nodded.

"Okay."

Before Annah turned to do Rebecca's bidding, one question came out. "What do I tell them?"

Rebecca swayed gently before regaining control. Her fists balled.

"Tell them I've found Elliot Peters and his assistant." Annah's eyes widened and she turned and ran towards the diner.

Chapter 18

Sometimes your most available avenue is to keep your mouth shut and hope for the best.

"If we need anything more we'll let you know."

Agent Kent fluffed and puffed himself up to his full five foot six as the real meaning of that sentence hung in the air.

Rebecca snatched the jacket she'd strewn on the uneven brick wall about an hour ago and stalked away.

"Don't leave the State - or country," he called after her, his shrill voice barely making it through the heavy heat.

She almost swung around and punched him. Her eyes stung from the dust, her cheeks were tight from the heat, and her stomach felt awful at the memory of the back seat passengers of the dark sedan. The only thing keeping her legs moving was the sight of Annah pacing back and forth, chewing a nail in front of that obscenely huge bloody jeep.

Annah jumped in the cab, flipped the passenger door open and fired the engine. Rebecca slammed the door, put the belt on and banged her head back on the padded seat.

Annah reached over, taking her hand, not squeezing or rubbing but just holding it as if to say, 'I'm here.'

"Drive anywhere. Please."

Annah let go, didn't say a word, and pulled them out of the lot.

Chapter 19

Be faithful in small things because it is in them that your strength lies.
Mother Teresa

Dirt and lime scale clung to every dip and chip on the bathroom sink. She shifted on the side of the toilet seat, dug another chunk of glass out of her sole and dropped it into the basin with the others. It clunked and clanked and circled for a while, like a roulette ball, before the plughole swallowed it whole.

She poured some hydrogen peroxide onto a rag. The sopping wetness made her hand cold. Her limbs stuttered a pause as they processed what that fluid plus an open wound would feel like. Muscle memory was Queen of this castle, but as with most royalty, there's always a time for revolution.

She pressed the rag to her foot and held it close. Pupils dilated, muscles tensed, and her neck arched as she silently screamed up to a ceiling stained with dirty watermark clouds.

Mascara tears cut down her cheeks. She carefully lay down on a thin towel on the bathroom floor, clutching the phone, waiting for instructions to answer her earlier text.

The ring tone filled the small bathroom. On ring three she pressed the cold plastic to her ear.

"Please confirm your identity."

Soothing soulless tones of the southing soulless female operator.

There was a slight echo. It was on a speaker. The room was probably filled with people trying to clear this mess up.

"White Crane."

"Hello, White Crane. Please supply the corresponding words: Foxtrot. Foxtrot. Delta. Echo. Alpha. Delta."

The training had been intense; her answer automatic. She watched the stains on the ceiling. Hexadecimal code.

"Navajo White."

"Foxtrot. Foxtrot. Delta. Seven. Zero. Zero."

She frowned. For God sake. "Gold."

"Please describe your situation, White Crane."

"I'm having a party and I've run out of dip."

"Please describe your situation, White Crane."

"Foxtrot. Foxtrot. Four. Five. Zero. Zero."

Hexadecimal for orange red. Mission failed. Operative temporarily safe and seeking extraction.

Voices in the background. It was hard to make out what was happening. There was a pause before the woman came back on.

"I have a negative on that, White Crane. Are you injured?"

She sat up, only then realising it was a very poor idea. She held her cool palm to her hot cheek. Her side twinged painfully. She lifted her dark top up to find a nasty long line of gapping red flesh. A bullet had nicked deep.

"Where's my handler?"

"White Crane..."

She got to her knees and then her feet, holding the phone in front of her mouth.

"Where's my handler!"

She slapped the phone on the edge of the bath and turned the speaker on. The wound needed closing before it got infected or just bled so much that it'd be impossible to walk around. Or worse.

She grabbed at a pull cord attached to a cheap bar heater above the mirror.

"We're getting him."

"Take your time. Not like this is urgent," she muttered, knowing it would be heard by the whole room.

The bar started to change to orange. She stood, just watching, focusing only on that colour and not more imminent pain. She'd had stitches, breaks, scrapes, gouges - pain didn't get less it just became a familiar encounter, one that you didn't run to avoid but simply greeted with gritted teeth and an infinitely bloodied determination.

Hurting foot on one end of the towel, she pulled sharply and ripped a section off. She rolled it between her hands. The bars were now red. It needed three good vicious tugs to get the cheap heater to come away from the wall.

"I'm here."

Her handler. Nick. He always sounded gruff, like a shaggy dog.

"Give me thirty seconds. I have a small problem."

"With?"

"A paper cut."

She bit down on the rag and held the bar to the line of flesh. It was like Sunday mornings cooking breakfast. It sizzled and fried, spat and hissed.

"What's going on?"

Searing, white hot pain that was unimaginable took hold. This time there was no silent scream but a very audible, deep, animalistic cry. Her vision snowed as all blood shrank back to covet vital organs due to the shock of what her body sensed as an attack.

She sat back down quickly, throwing the heater to one side.

"I need extraction," she rasped out.

Her hearing fuzzed and then it all went dark again.

Chapter 20

You had better live your best and act your best and think your best today; for today is the sure preparation for tomorrow and all the other tomorrows that follow. Harriet Martineau

Rebecca didn't know how long they'd been on the road for. The buildings, streets, signs, neons of the strip, it all blurred until she barely registered the fading light and encroaching darkness. They bounced to a stop, the jarring feeling familiar, feeling good. A warm hand took her own.

"Come on. Let's get inside."

Rebecca glanced out into the darkness. This was not the Hilton, unless they'd downsized to a two storey, white and delicately light blue stucco house. It was reminiscent of a maelstrom visit to The Catherine Palace in Russia, spent arranging the land purchase for a set of hotels.

"Where are we?"

"I have this place for the week. I hate hotels. I knew my way here so...."

Neither had enough energy to fill the pause.

Rebecca felt nothing other than the thumb comfortingly stroking the skin of her palm. After a while she nodded and exhaled deeply.

"Take me on the tour?"

"That I can do."

Large, airy and brick built, the temperature was as pleasant as the décor. The style was a smudged merge of numerous colourful cultures. Rebecca glanced about, trying to take it all in. The Baroque staircase would be of more interest when her level of energy dragged itself back from the depths of despair.

She put her case down and pulled her jacket off. She was getting more and more aggravated. She was exhausted, thirsty, she felt grimy, her hair was limp, even her hands felt filthy; she didn't want to look under her nails because she could feel grains of sand. It was like the desert was refusing to let her go, had branded her with the white heat it threw from every rock. She paused in the middle of the hall, on a brightly coloured circular rug.

Annah reached out, laying a hand on her arm.

"Go take a shower. You'll feel better."

Rebecca laughed at the irony of someone having known her a day, yet able to read her mind. However it was Vegas where Elvis could marry you in a drive-thru.

"I need today to end."

Annah sighed deeply.

"You and me both."

The house was simply set out and it was easy to follow directions to the large bathroom without incident.

"About time something went right," she muttered to her sorry looking reflection.

She was pale, tired...no, exhausted, and looked like she'd lost her entire fortune on the blackjack table.

She dialled Joy, getting the office answer machine. She looked at the clock and added eight hours for the time difference. She sighed and flipped her phone closed. She could phone Joy at home but it'd be too late to action much and she'd just worry too much.

She started to unbutton her shirt.

"If only today had been that easy."

The shower was heavenly. Hands planted on the tiles either side of the solid metal shower spray, the stream fell over her tired body. The shampoo smelt of mango, the conditioner of lemon, the shower gel was lime. The burst to her senses was invigorating.

She towel dried her hair but left it loose. She didn't know where the hairdryer was, and anyway, it just encouraged split ends. She paused at that thought.

"Amazing. Even in the most horrid times, the things that remain are fashion tips drummed in by years of reading tacky magazines."

The last thing she just had to do was change her contact lenses. Her head fell back as she blinked the new ones in. She almost groaned with delight at the feeling of cleanliness that was now complete.

She sat heavily on the bed, pulling the robe tighter. The thin cotton was soft, comforting, it felt like a protective cocoon. For the first time today her body let go of a little tension.

A knock at her door.

"It's your house," she forced lightly, teasingly, happy for the company that would be a welcome distraction.

Two emerald eyes sparkled as the rest of Annah peered around the gap. No longer in the sharp tailoring of a suit but dressed in well worn jeans and a loose grey tee-shirt, it was quite a difference.

"How are you doing - if that's not one of the most stupid questions you've ever been asked?"

Some deep part of Rebecca bristled, but instead of hiding it like last time she just let it out.

"You have this amazing ability to word your questions in exactly the same manner as my ex husband."

Annah grimaced.

"I picked a great day to be remembered like that."

Rebecca shook her head with a drained smile.

"You don't deserve any of that anger."

Annah set down a steaming mug on the side table.

"I took a risk on cocoa. I didn't know about sugar, so it's bitter rather than sweet."

Rebecca didn't need to be told. The aroma wafting through the room made her mouth water and stomach clench.

"Good choice." She regarded her companion closely. "You've done your homework, Miss Stevens. You know a lot of small things about me."

"My research didn't stretch to going through your rubbish bins."

"Thankfully."

Annah chuckled softly.

"Why, are you on a pack of Pop Tarts a day? Is there an addiction I should know about?"

Rebecca slapped her wrists together and offered them up.

"Caught red-handed."

She paused and lowered her hands with a scowl. She'd come pretty close to being hauled down to the station earlier. If Kent had one single strip of evidence on her, he would have. As it was, his hands were tied - just like the passengers of the dark sedan. An image of two pairs of cloudy vacant eyes appeared in Rebecca's mind. She'd known neither man was alive: pallid skin, milky irises, and of course, a long peeled apart slit along their throats. That was the giveaway. At the time her only instinct was to push Annah away so she wouldn't have it emblazoned in her nightmares for years to come. That she'd managed. She'd also managed not to pass out at seeing both Elliot and that bodyguard dead. It was a feat.

The tactile brunette brought her back to the present with a hand on her shoulder. Rebecca looked up into an open and honest face. Annah smiled down like a holy picture of serenity.

"Drink your cocoa."

Rebecca found herself staring.

"Join me?"

Annah donned a glitteringly infectious smile and carefully carried her full mug over to the long window seat. Rebecca started mentally categorising all the reasons she didn't want her to leave so soon. Many of them weren't easy to rationalise.

She sipped her drink, smiling at the taste of home. Annah watched.

"I'm never sure about making it for someone else. I'm normally competing with a mother's recipe, and that's always going to go bad."

Rebecca lifted her mug in cheers.

"Mine added cinnamon. But really, this is very good."

Annah inhaled the steam from hers and her eyes closed and lips lifted to a soft smile.

"We had it with nutmeg, but the kitchen here is kind of spiceless."

"I'm thrilled it's not instant," Rebecca stated simply, the creamy full flavour proving just as good as what she conjured up during sleepless nights.

"No way. Cooked on the stove with a pile of pans in the sink to prove it."

They drifted into a peaceful silence. Annah watched the view from the large window while Rebecca was just grateful to finally have some calm in the tumultuous day.

Annah pushed her face closer to the glass. Her eyebrows pinged up.

"We have a visitor."

Rebecca walked over quickly, pressing fingertips against the window, peering out.

"A burglar?"

Annah tapped a finger in the air, carefully stopping short of the glass.

"Only if you're a nut."

Annah pointed to the base of a large tree out back.

"Squirrel."

"They have squirrels here?"

Annah chuckled.

"And racoons."

Rebecca sat down on the bench, folding a leg under herself. She watched the little bouncing bundle of fur. It scurried about, stopped, froze, and then scampered off up another tree. There was something about that innocent little creature that reminded her.

"I have some in my garden at home. They're very amusing to watch." Rebecca smiled as a memory surfaced. "During quite a harsh autumn when I was a child, they filled a hollow with the most acorns I'd ever seen. My grandfather built a little shelter over it to keep them dry."

Annah glanced directly up at her with an easy smile.

"An acorn awning?"

"At Chez Cavendish, even the squirrels are treated impeccably."

Annah paused for a moment before pulling her legs up and resting her chin on her knees. Her smile fell.

"I want to check. I'm not going to quiz you, but how are you doing after everything?"

The honest question begged an honest answer.

"I've had better days." Rebecca snorted softly. "Although that isn't hard."

Warm and concerned eyes pulled more from her.

"You expect this sort of thing happens to other people, and when it happens to you?" A pause. "I have no frame of reference."

Annah nodded seriously.

"We've stumbled into something we need to stay very far away from."

Rebecca idly rubbed a thumb across the lip of the mug, calculating and spewing forth her findings.

"If we'd been on time for that meeting, I'd be dead."

Annah looked at her.

"Probably. And it's good you realise that. This isn't a crime series on TV where the good guys win in the end. This is real life, and the good guys bleed just as red as the bad guys."

"Are you saying this to scare me?"

Annah's expression became pained.

"Rebecca, I'm saying it to keep you alive."

"That's brutally honest." She sipped mechanically. "I'm not looking to solve a case. I will not end up like..." She shifted. "...the men in that car."

Annah frowned.

"I came in to take your mind off this, not drag it back. Sorry."

"Don't be. Not much can change what's happened."

Annah sighed deeply.

"Don't think about it."

Rebecca sipped the slowly cooling cocoa, cupping the mug with both hands. She knew what she needed to do, but between where she was and where she wanted to be was a seemingly impassable quagmire.

"That's easier said than done."

The foggy silence drifted. Rebecca looked towards the gardens, not seeing them, just her own ghostly reflection.

What a shocking mess this is turning out to be, she thought.

"I know what'll help."

Rebecca perked up a little.

"Should I be worried or eager?"

The younger woman's laugh was rich.

"Eager, I hope." Annah frowned. "Wait. Do you have a swimsuit?"

Rebecca smiled, her eyebrows dipping to a perplexed, but intrigued, frown. Sometimes Annah asked the most curious questions at the most curious times.

"We're going swimming?"

"Hot tub." Annah blinked. "I mean, there's a hot tub out back. It's fantastic."

"Hmmm," was all she could manage.

A hot tub?

Annah took hold of her face with soft fingertips and her twinkling eyes did the rest.

"Trust me."

Rebecca couldn't think of a single reason not to.

The hunt for the bathing costume was a quick one. She rarely used it but always packed it - a bit like her travel umbrella that had also accompanied her around the globe several times, even rolling along here where, she assumed, this month's rainfall could fit in an egg cup.

Rebecca glanced at the full length mirror as she grabbed a towel. Now she was glad she'd worked more after the divorce and not taken up comfort eating. The suit was high cut on the leg and low on the cleavage.

Sophia had made her get it one Saturday, saying, "Martin would turn in his grave. Buy it." She'd politely reminded her friend that he wasn't dead, but Sophia had just waved a hand, picked up a beach bag and muttered, "If you say so."

But she knew what Sophia meant. Martin wouldn't have approved. He'd have given her that look, the one equally of use when you needed to silently chastise a small child in a public place. Then he would have glanced away, any further comments being clipped and staccato. She smiled, taking a deep breath. Freedom was liberating.

"Every cloud has a silver lining."

She slipped a long black shirt on for a hint of modesty and padded down and out to the garden.

The scene that greeted her was a visual haven in a day that had dried her out like a sycamore pod. Under-lit by blue halogens, the octagonal wooden hot tub with its steaming, bubbling and rolling white water looked divine.

A head popped up from the water and Annah pushed flat palms back, slicking her hair off her face with graceful ease. And then came the rest: a steaming wet, bikini-clad body exited and stretched like a woken cat.

Rebecca stared. Objectively speaking she was a beautiful woman with distinctive cheekbones, athletically feminine body and especially the gemstone eyes. Those Chinese whispers whispered. They weren't so objective.

Annah pointed over to a large wrought iron table and raised her eyebrows, clearly waiting. Rebecca blinked.

"Sorry?"

"I said, can you bring the wine?"

Rebecca pushed those whispers far away, making sure all unwanted thoughts were barred for the moment.

"Of course."

She deposited her towel, shrugged her shirt, snagged the top of the wine bottle and climbed the stairs grateful the heat of the day had given way to the wonderfully cool evening. She groaned as the water ate her limbs.

"My muscles are going to adore you, Annah."

"That's the plan."

Rebecca sat on a step, water lapping her collarbone, and floated a hand in the escaping large bubbles. Annah slipped over and held two flute glasses out. She wiggled her eyebrows mischievously.

"Fill us up."

Rebecca did just that and then rested the bottle on the ledge of the tub. Annah held her glass up, her mouth opening and closing wordlessly before frowning then shrugged almost apologetically.

"I can't think of a good toast. My sister got me one of those silly idiot-guide books last Christmas on speeches and stuff, but..."

"You didn't read it?"

Annah laughed.

"If I did, I'd have managed something better than," Annah dropped her mouth open and pretended to fumble with her words again.

This is what I need, Rebecca mused as she chinked her glass to her lively companion's.

"Let me help you out. To less stressful times."

Annah shook her head with a smile and settled back.

"See, you make it seem so easy." Annah sipped the wine and pulled a face. "Unique year."

Rebecca swirled the liquid, trying to inhale the fragrance but just got mild chlorine instead. She took a small sip of the light and fruity wine and sent a playful glare over to the woman who was saluting her. She shook her head and laughed.

"I thought I was going to be drinking boat sealant. It's very good."

Annah winked.

"Of course it is. It's Australian."

Rebecca leant right back, sinking down, night sky watching. The stars were almost invisible due to the city lights, but still it was relaxing. The endless, hopeful expanse seemed limitless and beautiful.

Annah sat close, sighing deeply. Her soft voice drifted through the gentle hush.

"I'd love one of these in London."

Rebecca sank deeper into warmth that held her like a duvet on a cold winter's morning. She figured she'd need to be shoehorned out of this thing eventually.

"The water's delicious. Why don't you get one?"

Annah snorted a laugh.

"I live in SoHo."

Rebecca couldn't imagine anywhere in that tight square of bustling central London having enough room for even a quarter of the hot tub. She pushed up on an elbow.

"It's so noisy there, how do you get any peace?"

"It was nice a few years ago, but now..."

Annah shrugged a shoulder and looked around the quiet and very private garden, as if seeing it for the first time. Rebecca nudged her gently with a shoulder, the other woman's skin just as warm as the water.

"Now?"

"Now I want something different," came the vague reply.

Rebecca wasn't one to be evaded.

"Different, how? Less noise and more space?"

"I guess that'd be nice."

Curiosity peaked and she pushed Annah a little more.

"But?"

"Are you quizzing me?"

Rebecca played her ace quickly.

"I am, and it's taking my mind off of earlier."

Annah looked bemused.

"Guilt trip. Clever."

"Thank you. So. But?" she drew the word out.

Annah's fingers played with the rim of the tub.

"It sounds stupid."

"I trusted you and came out here and the night is wonderful. You should trust me."

Annah's gaze hid nothing. It offered up a pure sensory exploration that would have artists lining up to paint her, to capture that essence and condemn it to a canvas sentence.

"I want something more than a bachelorette pad." Annah's eyes darted away. "It sounds silly but I want to swap the revolving door I've been using, for something with at least a Yale lock, you know?" Annah paused and put her wine glass down. "The wine's making me blue."

Rebecca took a sip of hers, wanting to clarify one thing to the beautiful young woman beside her.

"I realise you know about my divorce. You got a seat on my flight, for god sake. You probably know every squalid detail." Rebecca's gaze went nowhere in particular. "But a serious relationship or even marriage doesn't always make things more stable."

Her vision was filled with two concerned eyes that even in this darkness she knew shone out like Chinese jade. Warm fingers touched her own.

"I read about it in the Times about five months ago. I'm not as good a hawk as you think. My research got me a skeleton, and as sappy as it sounds, I never thought I'd get the chance to flesh it out - but I have and I'm very grateful."

Rebecca searched those eyes, that face, for a hint of malice or something amiss, but the proverbial cupboard was bare.

She tutted, annoyed at her touchiness over that subject.

"Ignore me. I got custody of the grouchiness."

"What did he get custody of?"

She couldn't help the wide grin that broke onto her mouth.

"Nothing."

It was only then her hand was released as Annah burst out laughing.

Time vanished and carried them through the next hour as they had a bouncing discussion. Rebecca loved old noir films; Annah's favourite director was Hitchcock. Rebecca hated formal restaurants; Annah loved impromptu picnics. They sidestepped politics, and finished off on a bizarre jump to the economic stability of Japan. That's when both women looked at each other and smiled.

Annah splashed her face with warm water.

"I don't deal with wine well. My two glasses have gone to my head." Annah paused and stared at her fingers. "And I've pruned." Her thumb extended the index finger of Rebecca's hand. "You have, too."

Rebecca smiled as she was shown her own water wrinkled finger. She wiggled it. Annah didn't let go for a long moment before finally doing so with a perplexed frown.

"Sorry." Annah stood and wobbled. "That's the Jacuzzi waves not the wine."

"Sure?"

Annah smiled tightly.

"Maybe a bit of both."

Rebecca stood and linked arms. Annah's skin was warm and smooth and as they made it out of the pool, it felt…. Rebecca hunted for the word: comfortable. No, that wasn't it. They walked along. Intimate. That was more apt a description.

"Come on. Let's get you upstairs." Rebecca said.

There wasn't an argument. Annah turned off the tub and lights and waved the glasses and wine away until the morning.

Annah towel dried her hair as they walked up the cool stairs. Rebecca put her hand on the small of her back and let her lead. The last thing she wanted was Miss Tipsy here to fall over her own feet and take a dive down the stairs.

They neared the top, muscles flexing easily under her palm, smooth skin pulling taut with each step. Her thumb moved up the dip of Annah's spine a fraction and the younger woman slowed and glanced back, hitting Rebecca with a very intense look. The air almost crackled. For some unknown reason Rebecca pulled her hand away. It wasn't embarrassment or shame. It wasn't discomfort. Then she realised why. It was because that look made the Chinese whisper almost audible and she wasn't ready for that yet. Not tonight. Not so whatever oddity going on here would forever be tainted by the earlier events.

Annah kept walking and only her words fell behind.

"You didn't have to move your hand."

Rebecca didn't answer out loud, *I know, and that's why I did.*

They stopped outside Rebecca's room. The silence was heavy. Rebecca gripped her towel tightly, suddenly aware how little she was wearing.

It was Annah who spoke again.

"Did the tub help you relax?"

"Yes. Very much so."

"I'm glad." Annah smiled a light but genuine smile that made her eyes glitter. "Goodnight, Rebecca."

And with fingertips gently coming to rest on Rebecca's jaw, the younger woman leant in and softly kissed both cheeks, except in deference to popular tradition, it was not a superficial air kiss. The contact was bare but there, and it was that contact that thrummed Rebecca's heart rate. It was scarcely enough time to process the touch, the way all of that body heat felt, scarcely enough time to react before Annah pulled all of herself back, away, and added, "Sweet dreams."

Annah walked down the hallway, stopping for one moment before entering her room, whispering softly.

"At least tomorrow can't be any worse than today."

Fate just loves a challenge.

Chapter 21

All policies allowed in war and love. Susannah Centlivre

She awoke to white tiles, a blood soaked towel and that bar heater with remnants of burnt flesh on it. Little pieces stuck fast, held by charred stretches of epidermis. White, brown, multi-coloured.

The room smelt acrid, like that night in Turin trying to save documents from a burning Embassy. That had smelt acrid, of burning hair and burnt flesh, too. And when she'd found the safe she'd heard the sounds of crying, whimpering, gasping and rasping.

She'd walked out of the Embassy six minutes later with the file and that germ planted deep. And it had blossomed into a bright memory in her nightmares. She'd been there to get documents. Documents that saved many lives. It wasn't her job to rescue but to retrieve. You had to remember the task and stick to it. Rescue and retrieve. Not save.

Not save.

The motel bathroom was dark. Silent, as well. She took a moment to get her bearings and then got to work. A quick sweep of the room outside afforded some sense of security. The slithers of paper in the door and window jams were still there. No-one had disturbed her. Yet. But they'd be coming. Friendly or not. They'd be here soon.

It took ten minutes to clean the mess in the bathroom: the blood off of the taps; put the heater back on the wall so it didn't look too obvious; pick herself out from the filaments.

The shower was perfunctory. Just enough to get her dirty hair blonde again, and to clean away the blood from various parts. Pink water funnelled down the chipped metal plughole. After drying off she doused the towel in bleach and wiped all the surfaces she'd touched. That was better. Calming. Bleach was clean; it meant the end of a job in whatever capacity.

She got dressed and sat down on the bed. Time was not her friend. Whatever would be happening, she needed to move locations. Now.

The lights had been left off on purpose. She knelt down by a dirty window and watched the car park outside. It seemed okay, but really, you never knew these things until you opened the door. In Moscow they'd got close enough to almost garrotte her. Her nail clipped the dip she still had in her neck and on automatic she felt for the stiletto knife tucked into her ankle holster. The ceramic didn't set off metal detectors but could cut through a windpipe with a decent amount of force - which was the fate of the garrotter. He'd bled out like road kill in the gutter. She'd watched, not for pleasure but because you needed to confirm some kills more than others. Especially when the longevity of your own mortality had almost come to an end.

That needed a line drawn under it. She's drawn one on his jugular. Neat. Quick.

She grabbed her coat and opened the door forgetting what that sudden movement would do. Her wound screamed. She clutched her side. Slow deep breaths. Measured. Get control quickly when in the open and vulnerable.

She needed sleep, time for her body to repair. She needed somewhere safe.

Vegas was hot and intense, even at night. It never got any better, never a respite, never a dip, even when it rained. This place was like a heavy blanket on a boiling night. Just plain uncomfortable.

She rounded a corner and looked up. Bright lights and big city glare. It was obscene. It was beautiful. it was everything you shouldn't love but did. The right and wrong. The garish and spectacular. It was the effervescent pill in a flat calm glass of water.

"And this is why the ice-caps are melting," she muttered as she hit the strip.

Her phone vibrated.

"It's me. It's a secure line."

She stopped at her voice. Just stopped dead on the pavement. Tourists parted around her like she was a permanent and immovable fixture. This was the last person she expected to hear from.

The woman carried on.

"I'm sending your phone details now." The mobile pinged. *"Book into this hotel. Your name is Miss Walkenbach. Your room is paid for. You'll receive further instructions later."*

"Instructions you want me to follow?"

"Depends how much you like the prolonged existence of your life, I suppose," but there was a lightness to her words.

"You charmer."

There was a pause.

"Nina," She loved the way Diane never seemed to care about covers. *"Are you injured?"*

"I'm fine to carry on."

"I didn't ask that."

She stood still amongst a sea of moving bodies. Not one of them touched her.

"Minor and treated."

"How minor?"

"I thought you'd left the trade?"

"I have."

"So you understand how perplexing it is to have you call?"

"Nick couldn't get you extracted. They needed someone slightly...less conspicuous."

Nina squeezed the mobile, her fingers gripping hard. Made sense. Diane wasn't intensely monitored anymore - and her contacts were still immense.

"How minor?"

That remained hanging. This was a secure line, but still. One day someone was a friend and next they were swapping sides and stabbing you in the aorta. This game was only fair if you knew the rules - you have no true allies, only those who have not turned on you yet.

"Are you officially helping?"

"Whatever makes you feel better about answering."

"I'm not going to drop down dead but I'll need some stitches and antibiotics soon."

"I'll arrange it. This is going to hit the news soon. So, what happened?"

Nina sighed and moved to the edge of the pavement, back against the wall of a shop. This was more bad news added to a mountain of bad news that was already really bad news.

"God's children. At least three of them. Although it's safe to assume there are only two now." She pulled her jacket around tighter, not for warmth but because it felt like her cut was re-opening. "Grandfather didn't tell me where the information was before he passed."

"Did you...?"

"No. It wasn't me. But Brother Jehovah was overly stern. I only did what was necessary for me to stay pretty, because one of them had other ideas."

"I've arranged for a local to help you out."

Nina grimaced at that thought.

"I don't want..."

"It's not a request."

It never was.

She ran her tongue over her teeth, taking a moment to shrug that assertion of power off. From anyone else it'd be infuriating but from the woman who'd trained her it was tinged with a forgivable quality.

"Who?"

"No-one you know. Name of Nicholson."

"I can't be partnered with someone who doesn't even have a proper fake name."

"It's not a request," was chuckled down the line.

"Nicholson," she snorted, "She sounds like a golfer."

"Which is odd as she's actually your new local contact."

"A local will draw attention to me. It'll be like putting a flashing light on top of my head."

"The local agency wants it like that. This is their ground."

"And you're telling me you can't get me out of this?"

"Not exactly."

"Then what exactly?"

There was a long sigh.

"Sometimes I feel as if I'm working for you."

"I get that feeling, too." She smiled. "You know I don't play well with others."

Another long sigh. And she could see Diane shaking her head, smiling.

"Fine. I'll see what I can do. Await instructions and be careful."

"I'm still here aren't I?"

The low chuckle fuzzed the line, and she could see the laughter lines around those dark eyes as if they were in front of her.

"Keep it that way. I know you want a flight home to see grandmother but we have no other relatives in Vegas and we really need those documents."

She started walking towards the mass of casinos.

"I'll be good to go by the morning."

"Take care of yourself, Nina," was whispered down the line.

"The world's a better place with me in it."

She put the phone in her pocket and headed towards a soft bed and, hopefully, if they were doing their job right, some clean clothes.

Chapter 22

A ruffled mind makes a restless pillow. Charlotte Brontë.

Rebecca stared at the solid white expanse of ceiling. She sighed and rolled over, punching her pillow and flopping back down. Another half an hour went by. Her mind wouldn't quit clawing at the thin veil she'd rested over the images from inside the car - or the juxtaposed figure of a certain brunette who'd reverberated her emotional strings like a talented harpist. She growled angrily, flung the covers back and got up. Suddenly her mind was filled with the image of Kent, bumbling through things. She scrubbed her face with her palms, trying to get him out of her mind. Finally, with a firm squeeze to the bridge of her nose the pain instantly diverted that train.

"That bloody man."

Toes scrunching at the chill of the hardwood, she grabbed her robe and padded downstairs.

She picked her way through the hall, dodging ice cold tiles in favour of thick brightly coloured rugs. They'd be her choice, too. Deeply piled, the weave was comforting between her toes. When all of this was over, this house would be fun to explore thoroughly.

She squinted through the silvery darkness and carefully pushed open two heavy wooden doors. A solid wall of books greeted her. The library. She grinned and made a mental note never to stay in a hotel again.

"This is more like it."

She flicked the light switch, covering the room in a honeyed glow.

Head tilted, she examined each row of books. Leather bound classics sat amongst trash romances, crime novels, memoirs, historical journeys…. It was an eclectic but wonderfully familiar mix. Sophia always teased her about the lack of organisation in her own, but it wasn't for show, it was a working library, with each book having been read at least once, some five or six times.

Caressing the spines with bare fingertips she stopped suddenly, pivoting one book out of the row to confirm the title: *Wide Sargasso Sea*. It'd been her saving grace in a school where the wealth of her parents had left her rubber stamped as a little rich kid from day one.

Her English teacher had given it out in a lesson. It'd taken three pages before her imagination had embraced the vivid colours and deep sorrows the book offered up. Fifteen years later, after starting her company, she'd bought an autographed first edition as a reward. The book had remained in her library at home ever since.

She frowned and huffed on the cover to remove any dust.

"Some people don't recognise a classic."

She sat in a conker-red leather armchair, folding a leg under herself and opened it tenderly, careful not to crack the spine. She smiled and started on page one.

Warmth, a smell of citrus and a familiar feeling of safety helped to peel Rebecca's eyes open. She blinked tiredness away, trying to focus in the half-light. Moss green hues filled her vision. Instinctively she smiled. Annah smiled back.

"It's four A.M."

Annah knelt, leaning hands on the arm, her smooth black robe smelling of a comforting mix of fabric conditioner and the shower gel upstairs.

Rebecca cleared her throat and sat up.

"I couldn't settle."

Annah sighed.

"Me neither."

She glanced down sleepily. Only page ten.

"I must have dozed off quickly." Her brain processed a little more as it gradually awoke. It gave up a very truthful statement. "I won't be able to sleep properly for a while."

Annah sat back on the thick pile rug, legs stretched, crossed at the ankles.

"I wish I'd never suggested going back there. Then you wouldn't have seen what you did."

Rebecca refused that freeze frame again and pictured anything but the milky white irises of the two men. Instead she looked into two very vibrant and alive ones, focusing completely on the woman in front of her.

"Everything happens for a reason."

Annah snorted a soft laugh.

"You sound like my sister. She's into fate, chakras and..." Annah frowned, playing with the end of the cotton belt. "...you know, little pebble friends."

Rebecca blinked back the strange image.

"Pebble friends?"

Annah waved a hand.

"You know, healing pebbles. She has a shop in Camden."

"So, you work as a staff procurement agent."

Annah raised her eyebrows with a smile, "Diplomatic."

Rebecca winked, "And your sister is a New Age Healer?"

Annah nodded.

"It has its bonuses. I never run out of scented candles."

Rebecca pondered that for a moment.

"Do you like scented candles?"

"Not really."

They both laughed.

Annah peered at the book Rebecca was lovingly cradling. The younger woman's eyes lit up.

"Great choice."

"Lucky they had it stocked here. What a wonderful rental."

"Not luck. It's mine, I brought it with me." Annah shrugged and explained. "This place is rented from family so I can get away with dumping my stuff here."

Rebecca smiled. It felt nicer knowing it hadn't been filled with strangers before them.

"It's a beautiful house."

"I'll let my sister know."

"A new age healer decorated this?"

Annah laughed.

"No, my other sister Julia. It'd all be Feng Shui'd if Christie did it. We'd be surrounded by charms and every time you knocked into a piece of furniture some little knickknack would fall off." Annah quirked an eyebrow and motioned towards the books. "As you can see, the majority of my family has good taste."

"Yes. That they do."

Rebecca glanced down at the pristine copy of another example of that taste. There wasn't a crease on the cover or pages. She was about to make an off-handed comment about Annah not reading it much when she thought of what she always did with her favourites. She looked up at the brunette.

"You have two copies."

Annah got up, long legs carrying her to the book shelves. Scanning quickly, popping a copy out, it was handed over to Rebecca for scrutiny. Annah resumed her place, stretched out on the deeply woven rug.

Rebecca ran her fingertips over the terribly beaten up copy as if each crease and nick would offer up a story in Braille-like detail. It did. It sang of being actively loved.

"It's my favourite book," Annah whispered, gazing up.

"Mine, too," Rebecca added softly.

Annah's hands planted back and eyes closed.

"Books were the only way I could escape my sisters."

"Were they that horrid?"

Annah's head fell forward and eyes flicked back open.

"I'm the youngest of three. What does that tell you?"

"Oh, God, they were that horrid."

"Maybe not that bad." Annah chuckled lightly. "I learnt to give as good as I got. I was unexpected - although my parents deny it, of course - but I think by the time I came along they were sick of having kids and I was left to it."

"But that doesn't sound good."

Annah frowned.

"I'm explaining badly. I mean Mum and Dad were shell shocked by Christie and Julie so I had an easier time." Annah paused, deep in thought. "And my sisters made up for it.

"To get some peace, I used to go into mum's room and borrow her books. I'd hide one up my jumper, climb into our tree house and stay all day." Annah's expression was reminiscent and soft. "I bet I read an entire library up there."

"I wish I'd had a tree house. I just had a stuffy boarding school."

Annah's face fell.

"What was that like?"

"I didn't have a pleasant time."

"Bullies?"

"No, nothing like that; I was tall for my age. No..."

She paused, wondering if her next comment was too personal; they had only known each other a short time. She remembered what they'd gone through. Definitely bonds two people.

"I wasn't popular. My father was too rich, our house too grand and no one else had a driver take them to and from the building. The other children didn't like it."

"It must have been horrible."

Rebecca remembered back to the days and nights she'd spent there, the weeks and months, more often than not, alone.

"It was a mixture. I was deeply unhappy. That was a fundamental truth. However, my time there taught me to be self sufficient and also it drummed the shrinking violet out of me."

"But...didn't your parents take you out?"

The memories were old and faded but Rebecca could still feel the echo of intense sadness.

"My father worked away a lot. My mother often joined him. It's why I was in boarding school."

"Sorry. I'm prying."

Rebecca smiled easily.

"You're not. It's fine. It's not a skeleton in my closet."

Annah paused, thinking.

"So, you stayed in that school?"

"Actually, no, my grandfather found me crying in our attic one day and made me tell him the whole sorry tale. He moved me to the school down the road."

"He sounds like a sensible man."

Rebecca sighed sadly.

"He was. I miss him dearly."

"I did it again. I'm not cheering you up."

Rebecca rubbed her forehead, knowing the mood she was in and realised that she was being consumed by thoughts of loss.

"It's me. Sleep deprivation makes me maudlin."

Annah looked up with tired eyes.

"No more sadness today."

Laying the pristine copy down on the wooden table, Rebecca got up and stood over the brunette. She held a hand out and helped the younger woman to her feet.

"That's right. No more sadness. Come on, Sleepyhead. Let's try to get some rest."

Chapter 23

There is a beginning, middle and end to everything. However, the point at which we slip into a story is not always the point at which it started.

Rebecca hadn't slept well. Since lying back down at around five A.M., it'd felt like hours of interrupted catnaps all filled with dark thoughts and how she was going to deal with this situation...or how it looked like it was dealing with her with little mercy. That tended to make a situation worse, not better.

As she tugged at her lower eyelid, peering at her reflection, she knew she looked like she felt. Awful.

She sat back on the bed. A variety of conflicting and profound emotions fell at her feet. The unutterably awful last twenty four hours presented proudly, and she didn't have the energy to slap it back.

To say this was a ghastly year was an understatement of epic proportions.

A light rapping was accompanied by the cheery face of an alert brunette.

At least one of us isn't having it so bad, she thought.

"You're up," Annah asked.

On cue Rebecca yawned, eliciting a soft laugh from her hostess.

"Barely."

Annah crooked her finger.

"I have just what you need."

Rebecca's eyebrows scooted upward. Her mind perked at the suggestion. It managed to grab a robe to go over her pyjamas and get her legs working. They carried her over to Annah and followed downstairs like obedient puppies.

The scent of coffee and bacon curled through the air, creating a feast of a trail. Suddenly Annah spun around, holding a hand up.

"Halt."

Rebecca did but still felt an unquenchable urge to tease.

"And if I don't?"

Annah softly tapped the robe covering Rebecca's collarbone with a finger.

"Then you'll spoil my surprise."

"I hate surprises."

"I know." Annah sounded very smug. "Close your eyes."

Rebecca grabbed the first part of Annah's sentence.

"How do you know?"

"Because no-one as successful as you likes surprises. Now close your eyes."

Rebecca chuckled, shrugged, but did as she was told. A warm hand grasped her own, leading her on. The smells got stronger and rugs disappeared under her feet being replaced by cold tiles of the kitchen.

The body next to her was warm. It was something she missed, that feeling of energy bouncing off of another. Annah leant in slightly. It felt...good, secure, comforting. She leant in, too.

Annah's well clipped tones drifted through the silence.

"Yesterday was a bad day for both of us. I thought we could start today with something a little more..."

Rebecca cracked an eye open and was nudged gently with a shoulder. Her stomach growled as the smells wafted around.

"Sorry."

Annah carried on.

"With something a little more positive. You can open your eyes now."

She did. The kitchen would have gotten her attention normally - it was almost space-age in design - but that was eclipsed by the spread laid out on the family sized table. Her gaze flickered across bacon, hash browns, pancakes, and then the sliced fruit and juice and, and, and.... She turned and was ensnared by a warm smile and two eyes that called her into treacherous seas.

"This is a feast. How long have you been up?"

"Not long. I'm used to cooking this much. Big family, remember?" Annah shrugged almost shyly. "Anyway, it looks more than it is."

Rebecca arched an eyebrow slowly.

"Looks like we're going to be sleeping it off for a week."

"Lucky we have a gym down in the basement."

Rebecca glanced up. *And I didn't even have to sacrifice a goat.* She grabbed Annah's hand and pulled her forward to tuck into the sumptuous offerings.

It felt good to think of nothing serious. The last day temporarily sank into the background as she sipped a cup of very good coffee.

"I think I'll need to be rolled out of here."

Annah stretched both arms out with a yawn.

"It's America. There's probably a pulley and hoist system in here somewhere."

Annah finished putting the dishes in the washer and dried her hands on a tea-towel. Leaning back, crossing long legs at the ankle, a smile infused her features with a beautiful warmth. Rebecca was entranced, and worse still she knew it.

She stared into her coffee cup, trying to shake it off. Annah filled the long silent pause hanging heavily in the air.

"I don't think we should stay in today."

The black liquid sat darkly.

"I was going to go to the consulate."

"great idea. I can drop you."

Rebecca snorted a breath.

"But then I remembered that if I make this formal then my company's shares will probably be wiped out overnight.

"Oh."

"Yes. Oh."

"No consulate."

"Nope."

Rebecca settled back in a frustrated silence.

Annah spoke first.

"Let's go shopping."

Rebecca looked up from her coffee.

"Shopping?"

"It sounds crazy but it's mindless so it'll be a distraction and maybe along the way we can come up with a plan."

Rebecca chuckled in affable surrender. It was better than moping here.

"Fine. Let's go shopping."

Rebecca remained where she was - a fact that Annah only noticed when almost out of the door.

"I guess I'll get dressed and meet you down here in twenty minutes?"

Rebecca raised her coffee cup. Annah turned, grinned happily, and ran up the stairs. Rebecca listened to her door shut upstairs. She whispered to the empty kitchen.

"I think you're going to be very good for me."

She pictured those beautiful eyes, that smothering presence and charm.... She stared into the deep darkness of her cup not as confused as she'd like to be.

"And very bad for me, too."

She shook that out of her head and finished her drink.

I am a woman who enjoys herself very much; sometimes I lose, sometimes I win. Mata Hari

Hands deep in her trouser pockets Nina sauntered along the strip. It was hot. So much so that any sweat evaporated almost immediately. It meant she was still well pressed, and that was far more appealing than ending up creased and looking like a vagabond.

She pulled out the new phone that had been left for her. The casino had produced a nice generic room. A room with a view of lights streaming down the strip, and she'd been happy to sit for hours and watch people who were as small as ants. She felt like a God on a cloud; she'd pressed her thumb against the glass, squashing a tiny coach like it was a bug. Except when she moved her thumb away the coach drove down the strip, turned and disappeared. And in the end she'd fallen into a light sleep, curled in the chair with no blanket because blankets tied you into knots if you had to move quickly.

In the morning she'd wiped that thumbprint away and left the room cleaner than she'd gotten it. Nina was low impact and no residue; a tracker's nightmare and an agency's dream.

She thumbed the scroll wheel. The map pinged on the screen. She glanced up through throngs of brightly coloured tourists fluttering like noisy parrots, and followed her route.

Even dark alleys in Vegas weren't that dark. Staying to the edges so that one side was always facing a wall she picked up the breadcrumbs of the trail. And finally the prize emerged. A parked car with the engine running. She sighed at the politics of it all. Local agents to keep local agencies happy.

There were dents and nicks and scratches. What a heap. The back door struggled open and she slipped in. It smelt like a hinting effort of pine air freshener, trying to cover the other: the odour of a club lavatory towards the end of the night; all sweat and cigarettes and misbehaviour.

The balding man didn't turn around but caught her eye in the rear view mirror. He looked tired with deep lines cut into his tanned skin. She slipped sunglasses up and held her index finger out at the same time he held a box over his right shoulder. She pressed her print to it. The light on the box went green. She twisted her finger to smudge so it couldn't be harvested. She didn't trust the people closest to her. She wasn't about to trust this walking advert for the use of factor thirty sunscreen.

He passed back a briefcase. She took the handle.

"It's been nice talking to you. No, really, this moment we've shared has been so cathartic."

He grunted and mumbled a reply as she got out and shut the door; the metal didn't quite seal shut and, to be honest, she didn't blame it.

"Locals," she muttered.

It was one of those generically genetically germ-fest diners. It seemed that deviating from the strip by even a few blocks could really turn those glitzy lights off.

The seats were shiny plastic benches with high backs. She took one in a corner where she could watch the doors and no-one could walk behind her.

She cracked open the case. A laptop. Thin. Exceptionally so.

She closed the case then tilted it. It had deep dimensions; the laptop was slim. Her thumb ran along the seams, wondering which method they'd used to seal the hidden chamber. Clearly more exploring needed to be done—she glanced around—in private.

She pulled the laptop out and powered it up. A shadow fell across the table. Nina looked up.

The server was pretty and curvaceous. Her uniform was fitted enough for her not to be carrying a concealed weapon, either. Those small dangerous details.

"My name's Shirley. Can I take your order?"

Shirley had a nice accent. It was like oil on water.

Nina picked up the plastic wipe clean menu. Some of the dishes were as bad as injecting superglue into your aorta, but there were a few surprises.

"Well, Shirley. I'm going to have a free-range omelette, bacon and…do you do green tea?"

Shirley smiled. It made her cheeks dimple.

"Yes we do, ma'am."

Nina smiled, her face still aching from that slap. It had made the skin tight like a cheap astringent.

Shirley padded off, her lean frame taking its time in the heat that crept in every time the door was opened.

Nina's smile fell now it had no audience and she clicked open the folder on the laptop. Coded. She closed it, powered off and put it back in the case. Her phone shimmied noisily across the Formica. She flipped it open.

"White Crane Removals. We'll move what you don't want to."

"Always the joker," came the warm female tones.

She sat back on the barely padded seat.

"Helps the day go by."

"Nice to hear you took care of yourself and stayed away from trouble as I asked."

"I prefer breathing. It's surprisingly habit forming. Do you have the number plate yet?"

"I didn't have enough of it for a name, but that whole section is rentals."

"What a surprise. What about God's children? Do you have a location?"

"I'm sending it to your phone."

"Good."

"No heroics. Recon if you need to, but nothing else."

Nina sat back in the cheap seat.

"You're almost sounding like a superior and not someone lending a hand."

There was a pause and for a moment Nina wondered if Diane was on her own.

"Can't I profess my preference for you staying alive?"

Nina wasn't one for keeping her thoughts secret.

"Is someone there with you?"

A gentle laugh hummed in her ear.

"Do I sound like I'm talking in code?"

"Yes? No?"

"No, now please be careful - and don't fall over that paranoia on your way there."

Nina laughed just as her phone pinged, delivering the address of the Israeli nest.

"Got to dash. I have to see a man about a dog."

Chapter 24

To think is to practice brain chemistry. Deepak Chopra

Another quick shower helped to wash away the clinging jet lag. Rebecca dressed to help with the heat: light beige cottons were the topic de jour.

She'd resisted the urge to call Joy or her team of lawyers. If Annah had found out her flight details - there was a leak. She couldn't risk that negative exposure. Not with the next two months of huge deals on the horizon. It didn't take a genius to figure out she was in this alone.

Rebecca had almost finished securing up her slightly damp hair when a rapping at the door made a pin tumble from her fingers. She hunted around for it, feeling the floor with her palms for the insanely thin slither.

"Come in." She held it up triumphantly. "A-ha! Got you."

And glanced up at a veritable vision. Pin in hand, she blinked. Annah was dressed simply in a fitted white shirt, sleeves folded, and a nineteen forty's style linen skirt. Rebecca stood and dropped the now dirty pin on the dresser. She scrabbled for more than just a hair brush.

"That's a beautiful skirt."

"Thanks. It was a present. Jules claims I'm annoying but always gets me great stuff for birthdays." Annah picked up a bottle of perfume and lifted the top to her nose, inhaling just once. "I wondered." Then put it down, stuttering at the door, not in not out. "I'll wait downstairs."

It was half statement, half question. But Annah didn't move. Rebecca felt those green eyes track her whole body from head to toe.

"Help me with the last pin?"

Annah nodded quickly, letting the door close.

"Absolutely." Annah took the pin and after a long pause, seemed to flick back to life. "Sorry. Pin. Hair."

Rebecca turned, offering the final errant strand up. She waited as warm fingers caressed her neck, pushing the hair upward. The pin slipped in and she shivered. Those fingers didn't move but instead drifted over her skin for a moment. The warmth of the younger woman's body moved away sharply, and Rebecca turned to watch her striding out. Annah paused at the door, happier to examine the latch than look at her.

"I'll be downstairs."

And she was gone. It was then the Chinese whispers became audible, and what they said wasn't shocking.

She sat down, taking a few minutes. This was her rationalisation time. Before all deals she did it. Before mergers, important meetings, restructuring entire businesses, she did it. It was grounding, reaffirming. Like leaving a churned up puddle, the mud sank and water became clear again.

She glanced into the mirror and caught that heavy look in her eyes.

"At least you've decided to stop being coy."

She sighed deeply. Their chemistry was real, and getting more and more obvious. She couldn't pretend not to hear those whispers and she couldn't pretend an attraction to another woman was shocking. It simply wasn't. No, it was what it was.

She turned to her reflection.

"If you'd had half of that with Martin..."

She trailed into silence. But even that half sentence was too much. She grabbed the phone and dialled Sophia, pacing back and forth as it rang and rang. The blasted voicemail clicked on.

"It's just me. I'll call you later." She glanced at the clock and realised the difference. "Sorry. I forgot the time there. I'll call when you're alive - after you've had dinner."

She sighed and ended the call, adding this to a very large pile of things she didn't want to think about at the moment. There would be an avalanche waiting at some point in time. It wasn't an enviable thought.

Heels slipped on with ease, earrings slipped in with more, she dabbed some perfume on her pulse points, grabbed her purse and headed downstairs.

Parking was not an issue in Vegas. The whole city was designed to encourage people to stay and play.

Neither mentioned that moment but instead fell into a friendly banter as they perused the shops in the multi storey mall.

"This is bizarre." Annah looked around. "You have high class designer shops mingling with ones selling tat."

Rebecca laughed. She'd not heard that word in years.

"Tat?"

"Yes, tat. Low class..." Annah expelled the last word as if nothing else had offered itself as an explanation. "...crap."

"Ah, I know this isn't tat."

Rebecca pulled Annah into a jewellery shop. The younger woman glanced around then down at the display cases then leaned closer. Rebecca could feel her radiating warmth through her shirt, that silken smooth feeling comforting her skin. Thankfully Annah seemed oblivious. Rebecca gave her forehead a hard rub. She wished she was oblivious, too.

"I know when it doesn't have a price tag I shouldn't be in the shop."

Rebecca turned, determined to be her usual congenial self, a smile broaching her elegant features. She whispered, careful not to be overheard by the assistants who seemed to have digested the designer labels and general demeanour of the two women and found them to be acceptable enough to allow the new clientele to browse.

"I don't normally shop in places like this, but I need to get a birthday present."

Annah's gaze dropped to where Rebecca was gazing intently at a row of discreet but very feminine necklaces.

"She's a lucky..." A delicate pause. "...friend, lover, grandma, whatever."

Annah smiled easily. Rebecca caught the inclusion of one specific group and happily ran with it.

"I'd be loathed to spend this amount on a lover. A partner, perhaps, but I am definitely single. And my grandmother died some time ago."

"That only leaves...."

"Best friend. Yes."

"Then she's lucky you have great taste."

Rebecca caught the eye of a salivating assistant. She pointed to the row of breathtaking necklaces.

"Can we see these, please?"

He bowed, "Of course."

He slipped the padded display cushion out. Rebecca didn't need to look twice. She pointed to a robustly stylish chain with a Lalique cross. He handed it to her. She regarded it closely, holding it up to the light.

"Princess cut diamonds?"

He nodded. She handed it back.

"I'll take it."

Annah glanced at her, bemused.

"I've been thinking about it for a while. I'm not that impulsive," Rebecca winked.

It was boxed and wrapped carefully. Rebecca handed over her card. The transaction was completed in under a minute.

The assistant held onto the bag.

"You can take it now or we'll happily deliver it to your home address."

"No, I'll take it with me. Can you include a few ribbons? It's a present."

The assistant smiled and nodded, hurrying off to do her bidding.

"Deliver it? To England?"

"Did you see the price?"

"It didn't have a tag."

"Exactly." Rebecca chuckled. "They would have delivered it to Jupiter had I asked."

They walked out of the shop. Annah frowned as her mobile vibrated. It was dug out of her bag and her shoulders sank as the screen obviously showed the caller.

Jaw tense, eyes guarded, she turned, touching fingers to Rebecca's arm

"I have to take this."

Rebecca nodded, mouthing, 'Of course.'

She turned back to the shop and looked in the window. No, she'd made the right choice. She clasped the bag tighter. It was perfect; the chain, the platinum, the diamonds, the squareness of the cross. Of course, it was utter extravagance, but Sophia's birthday was coming up and this would match the earrings she got her last year.

Annah stopped by her side and stared off into the throng of people milling near a fountain. It wasn't hard to miss the visual signals.

"Bad news?"

The younger woman's body was tense and eyes like darts of energy.

"I'm working on a project and another group are interfering. I thought we'd got rid of them."

"That's not good." Rebecca squeezed her arm gently. "Do you need someone to bounce ideas off of? I'm available."

There was a long pause. Annah's eyes flickered, connecting intensely before moving away to some far off point. It was the nearest to anger that Rebecca has seen in the younger woman.

"I can't."

Rebecca tried to read the other flittering of emotions across her face but there were too many.

Annah forced out, "This is a really complex situation. I want to but..."

Rebecca patted her arm.

"We do similar work. I understand the need for a little secrecy."

"I wish you did," was the muttered response.

There were no more extravagant purchases but a lot of window shopping. They chatted for a while then went for - bad - tea.

It didn't take Annah long to shrug the heavy coat of preoccupation. It was nice to be out with someone able to turn the bright lights up and banish the shadows. It was infectious.

Rebecca felt completely at ease, something that hadn't happened in a long time. She was so used to her guard being up that at times it was a struggle to leave the current of the protective electric fence off. But whenever that urge came, Annah would do something like link arms and pull her over to some hilariously monstrous jumper and recount a tale of seeing something similar, or crack a terrible joke designed for nothing other than to give Rebecca ammo for teasing. All in all she was having a wonderful time.

After a couple of hours the mall was done. Rebecca looked at Annah and Annah looked back. Soothing, permissive, and delicate, the expression was barely whispering. It said nothing and it said everything. In part it was an acknowledgment of the fun they were having but...there was something else. It was the moments: soft yet fleeting. The glances: shy and charming. The touches: temporary but memorable.

Annah's gaze dropped as her cheeks flushed slightly.

"So, what now?"

It was a flash of an idea. Rebecca cleared her throat and pulled herself together. She didn't want to go back to the house and end up sitting around thinking about Kent, that car, poor Elliot.

"There's a fabulous private member's club not too far from here." She fumbled through one of the off-handed comments Annah had offered up, something to get a positive answer. "They have fantastic cocktails."

Annah beamed.

"Let's go."

Chapter 25

There is no such thing as chance; and what seem to us merest accident springs from the deepest source of destiny. Friedrich von Schiller

Boots connected with the baking asphalt. The motorbike engine idled. Nina kicked the stand, killed the engine and swung off.

What this machine lacked in security it made up for in sheer speed, and she always figured, you can avoid anything if you can move fast enough.

London had proved that point. The stories told she outran the bullet but that was ridiculous. You don't outrun a projectile. Really, it'd been a guess at which way to drop her body, a mountain of luck, and a predictable and amateur shooter who'd picked a S&W .38 - slow compared to a .204 Ruger that managed almost six times the speed. If he'd made a more educated choice then she'd be sporting a gravestone rather than a nick above her eyebrow as a souvenir.

She pulled the helmet off and ruffled dirty blonde hair. She looked at the warehouse in the distance and unzipped her leather jacket. Warehouses were very hard to protect and should only be used if you had to; if you had something big to hide. Otherwise there were too many entrances, exits, walls, doors and windows to protect.

"What have you boys got that you don't want little me to see."

The sun's heat covered everything, shade or not. It was like existing in the path of a high powered hair dryer. She kept the leather jacket on, though. It did afford protection from knives, blades; she'd just suck up the sweat dripping down her back.

She did a circle of the block. No cameras. Area pretty derelict. Just her, the sun, and a side door with a, now, picked padlock.

Eyes closed for a count of ten to adjust, then she slipped in, quickly and quietly, back flat against the wall.

Eyes open. Scanned. Clear.

Sounds. She cocked her head, pinpointing. Not in this section, but the next one. Accents. Israelis. Hard to tell from here if they were the ones from Elliot's offices. She hoped so, though, because a whole troop of opponents wasn't a pleasant thought.

She frowned at the vehicle in the middle of the warehouse floor. A large Hummer. Black, shiny and vile it wasn't exactly incognito.

How distasteful, she thought with a roll of her eyes.

Peering in the window there was a small laptop on the seat. Two ridiculously thick jackets in the back; a cheap looking briefcase; a half empty carton of cigarettes and some empty fast food packets. There were some loose pictures of a brunette getting into a big silver 4x4. She tried to get a better look but couldn't - yet. Still, at least this was a small cell.

"Oh, ye of little faith," she smiled.

A sharp prick to her neck and it pushed forcefully, breaking skin in the way a paper cut does - with maximum attention to pain. She winced.

"What do we have here?" came his low accented whisper.

He smelled of sweat and pizza with an attempt to cover with expensive cologne.

There was no planning, no detailed schematic of what to do and when to do it. Her neurons had gone over moves while she slept, while she walked, talked, ate, showered....

She twisted around and the knife slipped along her skin. Like a supercomputer producing an instant response, her brain whizzed: he was tall; gangly; his centre of gravity would be high; his hips were a little uneven; he was favouring one leg slightly more than the other. He also under-estimated her. They all did. She was a woman, and despite being tall her blonde hair and blue eyes always gave her an unmistakable aura of femininity that detracted from what she was.

What, indeed.

She slapped her palms on the knife, took a step back bringing the blade, too, and him by default. And with a twisting side step she had a knee to the back of his favoured leg. He jumbled to the floor; she stamped all of her weight onto the back of his head and neck.

A snap as his spine broke like a chicken leg.

She waited for a few seconds because lucky shots were hard to come by. There was a good test: she cracked his nose with the tip of her boot. You couldn't fake that.

His pocket was warm just like before. Some scrunched up, sweaty local currency; car keys which she dropped down the grate in the floor; a packet of cigarettes.

"Smoking kills but God forgives all, I hope."

She put them on his back, finding the large Maltese cross on the front of the packet prophetic.

Footsteps clattered loudly and she barely had time to roll before getting a kick to the ribs that lifted her in the air and back down with a crushing bang. And he was quick as his weight descended, pinning her body still. His fingers went to her throat; she quickly jammed a flat hand in the barely there gap, lodging it against her chin to keep her airway open.

And he was like a wild dog bearing down on her: snarling, spittle dripping from dry lips, this guy was stocky, shorter than the other. He shook her, trying to break her neck, or get her hand free, or maybe crack the bone of her windpipe or maybe just because that's what he felt like doing.

Years of yoga and Brazilian Jiu Jitsu paid off as she bent her leg up and managed to get it over his head and to his neck. But all the skill in the world doesn't change the fact that without a certain amount of brute strength, you cannot push off a grown brute.

Always have a back-up plan.

He squeezed, his nails ripping at her skin. And he picked her weight up a few inches and battered it down.

You don't see stars. You see blocks. Squares of black, like a television set detuning itself. Her hearing fuzzed as the body cut down on the systems running to maintain blood supply to the brain and other vital organs.

And it was like a red cloud descended in the crisis centre of her mind. Twenty seconds, tops. Ten before her vision went because that was the last thing to go.

And this was always the point where you found that extra strength; the moment your brain calculated it was losing and if it didn't release the last of its adrenalin...well, it wouldn't get another chance.

Her fingers felt like it was a cold morning in St Petersburg. Like the air was freezing her joints and shortening her muscles.

He growled.

Chances like this should be taken only when there are no more chances left.

She clenched at where she knew the hilt of her ceramic knife to be, pulled it out of the scabbard and stabbed and stabbed and stabbed and stabbed. Wild, flailing attempts, and some must have connected because hands loosened; air sucked in; she followed his body down and mounted back; and she stabbed and stabbed and stabbed. And it was absolute violence in the absolute.

A rhythm set as her hard wired brain performed the act that guaranteed it would survive. And then her hearing returned with a scream, and he was a partially gurgling mess of skin and muscle fibres and thick white fat pushing out of long thin slits.

Only when the ceramic knife slipped out and her fists started connecting with warm wet flesh did she pause, sucking in air through a throat barely able to handle it now.

A former prison gang leader once told her: when you make a move do so with complete conviction. If you plan on leaving the body as a message then make the killing horrific because your message needs to say:

Nina's voice rasped, "This is what happens if you challenge me. This is what I do to you." She rolled over, off, onto the wet concrete. "This is what I'll do to all of you."

Chapter 26

To tell part of the truth is more dangerous than lying. Minette Marin

The valet took Annah's keys. Rebecca led the way. She handed a mountainous man her swipe card. He fed it through a handheld computer, welcomed her with an autonomic smile and opened gilded doors of the next room.

The change was dramatic. Cavernous, the room resembled a stately home and was vastly different to the glitz and glare of the rest of Vegas. Baking air turned to an even temperature that instantly invigorated. Rebecca breathed deeply.

Annah looked around, turning a full three-sixty before catching her eye with a bemused expression.

Rebecca just laughed and whispered, "This city holds a wealth of other country's histories."

Annah glanced up at the elaborate ceiling; ornate, carved and high.

"How did you find this place?"

"My membership was a gift from a client."

Annah just stared at her for a moment before quietly laughing.

"No wonder you looked at me like I was a lost little kid when I came and accosted you that day - I didn't bring offerings."

Rebecca wiggled her eyebrows.

"Six crystal glasses and a George Forman grill would have secured me."

"I won't tell anyone you're that cheap."

Rebecca chuckled and gave the younger woman a friendly jab with her elbow.

They stopped at another set of doors. A tall exotic woman was the guardian here. Her high necked black outfit seemed only to be missing a dog collar - although what a juxtaposition to the woman's high cheekbones, sculptured eyebrows and dark, dark eyes, that would be.

The woman smiled, bowed her head and opened the door. The inner sanctum beckoned.

"Mrs Boyd."

Rebecca winced as they followed the hostess. It had been a while since she was here last.

"It's Miss Cavendish now."

The hostess' eyes closed for a brief second at the mistake.

"I'll have it amended right away."

Rebecca stole a look at Annah. Annah smiled tightly and glanced away.

The hostess beckoned with a hand.

"Please, follow me. We have your usual booth."

Annah leant in.

"Usual?"

Rebecca caught her eye, trying to ignore the drift of perfume attempting to hijack her attention.

"I've been here a few times."

"It's definitely private," Annah mumbled as they walked along, bodies close.

They stopped by a darkly lit booth. Rebecca glanced around at the luscious surroundings of dark woods and expensive fabrics.

"It's better than definitely public."

They slid in next to each other. The hostess smiled.

"Your usual, Miss Cavendish?"

"Please."

"And for your guest?"

Rebecca looked to Annah who raised both eyebrows with an amused smile.

"We'll have the same."

The hostess departed on her errand.

Annah shifted on the soft leather to sit side on, throwing an arm over the thick wooden lip of the back. Leaning her head in a hand her smile was effervescent.

"Does that happen a lot? The name thing, I mean."

The query took Rebecca by surprise. She'd been doing well not to think about Martin.

"It used to, but not so much now."

"Is it still hard?"

Rebecca could sense something else in that question.

"Sometimes it takes me off guard but that's all."

Annah digested that for a moment.

"So you got used to being Miss Cavendish again?"

There it was. She was impressed that Annah was so direct. She looked at that gentle smile, at the way it reached all the way up to emerald eyes.

"It was hard at first and still is at times, but I've got the rest of my life in front of me and I'm not wasting any of it."

"I'm glad." Annah's eyes glittered. "So, Miss Cavendish, what have you just ordered for me?"

"They serve marvellous whisky sours."

Annah leant across and gently took hold of her wrist. Rebecca's pulse jumped. Delicate fingers slipped along her skin, pushing the sleeve up to uncover her watch. Annah glanced at it.

"I suppose we can pretend to be on London time," Annah added softly before slowly letting go.

Rebecca cleared her throat and looked around for the drinks - and preferably an ice-cube to crunch through. What a mix of confusing feelings. Annah stared right at her and smiled. Rebecca massaged a temple. God, how did men cope with this?

On cue the drinks arrived.

"So." Annah raised the heavy tumbler. "What should the toast be to?"

Annah's expression seemed soft, reticent almost. Rebecca raised her glass and touched them gently. She took a calming, centring breath.

"To present company."

Annah's face lit up wonderfully.

"I'll drink to that."

Under a soft glow, light tones of a pianist permeated the room. Rebecca, head in palm, let the beautiful melody wash over her like a lullaby. Annah seemed to be in matching awe.

"He's amazing," said Annah.

Rebecca almost drifted off into the notes.

"My mother played like this. She loved what she played and it loved her back." She sighed wistfully. "I'm glad we came."

"Me, too. Did she play classical?"

"Sometimes." The memories were like warm sunshine. "She liked big band, too - not that you can recreate it well on a piano, but I think she aimed more for the happiness of each piece."

Annah really seemed to digest this news.

"Can you play?"

"Not even a bad version of Chopsticks. You?"

"London Bridge is falling down on the recorder," Annah smirked.

"Can I book you for a Christmas recital?"

"Bar mitzvahs and christenings only."

"If you change your criteria, you have my number," Rebecca sighed exaggeratedly.

Annah let out a low laugh.

"For sure. So, any more secret club memberships gifted to you? We could make a week of it."

"This is it. I'm a one trick pony in Vegas."

There was a glint in the younger woman's eye.

"And in London?"

"I have a wealth of secret handshakes and rolled up pant-legged introductions to get me into only the most exclusive of venues."

Somehow they'd slipped closer. It was only a fraction, but now Annah's fingertips rested lightly on her thigh. They were like scorching pokers, searing her skin through the fabric of her skirt. Somewhere in the back of her mind she thanked the hostess for taking them to this very private booth. Obviously she saw the need for...Rebecca pondered, scouring her slightly fuzzy mind. She found it: discretion.

The music lulled her muscles and the whisky sour helped her intolerably misplaced resolve. She reached down to where they lay on her thigh and ran her index finger along the smooth skin of Annah's knuckles. The other woman's eyes closed, as if blocking out visuals in favour of tactile stimulation only. It was then Rebecca fully realised how powerful, and mutual, this attraction was. The inevitable was sick of being delayed. Something was coming. She knew it like you knew the sun would rise and shine and sink, to rise again the next day.

Another club member walked by and reluctantly they moved away just enough to fracture that connection. Rebecca sipped her drink, savouring the burn as her eyes darted towards the pianist. She felt a deep need to change the subject - she glanced down at her glass - and the inhibition loosening drink.

"How about a fruit cocktail? They do what I can only describe as magnificent creations."

Annah nodded, almost absently.

"Okay."

The fruit cocktails were just that, perfect. Each layer miraculously held its shape in the glass, creating bands of bright colours. Annah had reanimated herself, ordering two, lining them up on the table.

"I feel bad drinking mine," Annah muttered, turning the glass gently so the colours merged a little.

Rebecca sat back and relaxed, her muscles finally giving up the rest of the tension she'd been holding on to. She knew it was a temporary respite, but my God, she was going to enjoy it.

She watched the younger woman running a finger over the condensation on the smooth side of the glass. Back and forth, back and forth. It was hypnotic. And then the pianist hit a series of notes Rebecca recognised. Then another joined another until they hijacked her attention. She tried to place the song but couldn't for a moment until it came rushing back in a fury of visceral memories.

Annah touched her hand.

"You're quiet."

Rebecca hadn't heard this piece in so many years. It did not bring back good memories.

"Sorry. I'm thinking."

Her tone was harsher than expected. Annah withdrew her hand.

Rebecca pushed her whisky sour away; it was still half full. Every note he played scraped, like the way new shoes rubbed with each step until you could take no more.

She remembered the night they'd played the piece. Of Martin bowing gracefully in his morning suit, of her curtseying in her wedding dress, and then taking the first dance as their guests applauded. It was an overwhelming slipping of emotions on a fragile piste.

Rebecca stood, unable to sit still. Her muscles had regained their tension and held themselves stiff and taught. She put a pitiful excuse of a smile on for Annah's sake.

"I hate this bloody piece of music. It was at my wedding." Slipping out from the booth, she patted Annah's hand. "I'm going to the powder rooms. Hopefully when I come back he'll have finished this God forsaken piece."

Not likely. As she remembered, it lasted an exorbitant length of time.

She gracefully dodged patrons and tables filled with chatting guests, and with unexpected social clumsiness, fled to the empty bathrooms. Heavy marble countertops, rolled edges and spotless brass fixtures did nothing to soften that unforeseen blow. She grit her teeth, bloody annoyed that this still has an effect on her. How long did she need to wait before it disappeared into the periphery? She held her wrists under the cold tap and stared into the mirror. Tired hazel eyes looked back.

"You can be surprisingly wretched at times, Rebecca," she muttered.

She glanced away, not liking the expression. It glowed weakness, something she was wholly not used to.

She leant on the cold marble. It was one thing after the next on this trip. She shook most of the water off and gently patted her face, the cool feeling good.

Squaring her shoulders she stood up straight, trying to relax a little.

"Time to face the music - literally."

She sat back down, looking curiously over to the pianist. He was now playing Beethoven. She frowned.

"What happened?"

Annah shifted stiffly.

"With what?"

"That piece lasts over thirteen minutes. I assumed I'd be tortured for another six."

Annah shrugged and poked an ice-cube with her metal stirrer.

"No idea."

The hostess approached, directing her comments to Annah.

"I hope this sonata is more to your liking?"

Annah forced a smile and nodded. The woman bowed her head courteously to Rebecca and left. Annah looked like she'd been found stealing biscuits before dinner.

Rebecca drew a hand down her arm to get her attention. Annah's expression was quite unreadable, but the little line between her eyebrows, the one that only showed when she seemed very tense, wasn't there anymore.

Face the music, Rebecca told herself again.

"Why did you do that? Don't over-analyse. Just tell me."

The answer was softly whispered as green eyes lifted to her own.

"Because this is our day, not his."

What a time for such a truth. It was brutal; it was beautiful. Rebecca sat back slowly. She watched the room not seeing a thing.

"Yes, it is."

Our day, she thought, *and it should be special.*

Too much of life was mediocre, passed by, floated through. She was always too busy, too rushed, too harried to take notice. She looked at Annah and Annah looked back.

"Wait there."

She stood abruptly and walked over to the hostess. It had been a while since her last visit, but this place wasn't a wine bar that just anyone could get into. It was expensive, exclusive and excluding; her membership got her perks and she planned to exploit them. Rebecca explained the favour she needed.

The hostess listened and finally said, "But of course. The room will be available now."

It was simple, really.

"Thank you."

"I'm here for whatever you need."

She watched the tall woman turn slowly, her long legs carrying her quickly over to a computer keyboard. Then the woman nodded and looked towards that room.

Ask and ye shall receive.

Rebecca returned to a perplexed looking brunette staring up at her with such a trusting expression. Rebecca held out her hand.

"Come with me?"

There was no hesitation. Rebecca guided Annah to her feet and led her away from the booth, through a heavy velvet curtain in a shadowed corner, and into another room.

The silence was deafening; the difference to the club, astounding.

Rebecca had seen it before and opened her palm, taking a step back. She hadn't arranged this for herself but for the beautiful young woman who was in a stunned silence.

Annah's hand remained where it was for a moment, lowering slowly, as if a graceful ballerina. Rebecca smiled and leant against one of the thick columns, waiting. Objectivity was harder and harder to come by. Annah had a murmuring charm and charisma that added fuel to a captivating fire.

She tried to justify it all, but kept coming back to the fact that she wasn't a teen and this couldn't be blamed on mere hormones, her failed marriage nor the incongruous situation Vegas and Elliot had dropped in her lap. Rebecca knew this attraction had been there from the moment they'd met - at least for her.

Annah turned and quirked an eyebrow.

"Are these real?"

"Very much so."

Annah turned back and approached a painting secured to the deep purple wall. Squinting, getting close enough to examine each brush stroke, her tone was incredulous.

Rebecca ignored the obvious masterpieces in favour of a living and breathing one.

"But this is Klimt." Annah moved across to the next. "And this...." One step back, pausing, then adding, "Is this a Mikhail Vrubel sketch?"

Rebecca was impressed. These weren't popular pieces shown in Sunday newspaper magazines.

"Even I had to ask about the Vrubel. You have very specialised knowledge."

Annah looked back to it, head tilting.

"I like Art Deco and Nouveau eras otherwise I'd never know." Annah moved on to the next, a soft cubist piece. "Like this, I have no idea."

Rebecca stood behind her to get a better look at the puzzling picture.

"I have no idea either. It's beautiful, though."

It was instinct, the automatic that brought her hands to rest on Annah's shoulders. Rebecca could smell perfume, could feel the warmth sink into her skin. Annah shivered slightly and crossed her arms.

"Cold?"

Rebecca's whisper was almost swallowed by the gentle hum of electricity illuminating the room.

Annah kept looking at the painting and shook her head.

"No."

"You're shivering."

"Tell me about the rest of these?"

It was a little prod; a little plea. Rebecca shook herself free and turned, focusing on anything else. Her hands felt empty so she clasped them behind her back and wandered up to another picture. Finding something pertinent to say wasn't easy.

"I only know details on a few. Some are on loan from club members and some are investments."

"Why would anyone loan a picture to a closed gallery like this?"

"Because it saves the owner insurance premiums, and if your little Klimt cost two million pounds, you can bet the security system, guards and insurance cover will come in at a hefty punch."

Rebecca examined an ornate frame. Gilded, elaborate, it was as beautiful as the canvas it protected.

"Oh, right. Of course."

Rebecca explained as many pieces as she could. It was better than silence, tempting that which seemed to be waiting in the wings. Finally, after they'd gone around the whole room, Rebecca turned on her heels right into Annah's intense gaze that regarded her almost like she was another piece. Annah didn't move, didn't speak, and those eyes carried an electric charge that hit her dead centre and followed her nerve endings too many places.

Rebecca struggled to find some words.

"You like my little surprise?"

Annah took a few steps closer.

"Yes."

And it seemed so natural to be this close to that scalding heat she wasn't sure was her own or Annah's. A hand rested on her arm, fingers moving upwards, magically making the material of Rebecca's shirt seem to disappear. They transmitted electricity directly to the surface of her skin. It was like turning on a light switch: bright and blinding hot, the effect was immediate. All air expelled from Rebecca's lungs in a slow exhale designed to try and ease back on whatever throttle the other woman had floored so successfully. An inane sentence came out.

"We need to talk about this."

It was like saying the sun was hot and water was wet.

Further elaboration was pointless as Annah proved.

"I know."

But the gunpowder had combusted and talking wasn't on Fate's agenda.

A blur as fingertips held her cheeks and the subtle strength of Annah's perfume overtook her nostrils, as yielding lips slipped over hers, as her eyes closed and palms pushed against heated material. Breasts against breasts, thighs against thighs, softness, hardness, warmth and cold. And then her hands were in Annah's hair, pulling her closer, and before she knew it they were kissing deeply, more of their bodies connected than not. A hunger she was only barely in control of surged forward.

Sense floated some place else as time disappeared and was replaced by...just this. Just them.

Slowly Annah pulled back, jaw set and eyes dark and heavy with an emotion Rebecca knew matched her own. They stared at each other. It was Rebecca who slipped first. Closing her eyes she sighed, and when they reopened her mind realised what had just happened; the enormity, the intimacy of it. The fact they were in an art gallery in Vegas and she was embroiled in a murder investigation that could well ruin her.

Her English accent surged staunchly as she whispered.

"This is insanity."

Annah seemed to rock backward fractionally from the blow then blinked then frowned and crossed her arms. Rebecca tried to backtrack a little, certainly not meaning Annah's obvious interpretation.

"I'm sorry. I didn't mean...." Except she was utterly overwhelmed and her next words proved it as she caught sight of a security camera that might not have captured it all but still raised her stress level even more. Visions of this tryst on CNN blazed into view. "We should go."

Annah did just that, leaving her in the room alone, the disorder and chaos she'd created littering her surroundings.

"Bloody Hell," she sighed.

Rebecca touched her tingling lips with a shaking hand, watching the billowing curtain for a moment before following.

Annah was sitting in their booth, staring into her glass.

Rebecca was more than a little dumbfounded. It was as though her life had been shaken and tipped out, like the contents of a handbag when you've misplaced your keys. It was a mess - although, as dangerous as it sounded, she suspected she might have found what she didn't realise she'd lost.

Annah looked directly at her. It was such an open and honest expression.

"I don't think this is insanity, Rebecca."

Rebecca sighed. Even in this shock one thing shone out like a lighthouse on rocky cliffs.

"No, me neither, and that's what makes it insane." She fished a pen out of her bag and signed the slip at the table, not caring how much it cost. "Can we go?"

She wanted to move, to walk, to get out of here so she could ground herself and think properly. She most certainly needed more privacy to explain her thoughts to Annah - except she didn't say any of that out loud. And she paid for it.

Annah nodded, "You call the shots," and walked away quickly.

"That went well," Rebecca exhaled sharply, quite disgusted at herself for managing to crash through things with the grace of a cow on ice.

Rebecca concentrated on the roads and light traffic as Annah drove them back to the house. The journey sped. When her brain finally rejoined her body she was standing in the hallway, looking at the woman who'd sent her spiralling like a stringless kite - and who now seemed to have erected a very large wall between them. She scowled. It's not like there was a single reason to blame her.

You kiss her then push her away? For someone so clever, you can be moronic at times.

The silence was ridiculous and needed to go.

"We have to talk about what just happened."

"No we don't."

"Annah..."

The younger woman's eyes flashed, her temper clearly frayed.

" Do you think you're the only person taking a risk? You do..." Annah struggled. "...that - kiss me - and then tell me it's all insane? Is this where you say how out of character that all was, and how we should pretend it never happened? If it is, then no, I don't want to talk about it."

Rebecca sighed. She deserved the burst of temper. Her own words and actions had been so completely topsy-turvy.

Now was the time for damage control. Now she had to take charge.

"Does that sound like something I'd say?"

Annah crossed her arms tightly.

"I don't know."

"Yes you do."

Annah's gaze was fierce and unwavering.

Rebecca sighed and gave it another go. She rubbed her forehead.

"This is a stressful time for me what with..."

She blew a breath out, trying to find the words but coming up short.

When in deep waters, lead with the truth.

She started again.

"Finding dead bodies is not the norm during my business trips. I'm not at my emotional best."

"Claiming temporary madness isn't very original."

She sighed.

"Just because I said this situation was insane doesn't mean I think *this* is insane. I don't. I'm not in my teens having a breakdown because my best friend kissed me before the school disco. I'm an adult and very able to see that chemistry comes in many shapes and guises."

Annah stayed silent but seemed to lose a little of her rigidity. Rebecca carried on.

"I won't deny this attraction between us, but I will deny it anymore purchase here and now. This place...?" She faltered. Her brain lagged as instinct took charge. She reached across and took Annah's hands, holding them tightly. "It's not a good environment. It's so negative that how can anything positive have a chance?"

The point was succinctly truthful.

"And when we get back to England?"

Rebecca looked away. Sometimes the truth wasn't pleasant.

"I don't know."

Annah's expression was crestfallen as she pulled her hands away slowly.

"Then you shouldn't have kissed me."

Unable to control her level of stress, Rebecca took the bait.

"And you shouldn't have kissed me back."

Annah sighed.

"Why? I'm attracted to you. I'm not having a moment because of it."

"I'm not having a moment," Rebecca said, having a moment.

"You normally act like this after kissing someone you're attracted to?"

Wasn't that a very good question.

"No." Her head was starting to pound. "No, I don't."

Annah filled the silence.

"I don't and won't regret it. But I'm not going to push you." Annah lifted a hand. "I'm tired. I need a coffee. Do you want one?"

For a moment Rebecca wondered if just brushing this off was the best thing. But was arguing any better?

"Yes, please. Let me help."

Annah shook her head, her expression decidedly chilly.

"No, I'll bring it into the library."

Annah turned and walked off. Rebecca sighed, standing in the miniature grandeur of the hallway. How had something so simple and wonderful gotten so awful and messy?

She waited for a moment before heading to the library. She sat in the sallow quiet as her memories skimmed the thin membrane holding the last few days back. Osmosis. The quiet dam broke. hands on her knees, head back, she sighed deeply, the magnificence she prided herself on deflating a little. She dug her phone out and stared at it - which was useless because who could she call? Even calling Joy could jeopardise her entire career; same with Sophia who she knew would call everyone from the Police, Army, Navy and even Coastguard; her lawyers - by their very nature would ruffle Kent. With a loud tut she jammed the phone back in her pocket. Distraction time. She examined the non-fiction row. It was a strange mix of war generals and ex-prime ministers versus religious leaders from the globe. She wondered what Christmas dinner must be like in the Stevens' household with the wonderfully diverse personalities. She sighed at that thought. Could she have messed this up any worse? She padded back to the kitchen.

Annah whirled around, a packet in her hand. Rebecca froze. Annah froze. Wide green eyes didn't blink for a second until Annah reanimated and walked across and locked the back door, the grinding of metal on metal loud. Annah turned and held the packet up. Rebecca frowned and took it. The Maltese cross stood out. Rebecca really froze this time. That brand.

"Where did this come from?"

Annah reached over the sink and pulled the window shut and locked it.

Rebecca flipped the tatty lid. One thin white filtered tube remained. A last cigarette. She felt her blood drain.

Finally the younger woman spoke.

"I found them on the garden stairs." Annah's tone held an unsettling quality. "The gardener smokes, but...I saw the brand."

A bell rang through the house. Both women jumped at the shock and stared at each other, puzzled. It was Annah who realised what it was first hence her deep scowl.

"Door. Sorry. I've stayed here five times and I never remember the chime."

They walked out, Annah pulling a hair-band from her wrist, securing a ponytail. Dark shadows danced with red and blues flashes on the walls via the glass of the door.

Annah opened it to a very serious Agent Kent. He held his badge up. Rebecca's feet stopped moving her any closer. She held back in the shadows.

"I know who you are," Annah frowned, nails digging into the doorframe. Two officers milled around the squad car behind.

"Is Rebecca Cavendish there?"

Rebecca took a step forward, almost crushing that cigarette box and offered a decisive answer in dangerously low tones.

"Yes, she is."

Agent Kent rubbed his chin.

"Miss Cavendish, can you come down to the station to answer some questions."

It wasn't a request. Rebecca suddenly felt very sick. Her business persona shuttered down as she straightened.

"I don't think I have much choice, do I?"

"No. You don't."

Chapter 27

A casual stroll through the lunatic asylum shows that faith does not prove anything. Friedrich Nietzsche

A booming television blared through the walls from the motel room next door. The benefits of a safe house in a shitty area.

Nina tore open the top of the addressed envelope she'd picked up from a dead drop on the way back. One pitted key. She checked the number on the front of the envelope again. Sixteen. The number one was missing on the door but at some point it had been there because the wood was bleached next to the weathered six. She stood in the blast of heat, still, breathing rhythmic but shallow. She hurt. Externally mostly. Mostly.

She squeezed the bridge of her nose, trying to reinstate the side of her personality that needed to take charge. She breathed deeply and let herself in.

Nina pulled off her bloodied boots and left them by the door. Socks, too. And then trousers with heavy hems, weighted with dry or clotted liquid.

And jelly red footprints on the wooden floor trailed behind all the way to the white tiled bathroom. For a moment she stood still, shivering despite the heat. The mirror created a portrait of violence: her blonde hair was flecked with smudged red streaks. A red welt raised below her eye. Her neck was a jigsaw of angry red finger marks. She didn't turn away. It was important to see what you were, that transformation from one mission to the next.

"I am a sum of my deeds," she whispered.

She stepped into the shower, turned the taps, not caring if hot or cold, and sat down and waited, hugging her knees.

From experience it took ten minutes for the water to run clear. Maybe it was quicker than that, but ten minutes was the safe cut off.

Once she'd pushed a guard into razor wire and used him as a shield to get across. That night she only waited six minutes and when she looked at the water it still had meaty sections of skin and hair that wasn't hers.

Now she took ten. Better to be safe because when the adrenalin stopped, seeing what you'd done wasn't so appetising. The water pounded her body, her head, her face, creating a blanket she happily hid behind.

The kitchen was a tap and a dirty sink. Fine. She hated gadgets. Too many electrical items that could hide bugs or be used to aid timer devices.

She poured out a large glass of cold water from a sealed bottle. In the early days she thought she'd been having an adverse reaction to killing, but then she'd realised that unless you dilute the adrenalin you'd spend the next two days being sick.

It took seven minutes for her applications to crack the passwords on the laptop she'd brought back. She clicked open file after file while she absently rubbed the ends of her hair with a thin cotton towel.

"It's all in bloody Israeli," she tutted.

She connected her phone to the laptop to transfer the files to the main offices in London. As technology did what it needed to, she went through to an extension she knew off by heart.

The call was answered by a generic woman with a hint of a Welsh accent.

"Secure this line," she ordered as she poured another water.

A series of beeps and a voice spoke.

"Confirm your identity."

They went through the code and answers.

"Line secured."

"Connect me to my handler."

The transfer was instantaneous and she interrupted him saying a word.

"You have the files."

"They'll take us a couple of hours to translate. Did you encounter any obstacles in obtaining them?"

"Two. Both removed to prevent accidents and incidents. I need a cleaning team."

"Consider it organised. I'm sending you a document."

And lo, it did appear. She opened it. With a picture embedded in the top, the brunette's details were listed: Rebecca Cavendish. British. Rich. Successful. Worked with Elliot over a period of three years. Was Cavendish the missing piece of this puzzle? Was she the UK contact?

She scanned the rest, taking in key words she'd process later, except for one that took prominence: current location is Las Vegas. Nina put her glass down.

Now, this was interesting.

She paused, staring. She dug around in the bag she'd returned with, flattening out a crumpled picture. She held it up. The woman was side on only and fuzzy. She held it up next to the one sent from England. Eyes flicking between the two, she stared closely. it was Cavendish. She quirked an eyebrow, glad she'd got rid of the Israelis now.

"She was set to meet with Elliot but...well. We're trying to arrange her return to London."

She nodded. They had more control in London.

"Does she have the documents?"

Nina looked at the picture again. There was someone else by the large 4x4. It was hard to see because of the distance. A slightly shorter brunette in sunglasses.

"We have no confirmation."

She took a picture with her phone and sent it. "But do we think she could have them?"

"Perhaps."

Her mind processed this new revelation. "Put me on the flight before her and have a team ready."

"You'll have a ticket waiting."

"Did you get the picture I just sent?"

"Got it."

"Who's the other woman with Cavendish?" There was a pause.

"We'll look into it."

"Quickly."

"Always."

Nina squinted down at the picture but it was no good. The resolution was

poor. She put it down, rubbing an eye with the heel of a hand. *"Safe trip and well done."* The line hummed as she leant forward heavily, dropping her forehead

against the cold wood of the table. She put her phone down, in her eye line, and waited. Seventeen seconds later it beeped. SMS details of her flight. Home. And the wait was lifted.

Chapter 28

Evil is not something superhuman, it's something less than human.
Agatha Christie.

It wasn't the same room as before but it felt like it - and smelt like it. Rebecca sat ramrod straight in a very uncomfortable chair. Agent Kent perched on the end of the grey table. He watched her; she watched the two-way glass. She watched the smears and fashioned stories in her head about their origins. She did anything but rise to his little performance of trying to make her uncomfortable, to throw her off kilter.

Too late, Agent, she thought perversely, *someone else already did it and his metier was far more impressive.*

"Why don't we go through it again?"

"I think four times is enough." She smiled up at him. It was the same smile she saved for tolerating fools. "The fifth time really should be with my lawyer present...or are you denying me legal representation?"

He straightened his tie. He smelt of cheap cologne.

"You have something to hide?"

She sat back, away from the aroma.

"This isn't a movie." She took aim at the huge expanse of idiot. "Innocent people are jailed by incompetent and inexperienced Agents all the time. I don't intend to be one of them. Now, either charge me, let me have legal representation, or let me go." She sighed. "It's up to you."

He smiled and left. Rebecca kept watching the door, wondering what he was up to. She didn't trust his abilities or methods, and he was a lousy interviewer. He'd asked all the wrong questions about the cigarette box not seeming to care it'd turned up where it had. It'd ended with a blasé comment about having it fingerprinted.

The door reopened. Carrying a small silver slither, his cheap shoes clumped back over. Flipping the screen up, the portable DVD player already had a picture showing. It was grainy, the quality low, but Rebecca knew that figure. Annah glowed in the middle of the screen, paused. She'd seen those horribly designed chairs somewhere before. Leaning closer, Rebecca squinted. Kent pressed a button and Annah silently started moving.

Annah looked left, then looked right, then looked rushed.

Annoyed at having to show her interest, Rebecca tried to remember where those chairs were. Her brain processed the horrible amount of blackened glass everywhere. She sat back. Kent didn't miss it.

"Elliot's office." He was smirking. "What's your friend doing in there, huh?"

He paused the picture just as Annah was heading back out through the door. Rebecca clamped down on her shock like a pit-bull.

"She didn't look to be doing much, to be honest. Clarify that with her if you feel the need. Now, about my legal representation?"

The pause lasted at least a minute before he stood up, glancing at the mirror. She guessed someone superior was behind there, watching, judging. It's the only reason she'd kept her temper for the last three hours. She had no intention of losing her cool in front of an audience.

"I've read your file, Rebecca." He leant back down, eye to eye. "Your influence won't help you here. You can't interfere with an investigation and hide evidence without consequences." He smiled. He had mediocre veneers. "I don't care who you are."

"Odd. I feel the same about you." She leant in closer, keeping her words private. "Remember, I came to you about this and you told me there was no crime. You hashed it all on your own."

He looked right at her.

"Your accomplice gave us the cigarette butt."

She looked back.

"When you start to use words like that, you start to make me insist on legal representation because of your obvious ineptitude."

He straightened, staring down for a moment before walking off. Kent paused at the door, trying so very hard to make an expression of arrogant calm.

Missed by a mile, she smirked outwardly.

"You're free to go." He leant against the door for a moment, scrutinising her intensely. "You're not free to leave the State."

She stood, stretched, and ran a hand through her hair.

"I'm enjoying your company too much for that, Agent." She walked across. He'd ruined her day so she intended to take a shot, at least. She whispered. "Next time you haul me down here with nothing, I'll make sure you're the one advised not to leave the State."

She winked and followed a burly officer out of the interview room. Finally free of that claustrophobic box, her bottled emotions almost popped their cork. Her temper simmered. Her fists tightened into rock solid balls.

Don't you dare lose it until you're outside.

It was a struggle because her resources had been sapped. Over and over he'd asked the same questions, "How did you know the car was there? Why were your prints on the glass? How did you know Elliot Peters?"

The only one to throw her, to make her clamp her mouth shut and insist a lawyer sat in was when he leant in and quietly asked if she knew about the others. Despite her better judgement she asked, "What others?"

And the nightmare had become corporeal.

"The three men packed into the trunk. That car was a holiday for five, Rebecca."

Initial crime scene pictures had accompanied this treat. Two ski-masked faces spared her no trauma with their cut throat smiles, but the third was Elliot's real assistant, the one who always made nice tea, who pulled her chair out at meetings, who wore a flower in his lapel no matter summer or winter. One bloody hole in his chest told all she needed to know.

Her stomach barely held on to its contents.

"That's Elliot's proper assistant," she'd offered up in a moment of unsupervised madness. Kent had shifted and fiddled with his tie. It was his tell, and if they were playing poker right now she would clean him out. As it was, her win was more discreet. And so he tried to bite back. He quizzed her over and over and over, trying to pull holes in her story. But there were none. Then she realised why they'd come to question her again. She was their only lead, the only one who'd seen every single person who'd ended up dead. She clearly wasn't that much of a suspect because the questioning, while annoying, hadn't been fierce. Rebecca also realised one important factor: it's one thing to tell the truth, but it's completely different getting someone to believe it.

Agent Kent had paced, had used every distraction he could, every trick, but she'd stuck to her story, to what had happened. Clearly he was satisfied or he wouldn't have let her go. She frowned. Or maybe he didn't have enough to charge her? That thought made her stomach knot.

Dressed head to foot in black, Rebecca spotted her immediately. Annah was in the middle of a heated discussion. Hair secured loosely and with her trademark sunglasses perched atop her head, jade eyes almost bore a hole in the desk sergeant's chest. As if sensing her presence, Annah spun around, blowing out a visible breath when their gazes connected. The desk sergeant was dropped like a discarded chew toy.

Before Rebecca knew what was happening, Annah was bare inches away. The younger woman's carefully crafted façade fell as her palms gently lay on Rebecca's shoulders, as if checking this was real and not some crazy apparition brought on by excessive stress. Her mouth opened but no words exited.

Rebecca smiled, covering warm hands with her own. She pushed down, grounding herself with that mere contact. Unspoken reassurances drifted between them for a long moment before Rebecca quietly spoke.

"Let's get out of here."

Annah nodded.

They walked side by side to the lot where the monster truck waited. It gleamed like a diamond, sunshine bouncing off of the body. Rebecca patted the side before slipping in to its safety.

For her own sanity, she needed one thing clearing up very quickly.

"They showed me security footage of you in Elliot's offices, Annah."

Annah stopped, key half in the ignition, half out and then sat back slowly.

"They showed me the same thing. Wanted to know what I was doing traipsing over police evidence."

"And what did you tell them? Why were you there?"

Annah frowned.

"You, too?"

"I'm just asking a question."

Annah's frown deepened as she looked out of the windscreen.

"I'll give you the same answer then. Kent had told us there wasn't a crime, even though we knew there was." Annah turned back, her frown lessening with a sigh. "I was looking for someone - anyone - while you were in the car park making sure no more murderers came running after us."

Rebecca winced.

"Oh. He didn't tell me when the footage was from."

Annah jammed the key in the ignition.

"When did you think it was from?"

The tone was colder than any air conditioning. Rebecca shifted. She deserved it. She should have known Kent would try and be underhanded. It was about his level of intelligence.

"I'm sorry. I've not had a lot of sleep."

Annah just shrugged., backing them out of the space and drove.

They carried on in silence for a mile before Rebecca spotted the younger woman's white knuckled hands gripping the wheel with enough force to bend it.

"Pull over here."

She pointed to a dirt lay-by on the side of the quiet road. Annah eased the vehicle to a bouncing stop. Rebecca couldn't help but smile. She reached over and ever so gently unpeeled the brunette's hands from the wheel.

"Annah?"

Two narrowed eyes turned her way.

Rebecca carried on.

"I'm sorry."

"It's fine."

Except it didn't seem to be as Annah remained tense, her hands still balled. Rebecca really needed things to be okay. They only had each other.

"I mean it. I shouldn't have fallen for Kent trying to get to me."

Annah's piercing gaze trapped her.

"This is how the police work. They give you half a story, let you go off and hope you fall apart. But that only happens if you're guilty. We've done nothing wrong."

"I know."

Annah sighed.

"He tried to scare me over the cigarette we took from the car park - it was still in the glove box so I gave it to him - but we ended up going in circles. He started on about evidence and I kept repeating we *told* him there was a crime. I said we forgot in the panic, which is kind of true."

The younger woman sucked in a lungful of air and then puffed it out slowly, leaning back against the head rest before carrying on, her voice dry and raspy.

"This is..." A pause. "Things are wrong. Really wrong."

Annah ground to an abrupt halt.

Empathy was not a problem for Rebecca. Her own levels of stress were enormous; she could see Annah's were about the same. She also bet Annah had gotten a worse grilling because of entering the offices, even if she'd only taken three steps in, looked around, and then came right back out.

Rebecca scooted closer, tilting her head, catching two green eyes.

"The police are just doing their job." Her lips curled into the best smile she could muster. "Badly."

Annah let out another long breath, clearly agitated.

"They came to my house to arrest you. Then they treat us both like we're terrorists." Annah's elbows planted on the steering wheel, hands dragging her hair back. "They kept on at me for two hours. I was in Elliot's place for thirty seconds, max. My feet touched the carpet and that was it. And then Kent was hinting you'd be kept for questioning all day."

Rebecca waited, giving the other woman some time to oust the stress build-up. After a beat she reached over and brushed a glossy lock of hair back from her shoulder.

"I'm here now, though."

Serious eyes turned on her.

"I have no influence here, Rebecca." Annah paused, her gaze skating off. "I mean, because we're foreigners."

The police can be insensitive bastards sometimes, she growled silently.

She was peeved with them, but also herself for involving the younger woman in this awful turn of events.

"I wish I'd taken a cab at the airport."

Annah turned, thick eyelashes fluttering in a stunned blink. Rebecca caught the hint of a scowl and she touched a hand to Annah's momentarily.

"I was apologising for involving you."

Annah frowned deeper, still holding onto a little of that hurt expression.

"You'd prefer to do this alone?"

Rebecca knew the answer. It was selfish but sometimes life is.

"No. I'm glad you're here."

Tentatively Annah reached out but that hand froze, mid-air. It hung, paused, as if unable, or unwilling, to go that final distance. Rebecca caught the flash in those fascinating eyes. It was powerful and alluring. Then it was gone. And so was the hand. It pulled back and gripped the wheel.

"Sorry. I don't like feeling powerless. No more tantrums." Annah shifted in her seat and then in the conversation. "That kid gets on my nerves."

One thing she knew beyond a shadow of a doubt, they had to have a long talk about a lot of things and soon.

"If it helps, he's not on my Christmas card list anymore."

The corners of Annah's mouth lifted a little.

"He was on it to begin with?"

"I'm nothing if not congenial."

"What do you want to do now? I'd sit tight, but it's your call."

"I agree. Kent won't be back. He knows we're not hiding anything. We obviously checked out or we'd still be there."

"Possibly."

Annah nodded.

"When I was waiting, some guy had a packet of those cigarettes. I saw the cross on the front."

"You think it was a coincidence?"

Annah thought for a long while.

"I don't know. It's a very subtle message and these people don't seem to be subtle, you know?"

"True. You don't go from killing people to hinting with a warning on the back step."

"Exactly. They would have shot us." Annah rubbed her neck. "I think Kent realised, too. It's just a pack of smokes."

"Well, I'm not going up against someone who killed five people."

Annah's eyelashes fluttered.

"Five?"

"Three more in the trunk. Kent let me know in his childish attempt to scare me." Rebecca shook her head. "If I'd just murdered that many people, I'd hardly be scared by a teenager in his dad's suit."

"Have you called a lawyer yet?"

Rebecca exhumed audibly.

"I can't afford the exposure, although I was pretty darned close in there." She opened her bag and rooter around for a card, handing it over to Annah.

"If I get taken in again then call this number. Jane will bring in the big guns and organise damage limitation."

Annah nodded, staring at the card, eyebrows dipping into a scowl. She didn't look pretty damn angry.

"His name sounds like what he is."

Not much you can do to that except laugh loudly. Rebecca did. Annah smiled sheepishly.

"I get crude when annoyed."

"I'll have to remember."

"Where to now?"

Rebecca tried to process everything but it was an impossible task.

"Let's get back to something more normal. Do you have a network at the house?"

The younger woman blinked, obviously thrown. Rebecca smirked and worded it again.

"Do you have the internet at the house? I need to connect my laptop and check some things out."

"Sorry. Yes. There's Wi-Fi." Annah scowled, almost talking to herself. "I need to call my sister for the alarm codes - just in case."

"I'll sleep better."

A thought manifested itself boldly to Rebecca. Joy always sent across work to wherever she stayed. It was probably sitting in her room right now. At least it would take her mind off of today. Distractions were the only thing that'd get her through this in one piece.

"Can we stop by the Hilton, first? There'll be work waiting."

Annah straightened up and nodded, seemingly able to focus more when given a task.

"Hilton then home."

Rebecca smiled at her choice of words.

Annah checked the already centrally locked doors, glanced in the mirror and pulled the 4x4 back onto the road.

Chapter 29

Life is a series of interlinking events that when viewed together, form a story. We can no more write our own than we can read that of others.

Check-in at the Hilton was quick. With a bank of desks and polite staff, Rebecca soon collected the innocuous grey key card to her room and some messages from Joy. Her courier packages were waiting upstairs as well as some faxes; the benefits of her fully loaded Hilton Honours frequent stay card.

They both padded along the thick carpets, dodging streams of uniformed tourists. It was a surreal moment in a disturbing day.

"I feel conspicuous because I'm not in three-quarter length, sand coloured shorts and a horrible Hawaiian shirt," Annah commented dryly and side-stepped another group of clones picking over piles of suitcases.

Rebecca chuckled as they walked into the shiny lift.

"It is a desert."

"And they're dressed for a cruise ship."

Rebecca glanced about.

"True. This is the city of sin where some people choose to look like gaudy baubles."

She pressed for her floor and the doors blocked the bright lights out.

"I need a long massage," Annah said, rubbing a shoulder firmly.

Rebecca knew what she meant. Her limbs ached and so did her mind. When all of this had sorted itself out, she was off on a holiday somewhere, perhaps a nice beach with clear blue waters and white sand and palm trees swaying in the cool evening breeze. She smiled at the thought.

"Earth to Rebecca?" A hand waved inches away, making her eyelashes flutter in the breeze, breaking that studious contemplation. "Your floor."

And that it was. Decked in deep reds, while being totally generic it was also rather pleasant - if you could ever think of a place like this as such.

"Sorry. My mind was elsewhere."

Annah gently nudged her with a shoulder as they followed the signs to her room.

"Just don't zone out when crossing a busy road."

Rebecca smiled, grateful their banter had resumed. It was a crumb of comfort.

She swiped them into the room. It was extremely large with a queen sized bed, heavy solid oak desk, and enough seating for a meeting. It didn't hold the charm or homeliness of Annah's house and never would, though.

Annah checked out the bathroom and large wardrobe. Rebecca smiled.

"Looking for miscreants?"

Annah shrugged, "I don't like surprises," then fell into a comfortable looking chair near the window and gazed out over the back of the strip, continuing.

"I'm sorry about earlier. I was angry and scared, I guess. I'm better now..." Annah put on a convincing southern American accent, singsonging the next sentence. "...I have expelled ma demons."

"I want this chapter to end. I'll be back to full strength when they catch the person who did it, too."

Rebecca sat at her desk and collected the papers at the fax machine. She paused, finger trailing off the smooth sheet and following a deep scratch in the wood. The person who did it? What does that kind of monster look like?

A swarm of memories buzzed. Her nail dug into the groove as stills presented themselves up for dissection, creating a macabre comic book: the car; the men in masks; the wall of an assistant at the police station; the bodies; pools of jellied blood collecting in folds of shirts and jackets; cloudy eyes open, looking, staring; those pictures of the contents of the boot. Nausea took her best shot. It was a killer right hook.

Elbows on table, she cradled her head with a hand. Like a missile finding its target, the last few hours exploded dead centre, catching her guard down.

The next thing she knew, a cup of coffee was in front of her.

"Latte, for madam?"

Rebecca frowned, the thoughts, memories and feelings having thrown her totally. She caught her reflection in the large wall mirror: deathly pale.

A warm hand reached across and fingers tangled with her own. Annah's palm lay on her forehead and two green eyes turned on her with a frightening intensity. Annah lowered to her level, kneeling in the thick, deep-red carpet.

"Your colour has drained. You feel hot."

At some point Rebecca had known the stress would realise. She didn't think it'd so vehemently strike, though. But it had, and like a venomous adder the poison was spreading, making her immobile.

"I need this coffee."

"I'm not so sure you do now." Annah stroked her cheek with the back of a finger. "It'll keep you up even more."

Rebecca's head lolled towards her caring companion. She sighed heavily.

"I don't know if I want to stay up or go to sleep. I'm officially thrown." She snorted a self deprecating laugh. "You can cut your losses and scamper out of harm's way, Annah. I won't think any less of you."

There was no pause as Annah answered.

"No."

"No?"

Annah's thumb stroked her palm.

"That's right. Unless you want me to go?"

Rebecca smiled gently, happy to be this close, to just sit and be reassured by her touch.

"No."

Annah ran a finger along her chin, along her jaw, slowly. It was a straightforward path of inexorable attraction and Rebecca's skin sang a lullaby.

"No?"

Rebecca breathed Annah's own answer back to her, "That's right."

The tension was strung taught. It garrotted the space, drawing them closer. Lazily Rebecca's fingers slipped through a mass of soft hair. Breath warmed lips, eyes closed. Close became closer, became closest. Instinct pulled them together. Fate drove them apart.

The fax beeped and the moment snapped, pinging both women back.

Annah stared at her with an unreadable expression. It wasn't anger or embarrassment, or any other singular emotion. It was a slight frown mixed with the clench of her jaw. It was a languid double blink. A deep breath. A lick of her lips. It was a shift, a turn away, then back. It was no words spoken.

Annah pushed up.

"I'll make the decision for you. You need rest."

Rebecca nodded, dazed and bewildered. Annah tugged her up and led her to the huge bed. Rebecca didn't have to be told twice. She kicked her shoes off, lay down and threw an arm over her eyes, blocking out as much as she could.

"I'll be fine in ten minutes. I just need to relax for a moment...."

Little black squares ate the rest of her sentence.

Chapter 30

The word perception is from the Latin capere meaning to take. The prefix per- means completely.

An unfamiliar ringing startled the figure sprawled on the bed. Rebecca reached over and got a handful of pillow. She sat up, rubbing her eye with the heel of a hand, realising she wasn't at home and the phone was someplace else. She reached the other way, grabbing the handset and throttling that noise.

Her voice was hoarse.

"What?"

"Got up on the wrong side of the bed?"

She glanced about, looking for the person who should have answered the phone.

"What?"

Laughter filled the earpiece.

"You're always monosyllabic in the - afternoon."

Her brain finally clunked to life and matched the voice to a face. A burst of relief erased considerable stress.

"Sophia. Sorry. You woke me."

"I gathered that. I take it that business went well?"

Rebecca fell back on the bed, staring at the ceiling. Sod business. Dealing with this alone was impacting other areas of her life in a considerably negative fashion. It was time to open that can and pout out the worms.

"Someone murdered him before..." No, not we. Not yet. That revelation would need to come face to face. "...I got there."

"What?"

She snorted a laugh as the tables were turned.

"It's a long story."

"Then you're lucky I'm still at work and have all the time in the world. Start at the start and don't skip a thing."

It could have been a quick run through of events had Sophia not stopped her after every sentence to ask a multitude of questions, few pertinent. At the end, Rebecca was awake and Sophia was in a stunned silence for more than twenty seconds, which for her was amazing. Rebecca always thought that silence for Sophia was just when other people stopped talking.

As if on cue.

"The boot? Was it a hatchback or were they all just very small?"

"Sophia!"

"It's not everyday you hear about a car with that much space, that's all." There was a long pause. "I'm still here. I'm processing."

Swinging her legs off of the bed, she stood and stretched. She frowned, looking around at the empty room and paused on the dip in the sheets and pillows on both sides of the bed.

"Snap. I'll be processing this for a while."

A foreign sound: cascading water. Rebecca blinked then glanced down at a pair of shoes near the desk.

"Has Colombo not solved it?"

She padded over to the bathroom door and listened. She could hear soft humming mixed in with splashing water. She smiled.

"We have Dougie Howser investigating. It'll be solved when he turns eighteen."

"I feel better already."

She rested her forehead against the cold wood door, letting the smooth tones of her showering companion wash over her. Annah hit a perfect note.

Her fingertips connected with the door; her mind dealt with her friend.

"You didn't get questioned by him for almost four hours."

Sophia laughed loudly.

"I expect as soon as you get home, you'll find a way to acquire his police station and have the replacement built halfway up a mountain."

"That thought occurred to me after hour one. His office will not have any windows."

"And, dearheart, why am I only hearing about this now?"

Sophia and her amazing accuracy.

"because if I'd told you, you'd have called everyone from the consulate to the Price of Monaco. I'm in the middle of some very..."

"Important business deals," Sophia clicked her tongue. *"Better you potentially languish in Rikers Island."*

"That's in New York."

"You've even brushed up on your prison geography. This situation is beyond bad."

"I'm not going to jail."

"You say that now, but I'm going on the hunt for cupcake sized files for your breakout."

The singing stopped and the handle rattled. Rebecca took a quick step back just as the door swung open. In a miniscule towel, Annah yelped, wide-eyed at the shock of the figure standing right at the doorway. Rebecca dropped the phone, her heart rate exploding. She couldn't help but notice the shapely long legs and the lucky water droplets clinging to them. Her cheeks warmed as she stuttered a turn then decided to grab the phone and stride off instead.

"Are you all right?"

Her words trailed. "No, I'm fine. There's someone else here..."

"Who?"

Rebecca fumbled, aware she'd left out mentioning Annah altogether. Technically it wasn't a lie but an omission.

"An assistant. Helping."

Okay, that was a lie. She rolled her eyes at the inadequate sounding excuse, but Sophia was obviously doing something else at the same time; with split attention Rebecca had an advantage. She held for a minute or two while Sophia gave a co-worker instructions before resuming.

"You need to come back before they give you the electric chair. When's your flight?"

"They won't let me leave the state, let alone country."

"How ridiculous!"

Annah walked by, now with the addition of clothes and caught Rebecca's eye, mouthing, "Sorry," quite shyly.

A slow smile lit up Rebecca's face.

Annah sat and looked out of the window. Rebecca sat and looked at her. Sophia popped her out of that bubble.

"I'll call you later. I have a client to see me. I expect to be kept in the loop from now on. Take care."

"You, too."

She ended the call, walked over to the relaxed brunette and lay a hand on her shoulder.

"Annah?"

Annah jumped.

"Sorry. I was daydreaming. You don't mind about the shower, do you? I felt gritty."

"Of course not."

Rebecca followed Annah's gaze out to the view of the strip.

"Looks like the back of a movie set, doesn't it?" She smiled down at her. "It's why I stay here. The view isn't so tinsel-y. Anyway, I'm famished. I'm ordering from room service so I can pick while I go through my papers.

Can I interest you in a mountainous salad or heart attack sized burger?"

Annah looked up, piercing the space between them with a personality that grabbed her and ruffled everywhere. Rebecca took control of those hormones for a moment and allowed the menu to slip from her grasp.

"I'll take a good look," Annah said.

The mood clearly needed lifting.

"It's only fair that you get the same opportunity I just had."

Annah went bright red.

"I temporarily forgot where I was. I'm embarrassed."

"Don't be."

She patted Annah's shoulder and walked back to the desk, easily sinking into a small pile of couriered envelopes. Work. This would keep her concentration in place for a while. She sank into contracts, queries and details with a dazzling determination.

Finally Annah got up and held the menu under her nose, and after five seconds Rebecca tapped Caesar salad with a friendly smile before turning back to some horribly complex inter-office politics that had stalled a very big deal.

She was vaguely aware of room service and the gentle humdrum of plates being laid out.

"Lunch, dinner, whatever, is served."

Rebecca glanced between the delicious looking food over on the table and at her papers. Annah laughed.

"You look like my sister's dog when I throw a treat in one direction and then rattle his lead in the other."

"You're a cruel tease?"

"Only when I have to be."

Rebecca caught the tail end of an intense stare. It was a loaded look, the glancing bullet containing a very mutual feeling. But experiencing and voicing are two different things. Neither woman said a word. Annah sat down and stared at her salad. Rebecca spun back quickly, fiddling with a file.

You need to get a grip.

Finally she sat down opposite. Annah noticeably struggled to find something to say, ending up with the inane.

"Balsamic dressing?"

Rebecca shook her head.

"No thank you. I'm not a fan."

Annah carefully put the little pot back down and picked up a piece of carrot, crunching it loudly.

"Me neither." Annah sipped blood orange juice. "Look, I was thinking. You know I have that huge house for the week. And we both think hotels suck." A slice of carrot was held aloft. "Although they do chop vegetables better than me."

Rebecca watched the swishing slither.

"Those are probably reformed. You know, mushed and then pressed into shapes."

Annah examined her salad. Rebecca carried on.

"Ignore me. I'm sure these were grown in only the finest of test tubes."

Annah's smile grew steadily and reached up to make her eyes sparkle.

"Can I enjoy my salad?"

"I'm sorry, are my partisan views littering your Romaine lettuce? I'm not going to be the one who points out all the leaves are very similar in shape and size." Rebecca kept her face straight. It wasn't easy. "I can see the assembly line now. Little lettuce cutters chopping the shapes out of huge sheets..."

Annah leant over and poked a small stick of celery into her mouth.

"At least I've found a way to keep you quiet."

She sat back, happily crunching through the thin stick.

"Quite a complex plan to steal your celery, wasn't it?"

Annah picked another piece up and deposited it into the bowl opposite.

"I hate it." A few more pieces joined the first. "You can have it all. I'll stick to my genetically modified salad and cloned salmon."

Rebecca happily corralled the stick, enjoying the gentle camaraderie .

"Thank you."

Annah's smile turned into a soft chuckle.

"I bet it controls your ulcer well."

Rebecca paused.

"You're very perceptive." She felt her expression shift for the worse, the wonderful mood about to be shredded at the change of topic. "Or perhaps it was just the research?"

Annah jumped in quickly.

"I don't want to talk about work when I'm with you."

Rebecca was scrutinised by a pair of intelligent eyes that flickered over her face. The owner looked very serious.

"That makes two of us." Rebecca's expression lightened as she waved a little celery 'flag'. "Celery is better than constant medication, so from now on, unload it all on me."

"Done deal."

They picked at their meal. It was hot in the right places and cold in all the others. It was why Rebecca always stayed here, because, despite it being a chain, this specific hotel had exceptional attention to detail.

Annah seemed to relax a lot more, seemed chirpy almost.

"Want to grab all of your stuff and stay at the house?"

Rebecca thought about it for a moment.

"I'm not sure, Annah. I don't think this is going to go away."

Rebecca sighed at the double meaning. She wasn't sure what was more dangerous, Kent or this attraction.

"It's better you're not alone, and I really like having you there. Don't rationalise. Just say yes."

Instinctively Annah reached over, lay a hand on top of Rebecca's and squeezed. After a moment's pause, Rebecca squeezed back. She answered two questions with her reply.

"Yes."

Chapter 31

Fascination is derived from the Latin fascinum, to cast an evil spell.

After arranging to courier a few signed documents back to Joy, Rebecca stopped at the check-out desks. She looked down at her key then slipped it in her pocket.

"Let's leave the room on the computer as mine. It's paid for."

It might come in useful, she thought.

"The police have my address, anyway," Annah said transfixed by the glitzy casino floor.

Rebecca's mood chilled as reality unexpectedly re-entered the picture.

"I'd hate to give them any trouble in finding me," she snapped, harsher than expected. It was a real reminder of the unique type of stress she was experiencing.

Rebecca started walking, needing her legs to be doing something other than staying put. Annah finally caught up.

"It was a stupid thing to say, Rebecca. Sorry."

She glanced across and saw the little lines of worry between Annah's eyes. Rebecca touched a hand to her arm briefly, trying to reduce the initial spike of her previous outburst.

"It's the truth."

Yes, it was.

They made it through the back of the hotel and out into the car park. Opening opposite jeep doors they both had to take a step back at the baking expulsion of air. Annah gave her a strange look. Haunting even; sad definitely. Annah didn't get in the drivers side, but leant on the heated metalwork.

"Rebecca, are you okay?"

What a question. What an answer.

She shook her head and spoke unedited words.

"This isn't a dodgy contract to re-write. I can't fix this by finding an angle to come at in the figures or by replacing management. I'm at the mercy of someone I wouldn't trust to investigate the case of my missing post-it notes. So, no, I'm not okay." She looked away. "Let's go."

Annah stayed still.

"Rebecca...?"

Rebecca massaged her temples as they started to pound.

"Please, let's go."

She hefted a bag of files into the rear, now fully realising how loose a grip she held on keeping it all together.

She was in ruins barely holding things together - and that feeling was so abstract that her coping mechanism wasn't...well, coping.

They made their way back to the house, along empty roads, busy roads, side streets that seemed untouched by traffic and others that were like motorways.

Leaving hadn't been a difficult choice on Rebecca's part. She really did dislike hotels. She really did like Annah's house...and Annah, too. She stared down at her hands. Could things be any more complex? She glanced across. Annah was watching for a gap in traffic at a crossroads. Annah was intelligent, protective and caring.... And also very attractive. Rebecca turned away, looking out of the window. Then there was the issue of how genuine this attraction was or if it was due to the latest dose of anxiety? It was another veritable can of worms. Her stress level rose.

A police car cruised by. She watched it as you'd watch a bug crawling over your skin.

I fought the law and the law scrunched me up like a scrap of paper.

Nausea jumbled her insides. To add to the influx of puzzling phenomena, the police car moved aside and was replaced by a shop opposite. It was a flashing beacon on a dark day.

She reached across and took hold of Annah's arm. Indolently beautiful green eyes turned on her. Muscles flexed gently under her palm and she lost her words for a moment.

"Pull in there."

Annah didn't look anywhere but at her.

"Where?"

Rebecca lifted that arm up and pointed the hand where she wanted the monster truck to go.

"There. That shop."

Annah leant over, looking. Rebecca could smell the hotel shampoo. It wasn't as nice as Annah's own.

It's bizarre. A week ago I'd never have thought such things, and now I'm all over the place.

Rebecca finally removed her hand. It felt empty. Her fingers flexed instinctively, wanting what they had held, back. It was proof of one fact. The attraction was real if even her skin believed it.

And her stress level soared.

Annah pulled the rearing beast around and did her bidding. Rebecca managed a small smile as they bounced to a stop in the lot.

Annah frowned a little.

"Your amusement is going to traumatise me."

For Annah's sake she hunted around for some cheer.

"And your braking is going to give me whiplash."

Annah chuckled softly.

"You're a harsh critic."

Rebecca shrugged, her mood having plummeted since their happy lunch. She hated this uncertainty. It was turning her into a mess, one minute happy and the other not.

She tracked an armed guard returning to his station, his badge glinting in her eyes just like that fateful moment when all of this started. She slapped the visor down angrily. It was as though fate was playing evil games with her nerves. She squeezed the bridge of her nose as if that would stop the images of the dead men floating back like ghostly apparitions.

"I know. I'm sorry."

Rebecca didn't move and at that moment she felt her body sag, every ounce of power, that spectacular animalistic authority, seep out. She couldn't help it. She was emotionally exhausted; this year had been carnage, this week, worse.

"It'll be okay."

The younger woman's statement was almost a plea.

It was a warm hand that took her own limp one, resuscitating it with the touch, making her fingers curl slowly. It was a peaceful embrace. Everything faded: the outside, the last few days, everything. She didn't resist as Annah lifted it smoothly; lips planted firmly; Rebecca sighed audibly. Annah replaced it back and let go. Rebecca's palm tingled from those lips. She looked at Annah for a long moment. Those Chinese whispers stood up to be counted again. They sang a song of sixpence, their message very wry.

"I need some air."

Rebecca stumbled out of the car into the stifling heat. The car dipped the smallest of amounts as she leant heavily on the door, sucking in baking air as the sun raged down. At least this place was constant. It was always hot as Hell.

She'd never been much for long pep talks. Her grandfather had told her after she'd lost an important cross-country race as a teenager: *you can do anything if you work hard enough. You don't need a cheerleading squad to razzle dazzle you on.* She'd pooh-poohed the statement to begin with, but with age came an appreciation for the things he'd told her.

She reaffirmed his thoughts, whispering to herself.

"You just need to pull yourself together."

She didn't move when the driver's door opened, or when Annah leant back next to her. There was a long heavy silence.

"This isn't how I saw this week going, Rebecca."

She turned and Annah's eyes blazed in the desert heat.

"Me neither. You're not seeing my best side."

"At least you haven't fallen apart."

The corners of her mouth twitched.

"I feel like some part of me is about to." She gazed off into the distance... "Divorce. Murder. Mayhem." ...but then turned her intense gaze back on Annah. "And then there's you." It was cryptic; it was straightforward; it was heartfelt; it was guarded. "This year hasn't been easy."

Rebecca added as a whispered afterthought.

Annah reached over, pushing a strand of hair back behind Rebecca's ear, making her shiver in the desert heat. Soft fingertips followed her jaw. Her body wanted this; her mind had no idea what it was doing. Rebecca held that wrist gently, stopping it.

"That's just going to make everything a lot more complex, Annah."

"Would it be so bad?"

Rebecca felt lost, as though she kept slipping from the life raft only to find it again as she took her last breath. It was exhausting.

"In general no. At this exact moment, yes."

Annah withdrew her hand quickly.

"I'm sorry."

Rebecca took hold of it and grasped tightly for a brief moment before letting go.

"Let's get out of this heat."

Annah flipped her sunglasses down from their usual resting place. They walked into the specialist cigar and cigarette emporium.

Chapter 32

All temptations are found either in hope or fear. English proverb.

Rebecca snuck furtive glances as she spoke to the man behind the counter. She caught Annah's eye and quickly looked away, pretending she hadn't turned into some fawning teenager experiencing her first confusing crush. She frowned. She was fawning; she was confused. All that was missing was a bad case of acne. With a chastising tirade in her head she reminded herself what she was here to do - and it wasn't to get derailed. She straightened her shoulders and sank into work mode.

At first the man fidgeted as her condensed focus hit him square on. It didn't take long for that fidgeting to stop as she proved how she'd closed so many huge deals. And then it felt better. She felt better. She vaulted the glitch outside and regained her poise, the elegance and assertiveness in which she moved.

The tall executive walked back, frowning. Annah looked away and grabbed a lighter.

"I don't know what I hoped to achieve coming here." Rebecca sighed, her statement remarkably frank. "No, I do. I was annoyed at being powerless and that kind of thing irks me."

"Couldn't he help with the filter markings?"

Rebecca glanced back at him for a moment. He smiled widely and waved. She waved back.

"He more than helped. It's an exclusive brand. He even told me where the factory was - that produces over thirty million packets a year."

"Oh. That'd be..." Annah's gaze slipped away for a moment before pinging back. "...about fifty-five thousand potential suspects."

Rebecca quirked an eyebrow at the human calculator in front of her. Such hidden talents. Annah shifted and carried on.

"It's ten packs a week. Five hundred and twenty over a year. Add a load of zeros. Fifty-five thousand, give or take."

"Any idea how long that would take to investigate?"

"I do, Miss Cavendish. A long time."

What a smart ass.

"Clever kid."

"I'm twenty seven," Annah's eyelashes fluttered.

Rebecca infused her reply with a gentle amount of wit, trying to lever the mood away from any potential offence.

"And I'm thirty seven, so I get to call you kid."

Annah frowned, a smirk hinting her lips.

"And using that logic I can call you grandma?"

Very slowly Rebecca lost the battle to keep her amusement hidden. Gradually her smile filled the space between them.

"Touché. I won't be held responsible for my actions if you do."

"That's almost enough motivation."

Annah idly fiddled with the lighter. Suddenly it flashed red and white and started to play a little tune that was completely unrecognisable due to the bad quality speaker. Both women looked down at the vibrating oblong. Rebecca's face glowed from amusement as she slapped her hand across the younger woman's, muffling the tune. Annah wiggled it free, allowing the wonder of the little speaker to reverberate through the other customers.

"Stifling such genius? Rebecca, you should be ashamed of yourself."

Rebecca glanced around and was rewarded with a few frowns, a couple of laughs and the beautiful intensity of two happy eyes.

"I am. In fact, I don't know how I'll sleep tonight - especially if it carries on."

Annah silenced it with a click and raised both eyebrows. Rebecca held her hand firm.

"Is it safe for me to let go?"

"I think so. My fun was short lived, and yet really rewarding. It's weird how that works."

Rebecca removed her hand slowly, adding, "Thank you."

"No, thank you for being a good audience."

The man behind the counter walked by and smiled widely again. Annah's eyes tracked him. Rebecca caught the curious look of her companion.

"What?" Rebecca queried.

Annah took hold of one of her hands and turned it over, then did the same to the other.

Rebecca blinked, "Uhm...?"

"Sorry. I'm looking for the pants you charmed off of him."

She laughed and freed a hand, putting it over Annah's eyes.

"You're too young to see that."

Annah pulled that hand off and quirked an eyebrow.

"You'd be surprised."

"I bet I would." Rebecca felt more relaxed as she tugged Annah's sleeve. "Come on, maestro, let's go. This is a waste of time."

The drive back to the house was quick. She felt better, a little lighter, more relaxed. She glanced across at her companion knowing why.

She flicked through some more papers Joy had sent. She tore up those which didn't meet her approval and dropped the pieces in a bag like she'd done ever since a competing firm had gone through her household rubbish seven years ago. They found some screwed up papers and stole a deal from under her. It wasn't a lesson to learn twice.

They bounced to another stop. Rebecca turned and laughed.

"You're never going to stop doing that, are you?"

"It's not me!" Annah laughed. "The brakes are very sharp."

They got out and climbed the gentle slope to the house. Sunshine bounced off of the path and mingled with the overhanging rose bushes thriving in this intense permanent summer. Rebecca stopped. Her mother had loved roses. Through-out the year the house would always have at least one vase, the rich scent permeating the air. She leant down, smelling a dusky pink rose. The fragrance was delicate, sweet and heady. Annah looked over. Their gazes met. She slipped her fingers from the petals.

"I love roses."

Annah walked back and sniffed a flower.

"It smells of Sundays."

Rebecca tried to process that but failed. She raised her eyebrows, begging an explanation.

Annah smiled.

"When mum used to do the washing."

Rebecca burst out laughing.

"Did you just liken this wonderful bloom to fabric conditioner?"

Annah had the decency to look embarrassed.

"Yes. Let's pretend you never heard that."

"At least you didn't say my perfume smells like deodorant."

Rebecca smiled widely and they resumed the short trek to the door. She locked the world out as Annah picked the newspaper up from the floor then glanced at the front page before folding it up and asking, "Are you hungry?"

Rebecca hung her coat up and stepped out of her shoes. She sighed and wiggled stocking feet. The heavy lull of jetlag was creeping through the adrenalin rush of today.

"I don't feel for food. I would love a coffee."

"Sit down in the library. I'll bring it in."

They parted.

As she pushed the library door open she stared at a large wall mounted television. She clicked it on and tried to find an interesting channel. It was a task. It was a long line of adverts interrupted by the odd few minutes of a scheduled programme. She flipped her phone open and called Joy, getting the usual greeting.

I signed the files you sent. I couriered them back today. If you have anything else, I'm not at the Hilton."

"Shall I cancel the booking?"

"No, leave it open. I'll e-mail this address across in case you need to send anything."

"Where is 'this'?"

"This is a private house where I won't be bothered."

"Good. One less thing for me to worry about. Oh, I caught the news."

Elliot was worth a lot of money and that demands attention. She bet the press were salivating to get an exclusive.

"Please tell me I wasn't named?"

Rebecca kicked herself for not making sure of the small detail. She was slipping.

"I dealt with it myself - privately. Jane's team have been looking after the case. She'll call you today or tomorrow. When are you allowed back?"

Rebecca sighed. Good question.

"I don't know. It's a waiting game now."

"I hate those."

"Me, too."

"Please be careful?"

Joy's tone was measurably softer. Rebecca smiled.

"Always."

After goodbyes she went back to channel surfing and hit a row of reporting shows. They were now all showing the same thing in glorious Technicolor. It was the epitome of not good news.

A primped blonde in a pastel pink suit spoke into her microphone with the battered diner in the background.

"Millionaire slaying of Elliot Peters, his assistant and three unnamed victims remains the topic of conversation in Las Vegas."

"He was a billionaire," she muttered, turning the blonde's volume down a little. "What a wondrous thing, reality. It always intrudes whenever it feels like it."

The woman went through other details. It was looking like a horrible game of Cluedo. Then more. The police have fresh leads?

"I hate to think what sort of leads," she snorted.

The door opened.

"The paper had the same headline." Annah said, standing next to her.

Pictures of the five dead men inhabited the large screen. Rebecca snorted.

"Maybe I should have asked for an Irish coffee?"

Annah's eyes stayed fixed on the screen.

"I could still make this all a pleasant blur for you."

Rebecca's expression softened as she divested her of the hot mug.

"It's safer if I stay sober."

Annah turned from the screen to her.

"Safer for...?"

The pause was long and heavy as Rebecca's smile turned wistful.

"For all those concerned."

Rebecca turned back to the screen.

This was what Rebecca termed as lounging. She was happily ensconced in the comfort of a large leather chair. Her fingertips drifted across a wooden arm polished by time. Annah was curled on the chesterfield with the newspaper but was clearly reading the travel section and not the murder extravaganza.

It was a comfortable silence. Martin would never allow her to settle. He'd always bother her with something ridiculous, something that could wait. Rebecca turned another page of her book, glad of the peace.

A shrill ring halted all of that. Annah hunted around for the phone, snatching the handset up. Annah listened, scowled, and held it out.

"Rebecca. Kent."

Rebecca carefully closed her book.

It was like a hit and run. The news was delivered quickly with a lack of emotion or apology, and then the assailant was gone. She hung up.

"It seems I'm free to go."

Annah didn't say anything for a moment. She looked utterly shocked before she managed a sentence.

"Have they found someone else to hassle?"

Rebecca ran hands through her hair.

"I think so - not that he'd tell me. Either that or they've found a witness who actually witnessed something."

...or Jane worked her magic? Some international lawyers were worth their weight in chocolate.

They fell into silence and remained like that for a while. Rebecca stayed on the same page. The paper lay folded in Annah's lap.

Finally, with a sigh, Rebecca put her book down, pulled her phone out and dialled, needing to do something productive. Annah went over to the bookcase.

Joy gave her usual succinct greeting and Rebecca wasted no time.

"It's me again. I need a flight out of Dodge."

"That was quick. What did you do?"

"Me? I thought it was Jane."

"I just spoke to her. She's in Antwerp; the team meeting about it was set to be in an hour. It wasn't her."

Rebecca frowned. Then who? Keyboard clacking sounded in the background, delaying her thoughts.

"I can get you out tomorrow morning?"

That wasn't appealing. Nothing about this was.

"Is there nothing later in the week?"

"Juan's coming in from Seville. It'd be great if you could be here. Corporate are sweating like pigs since the news hit."

"Can't you reschedule?"

"Sure. I can tell Juan he needs to wait so it seems like the news really is affecting our company."

Rebecca sighed at her own stupid question.

"If that's all they have, I've got no choice."

"You're on the flight out tomorrow. Direct. E-tickets at McCarran. I'll have a car waiting to pick you up here."

"Thanks." Real life intruded. "Did you organise...?"

She paused looking at Annah's back at the bookshelves. Joy finished for her.

"Oh, with Martin? I got the box myself. Your post is on the side table near the door."

Rebecca smiled. "And my plants?"

"Watered."

"I should have married you, Joy."

The line crackled at Joy's laugh.

"Yes, you should've."

She put the phone down and walked across to the bookshelf and Annah. She stood behind her, close, feeling her heat, her presence. There was nothing like it. It warmed her core.

"Seems I'll be leaving you soon."

Rebecca reached over Annah's shoulder to pull a book out. She slipped it into the younger woman's hands: *Dining in London.* Her forearm rested gently on Annah's shoulder.

"Pick somewhere. When you come back you can tell me about the fun you had without me."

Annah slipped the book from her fingers and turned in the partial embrace. Face to face, toe to toe, Rebecca stared at someone who had taken her by wonderful surprise.

Annah's words drifted softly.

"Do I have a price limit or can I get my revenge for you leaving me here alone?"

Those words floated over Rebecca's skin. She shivered.

"No limits."

"It doesn't feel like it."

She squeezed Annah's shoulder as if checking this was real. For a moment they stared at each other deeply.

"Please say you understand why I have to go, Annah?"

"Of course I do. But understanding doesn't mean I have to like it."

And she didn't move when Annah did, when they shared personal space in a very personal way. Not even when Annah's palm lay flat just below her shoulder. Especially when it slipped up, a thumb stroking her sensitive neck. What could be more natural than this, than being touched by someone intriguing, someone special, someone intelligent, amusing, sensual, beautiful, adroit...?

She didn't know when the kiss started but as that slow burn burnt, she knew where it would end if a modicum of control wasn't asserted. But as Annah carried on, her will softened and resolve dissolved and then all that was, was this, the soft lips, the warm compliant body in her arms. And it was everything she remembered and nothing she knew. It was like finding those lost keys or catching a contract loophole no-one else had seen. It was like an A in class; like getting something you liked at Christmas. It was like a kiss from the person you wanted to be with not the person you'd settled for.

They broke apart, slowly, the finale like a full stop to a classic novel. Annah cupped her face so softly before fingertips slipped away.

Rebecca was dazed, confused, and yet enlightened. It was like solving a puzzle but not quite understanding how you got there. She took a step back, letting go of both Annah's shoulder and the connection they shared. Her entire body was stunned.

"I should go and pack."

Annah just nodded.

Rebecca pivoted on her heels and left the room. She climbed the stairs and didn't stop.

Chapter 33

Always make the audience suffer as much as possible. Alfred Hitchcock

She felt better after a good night's sleep; during their last night she felt a deep sense of dread as she clock watched, feeling each second tick by. During dinner they'd talked about old movies and good books. Finally Rebecca had given up on food because her appetite was deserting her with every common bond she realised they had. Finally sleep beckoned and they said their goodnights awkwardly, neither wanting to leave each other's company, both knowing what the other alternative was - and Rebecca didn't want that to happen here. Not amongst the awfulness of Vegas. It couldn't, wouldn't be special here. Just tainted.

Rebecca picked up her suitcase and pushed it onto the back seat of the 4x4.

The whole time she'd been doing the final packing, Annah had been elsewhere. After Rebecca had finished, she'd descended the stairs and been caught up in the sounds of a tense, terse and, by the sounds of it, thoroughly disagreeable phone conversation between Annah and someone. She'd paused, half up half down, not knowing what to do.

Then, finally coming into view, the younger woman stormed from the kitchen and reared to a halt in the middle of one of those colour-explosion rugs. Eyes blazing, nostrils flared and hands on hips, it was Annah who swung around, looking up, her expression changing in a second - to include a peach glow to her cheeks.

Clearly off kilter, Annah was making an effort to hide it.

"Oh. Hey. I didn't see you there."

"Am I interrupting?"

"Me having a hissy fit?" Annah chuckled, the severity lifting in an instant. "No. Just work. Intermediate management always seem to have a pole jammed up their backsides." Annah dragged her hair up and secured it loosely, glancing at the last of the small cases. "Got everything?"

"I didn't come with much."

Her words felt staged and dull. Annah's answering nod wasn't much better.

Rebecca got in the jeep and leant her head against the glass, looking up at the cloudless sky. It should have been a beautiful day. As the other door shut all her enthusiasm wilted.

Starting the beast, Annah pulled out of the driveway and hit the short journey to the airport. What was normally a pleasant flow of words was now a solid silence as the journey's end neared.

They pulled into the short term car park, taking a handy spot near the doors. Annah bounced the car to a stop.

Rebecca lolled her head on the rest, smiling gently.

"Thank you."

"Like I'd let you take a cab."

Rebecca gave her senses a shake, knowing it was the last time they'd see each other for a while and as such, she should be more compos mentis.

"Not just for giving me a lift, but everything else. For putting up with the police nonsense, for letting me stay, for...being there."

"Easy choices."

Rebecca gave her hand a squeeze.

"You're very sweet."

Annah remained stoic.

"Is that how you'll remember me, as sweet?"

"It's one of the things."

Annah nodded.

"My dad used to call me sweet - and whenever he did Julia would slap me for being a suck up."

Her mood sobered as she felt their time disappearing like sand through her fingers. She grabbed at any subject just to have a few more minutes. Her words carried softly.

"It doesn't change the fact you are."

"You make me sound like a kid."

Rebecca frowned.

"I hope I haven't treated you like one."

"No, no, I mean...." Annah faltered. "I don't want you thinking I don't know my own feelings."

"I don't think that."

Annah's dejected expression sank lower still.

"Or that I'm some teenager with a crush. I'm not."

Rebecca was taken aback with the blinding honesty.

Annah continued.

"I know what I feel and why I feel it. Even in my organisation I'm the youngest person at my level."

Rebecca quirked an eyebrow and interrupted, taking the easier part of the conversation.

"Do you think I hadn't checked you out professionally?"

Annah sighed.

"I'm not sure your files reflect everything I do."

"They were very thorough. You sat on my bench, after all."

That got a slight smile from Annah.

"Your bench? You own it?"

"My name's on the brass plaque."

Annah blinked. Her eyes narrowed, clearly amused by all of this.

"Brass plaque?"

"Polished brass."

"And what did you have to do to get a polished brass plaque?"

"Not sell the park to a very rich man."

"And all you got was that?"

Rebecca shrugged.

"It's all I wanted." She paused for a beat. "It's where I go to relax."

"I remember." Annah didn't look away. "I watched you for a few minutes before I came over. I felt guilty disturbing you."

"My peace is precious, yes." Rebecca's expression sobered. "But I'm glad you did. There are few things worth cherishing." Her eyes flitted across Annah's face. She sighed and turned away. "I better go."

"Wait."

Annah held her hand softly and Rebecca turned into the intensity once more. Annah took a deep breath then leant over and kissed her, gently at first and then, as a hand pulled Rebecca in, with an expulsion of passion that knocked everything out of her mind. Confident yet yielding; soft yet powerful, Annah said everything that lay unspoken between them.

Annah moved away, her jade eyes dark like volcanic mineral rock that made Rebecca's internal compass spin. Finally her hand left Rebecca's hair, fingers lingering on the ends for a bare moment.

"I didn't want you remembering me as sweet."

Rebecca braced a hand against the fabric of the seat, trying to get her senses back. Her pulse pounded in her neck and her hand drifted upward, fingers laying on it not to hide but almost in disbelief.

With a slow inhale, she slipped out into a suffocating heat she didn't even register, and pulled her luggage from the back.

For a moment she stood, with heavy bags in each hand, rebooting her brain that couldn't even work her legs properly. Finally the haze began to shift, lifting away like muslin.

It was like a terrible countdown. Her muscles felt tight. Her thumbs rubbed the leather handles. She opened the door but stayed outside as couples, friends, children, and loved ones, walked by.

"Time has not been kind to us, Annah."

Annah stared out of the windscreen and then turned into her gaze suddenly.

"Can I see you off?"

Rebecca didn't move. Not a bit. The pause couldn't have been more than ten seconds but it felt like time stretched. Finally she exhaled.

"Of course."

What other answer was there?

They walked to the check-in desks. Row after row of long queues bode badly.

"Wait. Let me find out where I am." Rebecca flipped her phone open, speed dialled one, and held it between shoulder and ear. "It's me. Which check-in am I joining?"

She shrugged off her laptop bag, placing it next to her foot.

"Snobby first class," Joy joked.

She laughed and the tension seemed to leak away.

"Here was me thinking you liked the frugal me. I'll enjoy snobby first class and make sure I only authorise you going by economy next time. I'll see you soon." She closed her phone, smiling, shaking her head. "I'm over here."

She pointed to first class and picked her bags up.

"My assistant loves to give me a hard time."

Rebecca sat her bags down and gave the man behind the counter her details. She smiled. He smiled. Annah looked off at the departure gate.

With a ticket in hand and minimal time before boarding, they walked slowly towards security. The pair stopped. Rebecca glanced at the short queue. It was a horribly lingering feeling of loss that came upon her.

"The time has come to say goodbye, dear heart."

"Have a safe flight." Annah said flatly.

"And you have a pleasant time here." Rebecca cupped her cheek with a warm palm, laying a soft kiss on her other. She pulled back a little. "If your organisation wants me, Annah, then I expect to be wooed when I get back."

Annah spoke softly.

"And what if I want you?"

Rebecca wasn't expecting that. Years of dealing with tough questions did not prepare her. She floundered, aware this was a very public place, managing nothing in reply.

Annah sighed and looked away.

"You'll miss your flight."

Rebecca nodded. She picked her bags up and stared at the woman in front of her. Annah looked tense and so sad. She wanted to say more but could promises be kept when she returned to normalcy, to London

"I'd better go."

She walked towards security. She turned back at the last minute. Annah was still standing where she left her. Even from here, Rebecca was sure she could see the vivid greens of those eyes.

She turned and headed into the throng.

Chapter 34

Vision without action is a daydream. Action without vision is a nightmare. Japanese Proverb

Rebecca floated through security like a ghost. She emptied her pockets into a little see-through baggie and held it up. Keys jangled and glinted under the harsh lighting. One part of her was happy to have left all of that behind, but another...? She sighed.

Her heels were x-rayed. She was patted down. Her case was opened, laptop powered up to check it wasn't a slab of...explosive? Normally it was inconvenient but today it was just a blurring interruption from A to B.

She sat at the boarding gate, staring at her mobile. The urge to call Annah was intense but what would it accomplish? She turned her phone off and stared out of the thick glass, watching planes taxiing and refuelling.

"Final call for flight V44 to London."

She grabbed her carry-on and handed her boarding pass in.

Fate was a cruel hostess. Her seat was the same sort of positioning as before. She frowned and pushed the case into the overhead locker. As she sat, her eyes darted, almost expecting Annah to come strolling up in that relaxed friendly way and drop into the seat next to her. The captain made an announcement. The plane began to taxi. Rebecca stared at the empty space then just closed her eyes and willed the flight to go quickly.

The hours teased by. After zero success with a nap, she kicked her heels off, tied her hair up and watched a film. There was something to be said for Sandra Bullock and the ability the woman had for making everything seem a little less dark.

After finishing a business plan, she glanced across to see a tall glass with mineral water with half melted ice-cubes. The water didn't last long. Neither did the rest of the flight. Finally the seat belt sign was flashing, the pilot was announcing their arrival and London was approaching quickly. It was only a matter of time before the last week faded into a haze. The thought was welcoming and saddening.

As she waited for the others to disembark, Rebecca prayed Joy had a car waiting. The thought of getting on the tube in rush hour made her feel nauseous. Her grandfather's voice would not have permitted the luxury of a cab if the more reasonable public transport was available so close. It wasn't pleasant at the best of times, but crammed full of commuters and tourists with ridiculous size cases, all heading for prime working territories?

Well, that wasn't something to experience unless you had no choice. She had one and exercised it whenever possible.

Her feet knew their way out of the airport. She scanned people in the crowd outside the arrival gates. Clinging to their little welcome placards, their eyes hopped about. None had her name. She did a speedy double-take on one, "Millionaires only." Her eyes climbed the dark blue coat with the crisp daisy yellow shirt underneath. Then it was on to salon-red hair, feathered ends that hadn't been styled by anyone other than a hairdresser in the last ten years, wide friendly eyes and an excessively large grin. Her friend's voice boomed.

"Darling!"

Sophia enveloped her in a huge hug, not caring they were now blocking the exit. Several people tutted. Sophia just waved them away.

"Peasants. There should be a separate exit for them."

Rebecca couldn't help but laugh at the ridiculous statements her friend made.

"Is this another one of your jabs at economy class?"

"Being a peasant is not about wealth, it's about attitude. You can be poor in money and rich in spirit." Sophia motioned off somewhere. "Come. We must go. I'm parked in a police bay."

Rebecca blinked. Sophia just grabbed a bag and smirked.

"I'm parked in a space and even have a little ticket to pay. Look." Her friend waved one in the air. "See?"

"I can never tell with you."

"That's why our friendship shall last 'til we both can't remember each other's names."

What a thought. Rebecca squeezed her friend's shoulder.

"It's good to be home."

Chapter 35

Amor Fati: Love one's fate.

The drive back from the airport and through London towards her house was an experience Rebecca hoped never to be repeated. Yes, her friend was a skilled driver, but it'd been a long while since she'd had the pleasure of it for such an extended length of time. She gripped the seatbelt again and found her foot squashing an imaginary brake pedal. No-one took a roundabout like Sophia.

Rebecca turned her phone on and scrolled through the messages and e-mails. One jumped right out.

I think I've mastered the art of stopping without causing whiplash. I wish you hadn't missed it :) Annah

The cute smilie face was so Annah. She couldn't help but chuckle. Sophia picked up on it immediately.

"That's not a work e-mail. You're having too much fun with it."

Rebecca typed a reply: *I'll let you drive my new Jaguar when you return. The brakes are fierce. You'll prob. snap my neck.*

She read it through and pressed send.

"Stop being perceptive and watch the road."

"I was born to multi-task, darling."

"You can't even talk on the phone and put your shoes on at the same time. Please watch the road."

Sophia quirked an eyebrow.

"Secrets aren't friendly."

"Neither is vehicular manslaughter. I survived Vegas. I want to survive the drive across London."

Sophia clicked her tongue and stuck her nose in the air.

"You're horrid when you have jetlag."

Rebecca rubbed the tense muscles in the back of her neck.

"I know. I need a long bath and a nice home cooked meal."

Sophia gasped.

"Oh, fabulous! What are you cooking us?"

Rebecca pointed to the busy junction ahead.

"Get me home alive and I'll let you know."

Sophia took a corner like they were on ice.

"And when there, you can tell me, in detail, all about your time as a murderer."

She thought of Annah, her smiling face and the way her charisma sparkled. She glanced at Sophia.

"That wasn't the most troublesome thing."

Sophia's eyebrows scooted down to a frown.

"There was something worse?"

Sophia motioned impatiently with a hand so Rebecca decided to share. A problem shared is a problem halved.

"It was Annah - the head hunter who cornered me at the park. She got a seat on my flight out."

Sophia did a dramatic double-take.

"She did what? Wait, was this the 'someone' in your hotel room that you were astonishingly vague about? I thought you said that was an assistant?"

"It's a long story."

"Short version now. Long version when I can grill you without having to..." Sophia honked the horn and shouted at a Jeep they passed. "...navigate through *idiots!*" A trademark hair flick joined an eye roll. "Carry on with the taster."

"She bribed someone in my office for my travel plans and ended up in the seat next to me."

Sophia roared with laughter, slapping the wheel with a gloved hand.

"Fabulous. We must have her over for dinner."

"That'd be a problem."

"She's a bore?"

"Far from it."

"Short version, darling."

It would come out eventually. Rebecca took the plunge, too tired to evade.

"There was an - attraction."

Sophia's jaw dropped open and eyes bore into Rebecca for a moment before turning back to the road.

"She made a pass at you?"

"Not exactly."

"What exactly?"

There was a long pause until Sophia broke the silence with a loud tap on the dashboard.

"It was mutual."

"You hussy! Did you sleep together?"

"No, not yet."

"Not yet? Good god. Here I am with gossip about 35a's cat - who is ripping the edges of my newspapers because that silly child delivering them won't push the damn things completely through the letter box - and you're having a Sapphic sexscapade! Tell me everything."

"When we get back. I doubt your ability to listen..."

Sophia finished her sentence.

"And drive at the same time?"

Rebecca smirked.

"No, just listen."

"Is that lesbian humour? Is that why I don't get it?" Sophia smirked. "We're stopping off at the spa for tea and a shoulder massage."

Rebecca groaned.

"I am not..."

"You're just grumpy right now. It'll loosen you up after the flight."

Rebecca turned the heating in the car up and shrugged.

"Fine."

Sophia was right, after a forty minute shoulder, neck and head massage, her muscles were smiling, singing hymns and praising her name once more.

Rebecca stretched her arms out.

"You were right. I do feel better."

Sophia sipped her tea.

"Of course I was, and of course you do. You also look vaguely human again. You looked deathly earlier"

"Thank you so very much."

"It's my pleasure."

Sophia put the cup down.

"And now, tell me all about this woman you met."

Rebecca glanced around, making sure they were alone in the café area. She shifted, pulling her chair closer to her friend. Sophia laughed.

"Is it top secret?"

Rebecca tutted.

"Just because I want my business to stay that way - as my business doesn't mean I have a problem with what went on."

"I thought you said nothing did."

"It didn't."

"Nothing?"

Rebecca sighed.

"Sort of."

"Sort of nothing?" Sophia took her hand. "I love you to bits but you are infuriating at times." Squeeze. "Please spill the beans before I clock you with the antique sugar shaker."

"We...kissed."

Sophia's hands sprung to her gleeful grin like a naughty child.

"She kissed you?"

Rebecca shifted, fiddling with her tea cup. Her friend's eyebrows pinged up.

"Good grief, you kissed her? You temptress." Sophia sat back, motioning for more. "Once?"

Rebecca shifted.

"Not quite."

"What quite?"

"More than once."

Sophia blew a low whistle.

"Well I never. Come on. Tell me about her."

"I don't know what you want me to say. Everything was crazed in Vegas. It was emotional mayhem." She stopped, really thinking about her next sentence. "But in the middle of it all was this fabulous person."

Sophia watched closely.

"Are you sure she didn't try to seduce you because of this whole headhunting thing?"

Rebecca snorted a laugh.

"She's not stupid, and I'm not a man. If anything, it's less likely I'd think of a move now."

Sophia nodded slowly, before, with a narrowing of her eyes, throwing a question out.

"Describe her to me."

Rebecca frowned.

"What does she look like?"

Sophia held her hands up, her lips curling into a smile.

"Any way you wish."

Rebecca crushed the little paper square Sophia's sugar had come in as her mind retraced those emotional steps.

"She has amazing eyes. I remember them from when we first met in the park. They're like that jade figurine I picked up in Singapore." She smiled. "She's intelligent, witty - oh, she loves Wide Sargasso Sea."

"Someone has to," Sophia interjected. "It's maniacally depressing."

Rebecca couldn't let that old dig at her favourite book slide by.

"I'm sorry it doesn't review the latest Fendi handbag but it's what we lovers of good books refer to as a modern classic. Perhaps you could lobby someone to get them all burnt?"

Sophia grinned.

"I shall compose a letter of complaint to my local M.P. but that's not your concern. Yours is the matter of the Sapphic Seductress Annah. Carry on."

"We get on well."

"How well?"

Rebecca sighed, "Well. And..." Rebecca swallowed as she felt a pain deep in her chest. "There's something else." Another long pause. "The attraction, it's more intense than I know what to do with."

"Do you share likes and dislikes?"

"Of course, it's not only physical."

"Aha! So it was physical!"

"You know what I mean."

"You're a wriggly one. You get out of everything." Sophia digested what had been said. "I thought it was a mad - and temporary - crush, but I reserve judgement." Sophia grabbed her bag and picked her phone out of the mess inside, handing it to Rebecca. "Call her and invite her to dinner."

Rebecca blinked.

"What?"

"Clearly this won't be a fling so I need to meet her. Call her. We can go to that fabulous Chinese restaurant near Joy's place by Canary Wharf; the one on the boat. I adore their king prawns."

Rebecca pushed the phone away.

"I'm telling you all of this to claim some of my sanity back, not so we can bond as a family unit."

Sophia summed it up as only she could.

"It doesn't sound like you've lost your sanity." Sophia reached over and grasped her friend's hand tightly. "It just sounds like you've met someone who is genuine. Don't ignore chemistry because it doesn't zing often."

Rebecca frowned and sighed dramatically.

"I'm thrown over the whole thing."

Sophia pondered for a moment.

"When are you meeting again?"

Rebecca sighed.

"I don't know. Dinner maybe, when she gets back."

"And what's the problem, because I'm sensing one?"

"There are plenty of problems."

"She's a man!"

Rebecca gawped.

"No!"

Sophia tutted.

"I watched Oprah this morning."

"Clearly. No, I'm sorry, but she's a woman."

"So you realised?"

Rebecca frowned theatrically.

"At first I wasn't sure. But then I saw the name on her driving license."

Sophia burst out laughing.

"I like you sarcastic." Sophia rubbed her arm. "Anything else?"

"You're just mocking me."

"I am, yes, but I'm also asking a question. Anything else?"

It was like trying to stop molten lava.

"What if..." Rebecca paused. "What if she comes back and there's nothing there? What if it was all due to stress? What if that connection vanishes?"

"She's gay, not a magician."

"And you're mocking me again."

Her friend's smile grew.

"And you have jetlag so I'm taking you home." Sophia picked up their bags. "Come on. I have the basics now, and I shall interrogate you more when you can defend yourself properly. It's more fun that way."

Rebecca got up and shook her head.

"How did we ever become best friends?"

Sophia grinned.

"Fate, darling, fate."

Traffic seemed to have lessened. Rebecca smiled and watched familiar streets and buildings as they got nearer and nearer to her home. Suddenly she remembered the lack of basics in the fridge; there was no way Sophia would have thought to stock up on bread and milk for her.

"We need to stop off so I can get..."

Her sentence was enveloped by a bone shattered explosion of noise and movement. The windscreen imploded; metal tore, shifted into positions it wasn't designed for; twin airbags deployed as the car spun violently; the tyres heating and melting a path.

Rebecca's head snapped to the left; her skull impacted; transparent glass became a mesh of fractured squares. Rebecca stopped moving.

A blonde with high cheekbones watched from the curb. She caught sight of the circle of blood on the shattered glass of the passenger window. She smiled and flipped her phone open.

"MoneyGreen is out."

Nina turned, pulled her coat tighter, and pushed through the quickly building crowd.

Chapter 36

Speak softly and carry a big stick. West African proverb.

Rebecca's eyes cracked open. A wide expanse of white light filled her vision. It was blinding. Suddenly, as if a switch had been flicked, sound resumed with a bone juddering bang: voices, men and women, blurring movement, hands touching her. She tried to move. Something kept her immobile.

"Rebecca, you need to lie still for us."

Lie still?

Everything was foggy and hazy. Her right eye only focused enough to see bright white. Her words slurred badly, making the intelligent almost unintelligible. She cleared her throat and gave it another attempt.

"What happened?"

This time a blurred woman leant over. The woman smelt of ice-cream at the beach, of summers with her grandfather.

"Relax and in a little while we can..."

That was all she heard before she faded back out.

It was semi-dark. It was quieter, just beeping and whirring. There was more pain than before. Rebecca turned her head to the side. It felt like turning a screw the wrong way. Things did not want to move.

A little green line pinged up with a beep at every judder in her chest. Hypnotised she stared and stretched her hand out, trying to touch the machine. It all seemed so surreal. Maybe if she touched it she could...? The thought drifted away as the machine disappeared into a solid mass of grey. Her hand felt weightless. But then it felt warm, comforted.

"Rebecca?"

She knew that voice. All her energy went into concentrating and focusing. Grey sharpened into a thick knit jumper. The body descended. A face. This she definitely recognised. Everything would be okay. She closed her eyes as the hand squeezed her own.

She managed one more word before drifting out of consciousness.

"Annah."

Chapter 37

The mind heals that which the body cannot.

In just over forty-eight hours since her arrival, things were significantly different. Rebecca was sitting up, looking a little more coherent. A doctor was checking her eyes with a light. A nurse was fiddling with tubes that pushed fluids into her veins.

Sophia cracked the door open and came in first. The staff glanced across. If this were a normal hospital, guests would be asked to wait outside. But it wasn't. It was private, exclusive and expensive. The medical staff went back to their duties.

"Darling, you're alive!"

Rebecca blinked and grinned up at her visitor.

"I'm on morphine."

Sophia sat down on the edge of the bed, chuckling.

"Then you are going to be very happy for a few more hours." Sophia turned to a figure at the door. "If you need to know anything, ask her now."

Rebecca's eyes went wide as she realised there was another visitor. She looked comically shocked.

"You're real."

Annah smiled softly.

"I am." Annah walked over and stood at the foot of the bed, her smile falling. "I'm glad you're awake and talking. You had me worried."

Rebecca's brain processed chunks of those sentences. There was quite the time delay to it all.

"Worried? Yes, worried." She turned to her best friend. "Soph, we had an accident."

"Yes we did. We had a crash. The car's dead."

Rebecca's answer was delicately childlike in tone.

"But we're not."

Sophia patted her hand.

"No, we're not."

Rebecca waved her other arm encased in a chalky white cast. It felt oddly light. She stopped waving it and gave it a quick shake.

"I think there's a problem with my arm bone."

"I'm afraid it got temporarily dinged but it'll be fine in a few months."

Rebecca flopped back on her pillows. She felt extremely happy which she knew to be the morphine, but there wasn't a single part of her that cared.

"Good. Oh, Soph." Rebecca pointed to the end of the bed. "That's Annah. And Annah." She patted her friend on the shoulder. "This is Soph."

"It's okay, darling, we've had time to get acquainted."

"That sounds worrying. You didn't tell her anything horrid about me did you?"

Sophia laughed.

"Of course I did. And she's still here. Imagine."

A hand touched her blanket covered foot.

"She didn't tell me a thing. She did steal my salad."

"She always does that."

Sophia nodded.

"Other people's food always looks so luscious." Sophia's tone dropped to icicle standards. "Oh, I forgot. Martin's outside. Do you want to...?"

Rebecca's body managed to coordinate sitting up very quickly at that news and despite being dripped in morphine her brain functions still formed the shape of a big sharp spike.

"That bas-tard!"

"That'll be a no. Fabulous." Sophia stroked her hair. "Sleeping Beauty awakens and the wicked wizard is

banished to remain outside of the kingdom for a little longer."

Sophia leant closer and whispered in her friend's ear.

"She's been here since the early hours. I've kept her alive with coffee."

Rebecca looked directly at Annah. Dressed in jeans and a plain jumper she didn't look like she'd been here for hours. Despite her injuries, Rebecca was still rapt.

"You look wonderful if you've been up all night. That's good to know. If this is what your morning after the night before looks like count me in..."

Sophia burst out laughing and hugged her gently. The nurse finishing the chart smiled down at her paperwork and took the opportunity to leave them to it.

"With every low point there is an equal and opposing high. That was it." Sophia said.

Annah cleared her throat and shifted from one foot to the next. Her cheeks radiated red, "Glad I could lighten the mood."

Sophia leant back so her friend's view was no longer obscured.

"Look at me, sitting in the way of true..."

"Thanks." Annah interrupted quickly. "I think the medication is talking for her."

Rebecca grinned.

"No, I definitely think you look wonderful."

Sophia laughed, patting Rebecca's hand to get those eyes looking her way.

"Oh, sweetie, if only morphine were legal."

Annah almost paled.

"Thank God it's not."

Rebecca drifted out quickly. The last pain-free thing she remembered was a nurse doing something with her IV bag, mentioning meds and not to worry.

It seemed that not worrying was very short lived. Yes, the morphine had worn off. That was obvious by the stabbing pains she felt everywhere and the invisible vice crushing her skull. Rebecca awoke and glanced at a clock on the wall; only three hours later.

"What the Hell happened?" She growled up at the pair of them. "And where are my pain meds?"

Sophia waved her own bandaged arm.

"We were brutally crushed by a hit and run driver. And you, dearest, have been on pain meds for the last two days. I think your brain needs a rest before it starts telling..." Sophia glanced between Annah and Rebecca. "...everyone they look wonderful again."

Sophia fluttered her eyelashes. Rebecca frowned and glanced between her friend and Annah. Sophia just shrugged. Rebecca straightened with a grimace and snorted a deep breath.

"Pain medication can make you say strange things so I apologise." She paused, only vaguely remembering. Everything was so incredibly fuzzy. "Actually, who am I saying sorry to?"

Sophia frowned, tapping a finger to her mouth.

"To be honest, both of us. Annah because you announced the plus points of her ability to look wonderful - the morning after the night before."

Rebecca squeezed her eyes shut.

"And me because I was left out in the cold without as much as a mention."

And that got a hearty laugh.

"See, I must have been doolaly not to have professed doe eyes for you."

Sophia patted her hand gently.

"You're forgiven."

Rebecca compared hurt arms with her friend, taking any available source of keeping her mind off of the growling pains everywhere.

"Yours may be bigger, darling, but size rarely matters." A beat. "And now on to business."

Rebecca sighed.

"I have been crushed like a tin can. Can't it wait?"

Sophia instantly sobered.

"No, actually it can't. Annah?"

Annah unfolded the paper and held it up for all to see. Rebecca leaned forward a little, squinting.

"I take it I don't have my contacts in."

Annah smiled and walked next to the bed.

"They would have taken them out."

Rebecca was used to scanning for pertinent details but this didn't need a lot of brain power. The photo was of Elliot and his brother. Rebecca rubbed an eye as it blurred a little. The headline jumped out and slapped her into the here and now.

"His brother is dead?" Rebecca sucked some air in as her lagging brain computed the last week. "What happened to us wasn't an accident, was it?"

Annah perched on the edge of the bed, next to Sophia.

"I don't think so."

Rebecca nodded as the tension began to crawl through her body.

"Someone wants me dead."

Annah leant over and took her hand.

"Listen to me. I'm not trying to shock you, but if they wanted you dead then you'd be dead."

Sophia scowled at Annah.

"Can we leave this for when she's better?"

"No." Annah let go and stood up, biting her lip, eyes narrowed in thick concentration, before finally cutting the silence. "I'm going to speak to the police and arrange a guard."

Rebecca stared at the white ceiling, the blankness helping her overwhelmed brain. Her skull pounded and her entire left side hurt. Her arm was starting to scream as if it had finally realised what had happened.

"I need to...not think about this for a moment."

Two green eyes took her view.

"Rest. We'll stay here with you."

Rebecca's mind processed that instruction happily. She faded to grey.

When she awoke the room wasn't as bright. Sophia was curled in a chair, snoozing, and Annah was nowhere to be seen. Rebecca sat up with a lot of pain and a lot of difficulty. The door opened and the wandering woman returned. Annah twisted her hair up, looking terribly tired.

"You have a guard. He's outside for now. Where you go, he goes."

"How did you manage that?"

Annah blinked.

"I didn't. He was there when I got back from taking a walk. His bulldog of a boss let me know he'll be with you for the next few days."

"Great."

"Free protection. Don't knock it."

"I left Vegas and nothing got any better." Rebecca lifted her plastered arm up. "In fact it got worse."

Annah frowned.

"Yes it did."

Chapter 38

Life is short. Live not like tomorrow is your last day, but like today is your first.

Rebecca sighed and shifted. Her leg hurt, her back hurt, her neck, shoulders, jaw...even eyes hurt. She tried not to pull the IV out of her hand but it was hard. Shifting the laptop, she went back to typing her e-mail. The IV tugged every time she used the *T*. She slammed the screen closed.

Sophia glanced up from her magazine.

"Has her highness found she is limited in her powers?"

"Her highness is displeased, yes."

"Should I get the young and most beautiful Princess Annah to aid in your recovery?"

Rebecca groaned.

"Did I really say something like that to her?"

Sophia smirked.

"Loud enough for the nurse doing your chart to hear, yes." Her friend chuckled. "But you have an excuse of being totally stoned." Sophia paused for a beat. "Not that I've let up teasing her."

"Sophia!"

"Hush now. We've been here ages and I have asserted my right as your best friend to quiz your latest love interest. She's been taking it very well, even nipped me back at one point."

Rebecca scowled. Sophia carried on.

"What would you rather I did, just gloss over the fact? No, I made fun of it and put it out in the open..." Sophia walked across, flopped down, and squeezed Rebecca's hand. "...because there's nothing wrong with telling someone they look wonderful the morning after the night before."

Rebecca grimaced.

"Why didn't you stop me? Stuff a pillow in my mouth?"

"Because she likes you."

Rebecca flopped back on the pillow.

"I know."

"And more importantly, you like her."

Rebecca covered her eyes with her good hand, the other too damn heavy to even lift up.

"I know."

Sophia removed it and winked.

"She's extremely attractive."

"I know," Rebecca almost whispered.

"No, I mean she really is."

"I had noticed."

Sophia blew a breath out.

"You have superb taste."

"You sound incredulous."

Sophia smiled wildly.

"Not at all. Now, no tip-toeing through the tulips. Be brave. Embrace it."

Rebecca grimaced as Sophia carried on.

"Anyway, she seems nice."

"She is nice."

"Then carpe diem."

"How easy. Carpe diem. Of course. I don't know what I was getting worried about."

Rebecca's shoulder got a friendly squeeze.

"Worry about life, death, or the immortal realms of Fate. Don't worry about an attractive - and single - woman who happens to like you enough to have flown across the Atlantic to make sure you're alive."

Despite the pain, the confusion and everything else over the last week, Rebecca's brain chugged a thought out.

"How did she know?"

"Because you're all over the bloody news, probably."

Rebecca paled. Sophia carried on.

"I wasn't going to mention it, but you'll see it soon enough. I am afraid it all hit the fan blades rather messily."

Rebecca sagged. It was the last thing she needed. On cue Annah came back in with coffees and handed them out.

"There's a Starbucks downstairs. I got us something fancy."

Rebecca began to speak but was cut off.

"Apart from you. I checked with the nurse who said the caffeine was okay. You got plain filter with a little sugar."

Sophia sipped hers. Her smirk was large and obnoxious.

"It's just how she likes her morning coffee."

Rebecca narrowed her eyes at her friend then turned her attention on

Annah. It was niggling her so she wanted to know.

"How did you know I was here?"

Annah took a long sip of her drink.

"I'll tell you all about it when you get out."

The doctor came in. Suddenly, like giving a puppy a chew, Rebecca was a lot more alert.

"How are you today, Miss Cavendish?" he asked.

"Great. I'm looking forward to you signing me out."

He looked over the chart, took some readings from the machines and finally disconnected the almost empty IV bag. He pressed a cotton wool ball to that spot and got her to hold it. He talked her through what they'd done, the treatment, medication, and scan results.

"Don't do anything to excess, and that goes for eating, drinking, and working. Other than that, if you have any problems then give us a call and we'll have you back in."

He smiled and wandered out.

Sophia chuckled.

"As if anyone who hadn't been responsible for the funding of the new wing would get that explanation from a doctor."

Rebecca smiled brightly.

"Money talks."

A light rapping at the door and it opened to two concerned eyes that went wide as they connected with her boss. Joy sighed.

"I'm not trying to panic you, but you look bloody awful."

Rebecca had perked up at the news of her imminent departure and simply laughed.

"Thank you."

Joy walked to the end of the bed and pulled her gloves off, holding a hand out to Annah. Sophia chipped in.

"Joy, Annah. Annah, Joy."

Rebecca wasted no time.

"Did you reschedule my meetings?"

Joy sat down, crossing her legs.

"No. They're all waiting in your office now." A deft glance down at her invisible watch joined a mock frown. "I'm here because you're late."

Rebecca quirked her eyebrows and glanced at Annah.

"Everyone's a comedian."

Joy reached over and held Rebecca's hand.

"You look better than when you arrived." Joy squeezed at her perplexed expression. "You were doped up to the eyeballs and didn't have a clue I was here."

"Sorry."

Joy smiled.

"You're okay and that's all that matters."

Rebecca sighed. Yes, it was.

They chatted amiably, catching up. Joy refused to talk about work and instead recounted the tale of Rebecca's last hospital visit after breaking two fingers making jam. This was when Annah interjected with a plea for a lot more details.

Joy avoided Rebecca's glare and whispered loudly.

"As you may be aware, Rebecca is very competitive. She got talking to some of the corporate wives at a party we were throwing for a client, and I'm not sure how it happened, but of all things, they got into a home economics competition making jam."

Rebecca tried to cross her arms but failed because of the clunky cast. She grimaced.

"They insulted me because I choose to work, as though I wasn't a real woman."

Annah frowned.

"And she broke her fingers?"

Rebecca tried to catch Joy's gaze but her assistant wasn't having any of it and just carried on.

"Yes, she did. I bought books and all of the apparatus Ms Cavendish needed to perform the pectin miracles. All she had to do was follow instructions." Joy shook her head slowly. "She burnt the jam to the bottom of the pan, set all the fire alarms off and, in the rush to take the smoking pan out of the house, slipped on a wax paper lid and crushed two fingers on the way down."

Sophia laughed.

"The house smelled acrid for days. Martin was incensed."

Rebecca showed her stubborn streak off to a treat.

"It's my house. I'll do as I please."

Sophia took that and ran with it.

"Something to look forward to, Annah."

Annah blushed; Joy frowned, aware something was going on but not quite what; Rebecca willed temporary psychic powers to enable her to get up and slap her friend; Sophia just grinned.

Checkout was as smooth as a high class hotel. Rebecca struggled with the imposed wheelchair; Annah carried the cases; Sophia picked up the meds.

Joy handled the paperwork and hugged Rebecca goodbye, promising to bring a home baked cake next time.

Sophia turned to Annah.

"Her cakes are legendary. It's why Rebecca keeps her on."

Rebecca rolled her eyes while watching Joy's quickly departing taxi through the protective blackened glass of the hospital.

"No, that's why you would keep her on."

Joy had organised a smooth getaway via a back exit to miss the throng of reporters out front. They all got in the car waiting to whisk them away. It pulled away smoothly. Sophia glanced back noticing a police car following.

"It's like the Sweeny."

Rebecca crossed her arms stiffly and just stared ahead.

"I want my life back."

At last Annah interjected with sense.

"With protection you'll live long enough to do it."

The car stayed silent.

The convoy stopped at her house. Rebecca walked over to the police car that glowed hello on her driveway. The uniformed officer rolled the window down.

She leant her cast down.

"How long are you here for, Officer?"

He shrugged.

"As long as you are."

She nodded.

"Fair enough." She pointed to a small quaint cottage covered in ivy no more than thirty feet away. "The ground keeper's cottage. It's empty and unlocked. You can use the facilities in there."

He smiled.

She walked back to the house, mumbling.

"It's not your fault you were ordered to be annoying."

Annah was waiting for her in the hallway. Rebecca closed the door and turned to the smiling face of a woman who'd travelled across the Atlantic to be here.

"I thought you'd visit my humble abode under better circumstances. Can the tour wait until I'm not feeling like I've been crushed by a bulldozer?"

"Sophia said she'd show me around."

"Her tour is pointing out this is downstairs and that is upstairs." She laughed but pulled the sound short as a pain in her ribs started gnawing.

"My pills are wearing off."

Annah walked closer, gently placing her hand over Rebecca's ribs. Even crushed and bruised, tired and drained, the chemistry hummed.

"Annah, you remember asking what happens when we're back in London?"

"Yes," came the soft response.

Carpe diem, Sophia had said. Add that to Annah flying all the way back and what more encouragement did she need?

Rebecca leant closer and kissed her, holding it for a long moment before moving back. It made her lips tingle and heart pound.

"That's my answer."

Annah looked totally dazed, a slight smile making its way on to her lips eventually.

"That was a good answer."

Rebecca shifted. This was all so new.

"I don't know what to do now."

Annah smiled, her cheeks flushed.

"You need to rest." Annah took her hand and the smile fell. "At some point we have to talk about..." Annah faltered, looking very uncomfortable. "There's a lot I need to tell you. Not now, but later. Maybe tomorrow."

Rebecca frowned. She didn't do well with surprises.

"I'm not sure I like the sound of that."

Annah squeezed gently.

"We can talk about it later. For now come and sit down."

Rebecca's shoulders sagged. She was starting to feel dreary.

"I won't fight."

All three women relaxed in the large expanse of kitchen space. Annah, the most agile at the moment, proved her worth by serving up marinated Greek olives and feta, and a tomato salad that had survived well in the fridge. Occasionally Sophia caught Rebecca staring at the younger brunette. A mere raise of an eyebrow would be all it'd take to express her amusement.

The meal ended. Annah popped the dishes into the machine and made tea.

Rebecca and Sophia ambled towards the conservatory.

"So," asked Sophia.

"So?"

"Something's gone on - or else you making doe eyes at each other is perfectly normal."

"I'm on pain meds, my arm is broken and I've not slept properly in a week. It's not doe eyes. It's barely sane eyes."

Sophia smirked.

"Claiming an imminent breakdown. You've learnt so well, grasshopper." Sophia sniffled. "I'm terribly proud."

Rebecca jabbed her. There was a knock. Sophia paused.

"Who is that tap, tap, tapping at your mansion door?"

Rebecca opened it to find the officer escorting a blonde in a beautifully tailored nineteen-twenty's style trouser suit. A crisp white shirt finished the juxtaposition between the masculinity of cloth and smooth femininity of her.

The blonde glanced between the officer and Rebecca.

"If I'd known it was such a formal reception I'd have worn a gown."

The policeman piped up.

"I'll escort all visitors and check with you."

Rebecca nodded then addressed this surprise guest whose arctic blue eyes never left her.

"And you are?"

"I'm part of an art syndicate, Miss Cavendish." The blonde took a step forward, extending a hand but when out of view of the officer, her expression fell; her voice remained light and chirpy; her eyes blazed their message loud and clear. "You may have seen my work in Nevada."

Rebecca caught the hint and let go of that hand. She looked the woman over. She was surprisingly free of malice and yet...there was a darkness. It was subtle but there. Never one to shy away....

"I remember." She turned to the officer and dismissed him with a smile and nod. He plodded off.

Rebecca did have enough sense to minimise any possible negative impact. She turned to Sophia.

"Business calls."

Sophia frowned.

"Make it quick. Doctor's orders." Sophia rubbed her arm and flounced towards the kitchen. "Anyway, the longer you leave it, the more time I can spend grilling your lovely companion."

Rebecca's attention focused and mood chilled as she faced the woman.

"Come into the conservatory."

Rebecca led the way, glancing in the long mirror that stretched along the hallway. The woman was just following, hands casually in pockets. Rebecca had wondered about the odds of getting a knife in the back.

The woman took a seat in the sprawling glass room. Rebecca spun around and held her cast up.

"Did you do this to me?"

"Yes," was the perfunctory reply.

"There's a policeman outside."

"Don't make us dispose of him, Rebecca."

Being good in business and with money is one thing. Having your life in peril is a distinct other. Rebecca remained silent so the woman continued.

"You're caught in the crossfire and for that we're sorry."

When in doubt, repeat what a person has just said as a question.

"Crossfire?"

"Do you want to be involved?"

"I already am!"

"Elliot Peters was involved. His brother was involved." The woman paused "You're not involved."

This was like a nightmare she couldn't wake from. There was no other explanation. Real life wasn't like this. Rebecca exhaled a long breath.

"So, what are you here for, to intimidate me?"

That brought the blonde to life a little: her smoothly curved eyebrow smoothly curved.

"Is that what I'm doing?"

"No, you're not."

"Then no, I'm not."

She didn't want to say it, but...

"Then you're here to kill me."

The blonde's hard stare took hold of her.

"It'd be noticeably easier, but due to reasons still oblivious to you but obvious to me, no, I'm not."

Rebecca waited. It made no sense but what did? The blonde stretched her legs out.

"Elliot Peters kept documents in your safe. I'd like them."

No please. No hint of a request. It was a distinct order. Rebecca bristled.

"I keep my documents relating to my business transactions."

"May I see them?" The blonde leant closer as the silence carried on. "I'm giving you an opportunity to remove yourself from this pursuit. You can treat this as a game, but we both know you understand how serious we are."

Rebecca couldn't deny it.

In all business deals there came a time to either show your hand or bluff. Sometimes it's all about risks.

"I want to know why I shouldn't call the policeman in and have you arrested?"

It was like threatening to set a field mouse on a mountain lion: Rebecca got about the same reaction. No reaction.

The blonde's face remained blank.

"I'm going to tell you a story."

Her voice was a monotone.

"Over sixty years ago, there was a businessman called...let's call him Elliot. He was based in Paris. They were dark days. An evil war raged. Families were torn apart. Men, women, children were transported to camps where they were killed like cattle. Those were the lucky ones. The unlucky ones were taken to other places. Special places. In these facilities, the Devil walked freely in the sunshine."

The blonde's blue eyes shone clearly.

"These facilities were made possible by teams of men and women who collaborated with the Nazis to run them in secret.

"Elliot was the golden child. He ran eleven facilities spread across France and Germany. He made his fortune through the torture and murder of over fifty thousand men, women, but mainly children.

"As the tides of the war turned, as the locations of his other facilities were being discovered, Elliot razed what remained and fled to America as a war refuge.

"He had enough money to buy whatever papers he needed to make the transition simple. Elliot purchased a new life. He left the horrors behind and started again. His victims were not so fortunate.

"Mass graves were discovered. There was a lot of evidence, a few witnesses - and then a series of deaths and fires left the prosecutors with nothing.

"In nineteen sixty three the governments remaining that were chasing Elliot -the ones who cared - formed a group with a select few operatives from each country involved. It won't bore you with the name or details. It was designed to hunt war criminals and bring them to justice."

"By killing them?"

"Justice comes in many ways."

"What has this got to do with the papers in my safe?"

The pause hung.

"The papers detail the plans of his last building: Peters Towers. In that building is a safe. In that safe is the evidence that can bring many to justice."

"How do you know?"

"It's my business to know," her slow enunciation was quite chilling.

"You trust me enough to tell me all of this?"

"At times obstacles are placed in our paths. These obstacles can be moved in a variety of ways. This is how I choose to move you." Her tone dropped. "But you need to understand that there are forces at work whose goal is to keep the papers hidden except they move obstacles in a different way."

"Did you kill Elliot Peters?"

"No. He was valuable to us alive."

"Why should I believe you're the good guy and not the bad?"

The woman smiled, slipped a hand into her jacket and pulled out a sleek gun with a silencer. She placed it on the arm of the chair.

"Because you're not dead."

Chapter 39

***Status quo ante bellum*: let's pretend this war didn't happen.**

There was something to be said for seeing a lot of your life flash before your eyes. It gave a distinct appreciation for doing whatever was needed to maintain the equilibrium of a heart beating and all of the blood staying in all of your body.

Rebecca glanced down at the gun. She glanced up at the owner. So, this was possibly the judge and jury for the five men in the car? When in doubt, blag it.

"Should I be impressed at the implied threat?"

"If you weren't I'd be worried." The woman rose slowly, regally. "They'll be coming. You need to give me the papers."

Rebecca blinked.

"What keeps me safe when you have them?"

The blonde picked the gun back up, sleekly holstering it.

"I do."

It was a split second decision. The alternatives were non-existent.

Rebecca walked over to the wall, opened a door covered by a large picture and placed her finger on an illuminated square. She paused but no grand plan materialised.

"Damn it," she said.

Speaking a muttered series of Greek letters, numbers, and words, she pressed a sequence of buttons. She sent a glare over to the blonde who was now lounging against the back of a chair. The blonde raised both eyebrows and smiled.

"I don't like you." Rebecca stated simply.

"Lucky I'm not sensitive then."

Sliding metal; clunking mechanism; hydraulic systems did their job. Three two inch bolts slid back. The safe door opened.

Rebecca took a file out and opened it. She flicked through the various coloured pages and pulled away a handful. She held them out. It took absolute concentration to stop her hand from shaking.

"The plans."

The woman seemed quite amused.

"You have three safes."

Rebecca pulled the papers back forcing an explanation.

"We checked your other two - which is why I'm here, and why you had to be delayed from returning home, hence the small crash. Sorry about that. I had no choice with the timeframe."

Rebecca clenched her good hand.

"How honest."

The blonde's smile grew.

"At times my pleasure does come from telling the truth."

"What a surprise, I thought it'd be from when you murdered people."

"Good guys and bad guys. It's hard to tell them apart from just reading two pages of the book, Rebecca. You've got to turn that final page to fully appreciate who is who."

The papers were slipped from her grasp and the blonde bowed graciously, turned and began to walk out. Rebecca frowned, perplexed.

"That's it?"

Paused at the door, the mysterious woman winked, "I'd stay longer but you look like you could do with a rest."

The blonde left. The front door opened and banged shut.

Rebecca was dumbfounded. Her fist unclenched; she wiped it on her top and walked quickly to the hall, to a small window. She watched the woman get into a dark car. It pulled away with arrogant calm.

She stood for a moment. This was far too easy. She glanced out again. The car took a twist in her drive and was gone. The policeman got out of his vehicle and stretched like a moggy taking up space on the sofa.

That really was it.

She went back to the library. She pulled a manila folder out of the safe, opened it up and examined the building plans. She slipped out a security pass to Peters Towers.

"Let's see what you really want before you realise you've only got the preliminary drafts and come and shoot me."

Chapter 40

If no-one tells the truth, is it really a lie?

It wasn't easy getting out of the house. A barefaced lie of, "I'm tired. I'm going to lie down," was met with a jokey tut from Sophia and a glittering glance from Annah.

She felt a twinge of guilt but the less people who knew about this the better.

Rebecca silently made her way out of the conservatory. She slipped through the gardens and, turning the flashlight on when she was far enough away, took a path to the side entrance of the gardener's garage. She slipped a key fob from a hook on the wall and slid behind the wheel of the vehicle. It quietly purred to life.

She rested her cast on the steering wheel.

"Thank God for automatics."

She tapped it in to drive and, with lights on dipped, slowly set off down the barely used path to the back gate. It wasn't easy during daylight hours; it was extremely unpleasant now, in the dark, with a broken arm, pounding head and vision like a pair of cracked binoculars that created a fuzzy halo around everything.

The journey to Elliot's building was slow, sweat-inducing and made her realise how fragile mobility really was; each roundabout or tight turn was vilely painful.

The Peters Towers loomed large. With no soft curves, too many mute colours and geometric angles, it was reminiscent of afternoons spent reading Batman comics. Rebecca frowned.

"You, Mr Peters, had a strange fetish for glass and oddness."

She manoeuvred down a concrete ramp, making sure not to knock her cast on the wheel again. That was something you didn't experience twice if you could help it.

Holding the pass against the security device, the doors of the underground garage cranked open.

One thing Rebecca knew, you didn't hide the obvious. It's what people expect, and it's always best not to do that when you don't want to draw attention to yourself. So she didn't look for the staff lift, or duck her head down; what exec would do that? No, chin up, shoulders back, her shoes echoed a rhythm across the concrete floor. The CCTV cameras blinked red eyes all around.

She swiped for entrance into the basement lobby, and again in the executive lift, and pressed for Elliot's offices. After a pause the light went green, the doors closed, the lift climbed.

Her thumb rubbed the raised text on the little oblong of plastic.

"The benefits of an old man who hates opening his own doors and forgets to take his pass back."

She massaged her forehead. It hurt. She hurt: muscles, skin, bones, everywhere. She felt like one of those stretchy toys you gave to children, the ones whose limbs grow exponentially and never snap.

The lift barely bumped as it stopped. The doors parted. Elliot's offices glowed a dull low hello. For a moment she didn't move. Breath held, she listened. There was rarely true silence. There was always some sound. Here it was electricity; minimal air conditioning; perhaps the odd computer left on.

"Don't try to hide the obvious," she repeated.

She strolled out, directly towards that place she knew very well. Elliot's private office. A wall of a security guard sat at the front reception desk. He frowned as she approached. A novice would smile, engage in some friendly chatter. A novice would have their arm dislocated as they were thrown down the stairwell. These were Elliot's offices, and as such, only Elliot's people would be here this late.

She dug the pass out and scanned it through the unit on the desk. The guard stood.

"Can I ask your reason for being here so late?"

Rebecca stepped out off her shoes and hooked them up with two fingers in the backs.

An important point she'd learnt early on in her career was, sometimes all you need are words. In the eighties, the early hackers used their wiles to call offices up and talk passwords and exploits out of workers. Technology had changed that, but, still, it held water in certain instances.

"Because, despite Elliot's bad case of death, it seems I am still able to be called from the hospital..." She waved her cast. "...to pick up inconsequentially unimportant documents at this time of night."

That added to the pass did the trick. The guard blinked and sat back down. His smile rested awkwardly on his lips. Social engineering opened so many doors.

It hadn't changed much. Her stocking feet sank in the expensive pile; same carpet. She padded closer and closer, just wanting this over with. If memory served her right, the preliminary plans had his offices on the top floor, protected by a complex set of security doors. That entire floor was now an apartment used by whomever for whatever. It'd certainly take a while to get in to.

Rebecca swiped her card at the heavy dark oak doors. They beeped entry.

And she was in.

She had spent a long time researching safes for her house. She'd poured over books, recommendations and had meetings with many specialists. It wasn't that she didn't trust them but that she wanted to know her true options, unfettered by bias. It'd taken a month, fitting the appointments in-between work - and Martin - but she'd finally picked what she wanted and where she wanted it. As she glanced around this bare office, she was thankful for that mini obsession, because if she knew Elliot, he, like her, didn't hide his main safe in an obvious place, either. There was one difference. He didn't like conventional ones. She knew because she'd asked him when choosing, and thank God for his chatty nature.

He'd talked about ideal places to hide things. Put your safe in the floor, or the leg of a desk - even in concrete pilings or ceilings. She looked around. He'd also mentioned disguising what was out of the ordinary by that which was in the ordinary. She went over to a refrigerator. She pulled the brushed aluminium handle and was greeted by a metal filing cabinet where chilled shelves should be. A security swipe box blinked. Nothing ventured, nothing stolen. She swiped the card. Clunk, click, it did the trick. What she saw made her smile. A small pile of dusky red folders.

She flicked through them quickly, biting back the pain of every page that flapped against her cast. Nothing that important. She flicked some more. New employees. Land rights. Company formations. She closed the door and sighed, chewing her lip.

"Come on, think. Where do you put important things that you either need constant access to or are confidential enough to get paranoid about?"

A memory pinged about their last meeting and the transfer of data regarding hotel plans. She looked over at his desk and the computer tower sitting underneath it.

Elliot's voice sounded in her mind: *I'm always forgetting it.*

"These things should have a beeping alarm on them so we don't..." She ducked down and saw the little oblong in the U.S.B port. "...leave them in our computers."

Bingo!

"Elliot, you were as lax as most rich men."

While the lift descended, she slipped her shoes back on. Doors opened to the garage. Her fingers gripped the dusky red folder tighter just as a cold metal cylinder gently pressed her temple. She froze.

"Miss Cavendish, you are terrible."

Rebecca turned slowly, carefully, the cylinder slipping to the centre of her forehead.

"Sending us on a fake trail, you naughty rabbit."

The blonde smiled back and divested her of the folder. She tapped Rebecca with the barrel of the gun.

"No funny stuff."

The blonde pivoted; a black car pulled up; she disappeared with a distinct lack of drama, tyre squeals or assorted nonsense.

Rebecca expelled that held breath and opened her other palm. The pen drive stared back.

"I suppose this would be the epitome of funny stuff."

Chapter 41

All things appear and disappear because of the concurrence of causes and conditions. Nothing ever exists entirely alone; everything is in relation to everything else. Buddha.

Traffic was light. Rebecca drove through the Limehouse link towards Docklands. She knew the route off by heart, slowing for the yellow banding across the lanes that shouted the position of the speed cameras.

She emerged from the tunnel. Huge city buildings overtook the skyline. It was like an infestation of technologically advanced termites preferring glass and steel to rock and dirt.

Rebecca slipped down into the underground garages of Joy's building. She handed the keys to the valet and made her way up in the lift. She leaned back on the sturdy rail. Something about this building was very likeable. As the lift smoothly rose Rebecca pondered her affections. Polished steel, solid buttons, heavy woods, sturdy handles, thick, well cared for carpets. Yes, that was it. It wasn't a flimsy weak design. It was one to be proud of, unlike the detestable new wave of paper thin apartments with half a million pound price tags.

What a foreign idea, to pay that much for a glorified cupboard where you can hear your neighbours coughing.

The doors smoothly opened to lush carpeted floors, deftly dimmed lighting and a tasteful walnut door.

She knocked. It was opened and Joy's eyes almost fell out. Rebecca smiled.

"When I hired you I said it'd be a twenty-four hour job."

Joy's fingers reached across, laying on her cast. Joy scowled deeply.

"You're unbelievable. In."

Joy pointed through a soft arch. Rebecca didn't argue.

"In there. Sit down. I'll get tea."

Tea was the English equivalent of having a palm filled with sedatives. Rebecca flopped into the soft mass of the leather couch. She fished the short oblong out of her pocket and rested her cast on her thighs. Palm open, the USB drive lay there, innocuous. For now.

Joy came back with two ceramic mugs. Steam billowed out. With a shake of her head a mug popped down next to Rebecca's good arm.

"I hope you took a cab here."

Rebecca held the pen drive up.

"Have you got a laptop?"

Joy remained still for a moment then sighed loudly.

"So many years as your assistant means I know when to fight and when not to."

Joy went into a room opposite, shouting back, "Who was the woman at the hospital?"

Rebecca chuckled. Joy commanded not just small details but all details. Rebecca shouted back.

"Annah Stevens. You did a dossier on her for me."

She stood and picked the mug up and went to stand by the floor to ceiling windows. The balcony looked inviting but the lock gave her trouble on the best of days, and now with one working hand? She resigned herself to being on the inside looking out at the huge expanse of balcony banking the river. Moonlight shimmered and reflected as if the water was a smooth slab of glass.

She sipped the milky sugared tea, warming her hand on the cup. The Thames path was lit with miles of fairy lights. Strings and strings guided you from Docklands through to Wapping and the Tower of London. With only a few detours you could walk from one end of London to the next.

Once, Sophia had dragged her on such a trek only to give up halfway through and divert to a Tapas bar, claiming surgery grade cramps to her calves that miraculously cured themselves after two margaritas and a plate of marinated seafood.

Joy returned. Rebecca tore herself from the view.

"Annah Stevens the head hunter? She found you at the hospital?"

Rebecca told her the work related details. Joy didn't say a thing for a moment. Then her eyes narrowed a fraction.

"She seems nice for a corporate raider."

It was an innocuous statement but phrased slowly and carefully.

"Are you putting your feelers out, Joy?"

Her assistant laughed.

"You obviously like her and so she seems nice."

"Ever the diplomat."

"Why, is she not nice?" Joy smiled.

"She is. Very much so."

"Well, then."

Laptop powered on the table in front of them, Joy sat, cross-legged on the floor.

"What do you need me to do?"

Rebecca handed over the drive.

"I need to know what's on it."

Joy looked up.

"Did you get a taxi here?"

"Honestly or not honestly?"

"You drove with..." Joy pointed to her plastered hand. "...that, to find out what was on a USB drive?"

Rebecca nodded. Joy tutted, plugged it in and clicked to open the files. A box flashed up. Rebecca sat down next to her and leant back on the sofa.

Joy stated the obvious.

"It's protected."

"So?"

"So, can you please give me the password?"

"I don't have it."

"Why not?"

"Honestly or not honestly?"

Joy sighed, shook her head and got back to it.

"Fine." Joy clicked open a few applications, connected to the net, looked at some links, and then went back to the protected folders. "This is standard protection you get with the drive. I'm not a hacker but I think I can get in. Praise warez."

"What?"

"Never mind."

"He probably thought hiding it was good enough which was negated by him then leaving it in his computer's port."

Joy glanced at her.

"I don't want to know, do I?"

"You definitely do not."

The boxes flashed off. Joy opened up the folders and another box flashed up. She ran another application and sipped her tea. She tilted her head and looked at her boss.

"How's the arm?"

Rebecca shifted.

"Painful."

"Did they give you pills?"

"Yes, but I've not had a chance to take them."

A box flashed up recalling Joy's attention.

"I've removed the protection. There's nothing here." Joy paused. "Wait a minute." Her brow dipped. "Lucky I'm resourceful." Another application started to run. "When you delete a file, all you remove is your link to it; the information remains until you physically overwrite it." Joy smiled. "This recovers the pseudo deletion."

"I'm glad you're on my side," Rebecca muttered.

Joy opened up some spreadsheets, clicking through five or six of them. It didn't seem to make anything clearer.
"What am I looking at?"

"I have no idea."

"Can you give me a clue?"

There was a bare hesitation as Rebecca wondered if she should involve Joy, but she knew she needed help. Better a bold truth than a bare faced lie she'd have to cover up later.

"They're Elliot Peters' files."

"The dead Elliot Peters?"

"That'd be the one."

Her assistant blinked.

"What are they, his financial accounts?"

"I have no idea."

Joy scrolled through sheet after sheet. She copy and pasted some names across to Companies House website. The details of the directors flashed up.

"I'm not one hundred percent sure but something is going on with these companies. Look at the names."

Rebecca did. She couldn't put her finger on what was making her curious until Joy pointed it out.

"The names mostly begin with S's and B's. Stephen Bragger. Susan Blends. Sarah Banks. Odd coincidence when you put them all on a spreadsheet and even odder when they own companies beginning with W. West Gyro Expanse Limited. Williams Blends Limited. Wicker Plants Limited. Then they go to animals as names." Joy shifted and stretched her legs out slowly, massaging her thigh muscle with a grimace. "Looks like they were picked quickly by someone in a rush with no imagination."

Joy concentrated on various pages for another few minutes before continuing.

"They're all controlled via two shell companies owned by another that is run by - Elliot Peters' brother." Joy looked up at her. "And you know he's dead, too?"

"Not seeming so rosy is it?" Rebecca tried to figure out the screens but there were too many. "What are they up to?"

"The main shell companies are drawing down money from the smaller companies; office cleaning contracts; building maintenance; staff procurement. Except, why do you need all that for all these businesses that don't really exist?" Joy paused and clicked through more sheets. "Okay, I've seen this somewhere before. Don't quote me, because I'm not an expert - I only did a short course at uni - but it kind of sticks out even to me. I think this is laundering."

Rebecca frowned and Joy clarified.

"Money laundering."

Just because you don't understand it doesn't mean it's not happening.

Rebecca sat in the front seat of the car. She tapped the pen drive on the steering wheel in time with the thumping in her chest. *Focus*, she told herself. However, with a lack of sleep, an aching body, and thoughts of murder and mayhem swirling around, it wasn't easy.

"Why would it be simple," she muttered

Her phone chirped abruptly. Caller ID made her brace for impact.

"Hello?"

"You're alive then?"

Sophia's voice held a distinct chill. Rebecca slid down in the seat and leant her head on the window.

"I went for a drive. I needed to clear my head..."

"From brain aneurysms or murder attempts? I don't think it works like that, Dearest. Click your heels three times and come back right now before constable plod notices you're not here."

There was no point in arguing.

"I'm heading back."

The roads were eerie. It was strange the way traffic changed as darkness fell. Gone were the snaking lines of cars and lorries, the speeding bicycle couriers, motorbikes weaving in and out of static queues, pedestrians ignoring all sense and danger as they crossed at inappropriate places. Now there were obscene amounts of taxis - mostly empty - and slow moving rental vehicles full of tourists stumped by the legions of one way systems and blocked roads designed to filter you through police checkpoints. She bet they were quite annoyed at the lack of horse drawn carriages.

She checked for oncoming traffic three times before moving off; it'd make any driving instructor proud. Her nails dug into the hard steering wheel. It was sweat inducing and painful. Driving was no longer relaxing or calm.

Finally the gates closed as she cut a path up her driveway. Anxiety leaked, shoulders relaxed, grip loosened, heart rate eased. Home.

Rebecca pulled in next to the police car and smiled at the surprised look on his face: paused to take another big bite of his sandwich, his eyebrows went skyward. A piece of tomato tumbled out as he lowered the window.

"You...?"

Rebecca shrugged, "Are sneaky. Yes I am," and walked towards the now open front door.

The towering figure of a woman in white was framed by halogens from the hall. It was an impressive halo.

Sophia's eyes narrowed into laser beams as she planted hands on hips. She puffed up.

"What time do you call this, young lady?" Sophia wagged her finger, scowling. "Wait 'til your father hears about this."

Rebecca walked in and kicked off her shoes.

"But Stacey was having a party and Dani and Katie were there and I sooooo couldn't miss it because Trent said he liked me and I've gotta have a date for the prom or my life is over!"

She was swatted as she passed.

The next set of eyes didn't cut her any such slack. Arms crossed tightly, Rebecca got a piercing stare before Annah offered one thing.

"I was worried."

Rebecca opened her mouth to apologise but Annah just walked off. Sophia nudged her.

"Is this your first official fight?" One of Sophia's beauty salon sculpted eyebrows drifted upward. "She's very attractive when angry. It makes her radiant."

Rebecca sighed and took the stairs to her room. Sophia wasn't easy to shake off.

"I heard..." Sophia's tone dropped to a throaty whisper. "...you girls like to make up for a long..."

Rebecca stopped, spun around and pushed a finger onto her friend's mouth.

"Sometimes you are proof that even the sanest of people could do with a little medicating. Now, I am tired. I am going to...." She paused, remembering a very valid point as she lifted her plaster cast arm up. "I can't have a bath." She took an audible breath and carried on to her room. "I'm tired. I'm going to have a quick shower and lie down for a few hours. Then I need to show you something." She preempted Sophia's scrunched face. "It's important."

Sophia nodded and pushed the bedroom door open with a flouncing bow.

"Madame, your palace awaits."

Rebecca smiled. On the stand was the little pot of spiced orange potpourri that was still infusing the room. She ran fingertips across the soft thick duvet along to the fleece blanket at the foot.

Sophia bounced down on the bed, clicking her heels.

"There's no place like home. There's no place like home."

Rebecca sat next to her.

"It's only now I fully appreciate my little nest."

Sophia threw an arm over her shoulder and gave her a gentle squeeze.

"Lie down. I'll organise a fresh robe and some warm towels for your shower. I've bolted the bathroom window, so no sneaking out to neck with...."

Sophia frowned, clicking her fingers. They replied simultaneously.

Rebecca: "Trent."

Sophia: "Annah."

Rebecca exhaled slowly.

"Will this teasing go on forever?"

"I hope so."

Rebecca crawled into the middle of the large bed, put her arm on a pillow and lay there, star shaped. She yawned.

Sophia patted her thigh.

"I shall have towels and a robe coming soon, your highness."

Rebecca didn't sleep. Her mind fired rapid questions, scenarios, whipped through hundreds of possibilities but couldn't pull all the yarn ends together. There were clues but nothing made sense. Nazis, money laundering, transatlantic murder.... It was like a Ripley novel. Finally, giving up, she leant against the headboard, put the pillow on her lap and rested her throbbing arm.

The door opened. A hand, a steaming mug, an arm and then a gentle face and smiling eyes followed. Annah deposited the drink and sat on the bed.

"My dad said tea cured everything."

Rebecca smiled as she took a small sip. Now she really felt at home.

"My grandfather said the same."

Annah's fingers traced the smooth alabaster cast.

"Hurting?"

"It's starting to get uncomfortable, yes."

"That's even more reason why it was stupid to go driving...wherever." Annah frowned. "Where did you go?"

And there it was. Trust or not? Lie or truth? Not much was black or white but this was.

"I went to Elliot's offices. I wanted to get something." A cartoon light bulb pinged on in her mind. Annah used to work for a bank in the fraud section. She fished the pen drive out from between her cast and skin. "Can you take a look at this?"

Annah looked incredulous.

"You went to his offices? Alone?"

Rebecca nodded.

"We can discuss the finer points of my insanity later." She waved the drive. "Please?"

Annah pincered it away with her thumb and forefinger.

"Now?"

"Please."

Annah set Rebecca's laptop up, opened the files and skimmed through them. After a minute or so she shrugged

"No idea, sorry. Not my field of expertise."

Rebecca remained expressionless.

"Nothing looks familiar?"

"Should it?"

Rebecca smiled tightly.

"I guess not."

Annah pushed the laptop shut and smiled.

"Sophia said you needed towels? Point and I'll fetch."

Something her grandfather had said resurfaced.

Everyone lies. Some are harmless but others can burn you.

Rebecca forced another smile.

"Sounds fantastic."

Annah left and Rebecca sat, still, on the bed. She couldn't say what made her get up and go to the door and peek around it carefully.

Annah was walking down the hall toward her room on her mobile, her voice a hushed whisper. Annah suddenly ground to a halt, shaking her head, her words coming quickly. The only thing obvious was the urgency and seriousness of her tone.

Rebecca took a creeping step back in the room and closed the door.

All of our unhappiness comes from our inability to be alone. Jean de la Bruyere.

The shower was a tease. It was too short and too cool. Rebecca twisted her head under the spray, knowing time was limited. After a few minutes - all the time holding her cast out of harms way - she reluctantly pushed the door open and grabbed a towel. She held it to her nose. It smelt too fresh to have been in the linen closet for any length of time, and Sophia didn't even know where her machine was. She clicked on the light over the mirror and her smile fell. She looked back at herself. Why didn't Annah know about the spreadsheets like Joy did? Especially since the dossier on her had shown experience in working fraud cases.

She grabbed a robe, slipped it on and left her en-suite. Emptying out her bag on the bed, she grabbed her phone and dialled Joy.

Her fingers drummed on her thigh as she waited.

"Come on."

"What?" came the sleepy reply.

She tipped the clock back with her good hand. It blinked one in the morning. She grimaced.

"It's late. Take the day off tomorrow."

"I will."

Rebecca got to the point. "Did you find the leak who sold my flight details?" There was a pause and rustle of sheets. *"Uhm. Give me a moment to wake up."* A breath fuzzed the line. *"There wasn't a leak. Only I knew."*

"Are you sure?"

"I booked it through a secure line. There was no one else in the office."

"Then how did she find out?" There was a pause. *"Why don't you ask her?"* Joy enunciated each word carefully. "She won't tell me."

"When's that stopped you?"

"Good point. Okay, you can sleep now."

The phone clicked off and Rebecca sat staring at the black screen. How could Annah have known? She processed and crossed through various possibilities. Was Joy the leak? No reason to be. Money/power/hatred made people turn. There was no motivation for her friend to betray her. Followed? Annah had luggage. It was planned. Hacked the server? They had military grade encryption, the same as banks. The airline? They wouldn't give that information out to just anyone.

The door swung open. Rebecca looked up from her phone. Sophia bounced into the room.

"I hope you're decent."

Rebecca smiled.

"And if I wasn't?"

"I'd have a lot of explaining to do to your girlfriend."

"You're like a child with a new toy."

Rebecca sighed as she processed what she'd said and what the reply would be. Sophia opened her mouth and closed it again, shaking her head.

"Far too easy a retort. I can't degrade my quips with jokes about toys." Sophia put a bottle of pills in her hand. "Pain medication. Take two now, please."

Rebecca read the label.

"It says they'll make me drowsy."

"It's one in the morning. And it doesn't say they'll make you drowsy, it says do not operate machinery." Sophia paused. "Oh, were you and Annah thinking of - you know, accoutrements?"

Rebecca growled.

"Out!"

"These moods of yours." Sophia was almost in the hall, but paused. "Take two of those pills now. I'm waiting."

Rebecca cracked the lid, poured two pills into her palm and swallowed without liquid. It was a trick she'd learnt when taking her ulcer medication in meetings. She didn't like giving the sharks anything, especially not a weakness like that. One whiff and they'd be laying on chilli buffets.

"Happy?"

"Very."

"I'm getting a book and reading myself to sleep in my own bed."

"You know where I am if you need me. Annah is in the room at the end"

Rebecca lifted her cast.

"I'll be sure to ravish her."

"There, I knew you had some fight left in you."

Sophia winked and was gone.

Rebecca got up. The shower had loosened her muscles but now they were starting to tighten again. It was going to be a very painful road ahead. She pulled her robe tighter, trying a knot as best she could, and padded downstairs. The lights were off. There was a peaceful blue glow. It was good to be home. It felt right. It felt safe.

She wondered what book would lull her mind into rest. She pushed the library door open.

A smiling blonde crossed her long legs and reclined in the Chesterfield.

"You keep me on my toes, don't you, Miss Cavendish."

A hand grabbed the collar of her robe and pulled her into the room, pushing Rebecca towards the fireplace. The six foot brute growled and moved closer. His entire frame filled her vision.

Fight or flight.

Her back hit the cold marble surround. It was pure instinct that helped her find the metal poker. She grabbed it and held it up. He pulled out a gun. Instinct or not, that was a top trump.

A bang made her ears ring and shifted the next scene into a partial silent movie. His eye socket exploded, throwing out a mass of skull, skin, blood and brain. The poker bounced against her thigh. She froze as he dropped like a dead weight with a dead thud.

Annah frowned, gun held out, a curling snake of smoke extending from the end.

The blonde uncrossed her legs and quirked an eyebrow.

"You're such a thorn in my side, Annah."

Annah glanced at the blonde.

"Shut up, Nina."

When the chaos finally begins, we'll see - we cannot eat money. Cree Prophecy

Nina got up, commanding the space with the demeanour of someone not often ignored.

Rebecca wiped her face with her cuff. Her robe turned from white to red, pure to tainted. She picked a piece of hair on bone off and dropped it to the floor as if it were a loose thread.

Her eyes met Annah's. The young woman opened her mouth but clearly thought better and closed it again. Annah lowered the gun.

Rebecca's head was swimming and she wasn't sure if it was from the dead body, the pain-killers or a mixture of both.

The library door swung open and Sophia rushed in, instantly stopping when her brain processed enough of the scene. Her mouth was agape. Sophia looked between Nina and Annah, the body and Rebecca.

"What's going on?" Sophia paused on Nina. "Who are you?" Then swung her attention to her friend. "Rebecca, are you hurt?" Sophia grabbed the phone. "I'm calling the police."

Nina walked over to the body, pushed it over and pulled some papers from his inner pocket as if it were a bag and not a still warm human.

"No need to press a single button." Nina stood, turned and bowed deeply at Annah - whose expression hardened like steel. "Officer? Aren't you going to arrest the criminals?"

Sophia's eyes darted around.

"Why did she call you officer?" Sophia put the phone down then looked at Annah, totally perplexed. "What the bloody hell is going on here?"

Nina just quirked her eyebrows with an amused smile.

"Annah, shame on you, you didn't tell them?" Waving a hand, her deep chuckle sounded out of place in the silence. "Do you need a moment?"

Annah's shoulders lifted with a deep breath and didn't drop much when it was let out loudly.

"Sit down," Annah said tiredly, flipping her phone open and turning away, obviously needing some privacy.

Rebecca glanced at her feet. They were drowned in a damson red puddle of warmth. She wiggled her toes. It squished. It was thick and velvety. A hand lay on her cast. She looked up into green eyes she no longer knew.

"Rebecca, sit down." Annah's voice lowered to a whisper between them. "I'll explain later. I promise."

Rebecca's mind began to lose its grip on what was happening as she gently drifted, as the sharp edges of reality hazed into a soft mass. This was definitely the painkillers. They were pausing her ability to process - she glanced over at the body - not such a bad thing.

A warm hand gripped her own. Sophia rubbed a thumb over her skin and leant closer.

"I don't think we're in Kansas anymore, dearheart."

"I'm not sure we ever were."

It was Annah's voice that was raised as her phone flipped closed with a loud clack.

"My office is sending a team."

Annah leant on the fireplace and stared dejectedly at the body. Nina sat back in that chesterfield, looking decidedly comfortable.

Nina smiled directly at Rebecca. It was chilling.

"If you knew her office like I do, that'd make your flesh crawl."

To say the next half an hour was a foggy shade of the here and now, was an understatement. It was Sophia who took charge of all sense and talked to the three men in dark, perfectly fitted suits. To Rebecca they just looked like high class waiters.

People came and removed the body, leaving an abstract work of violence soaking into the flooring.

One of them shone a light into her eyes.

"Have you taken anything?"

"I took the red pill." The film reference fell flat. "Just standard painkillers."

She lifted her cast up and he nodded.

"You need to come with us."

Now was as good a time as any to rejoin the proceedings, she thought.
"I'm going upstairs."

He shook his head.

"You need to..."

Compartmentalising the last hour, Rebecca leant down so their noses almost touched.

"In the last week I've seen three dead bodies, been arrested, threatened, almost imprisoned, lied to, cheated, followed, and now I am covered in some dead man's blood." She straightened up, glancing at the room of attention she'd secured. "And so, I am going upstairs." Her lip curled into an angry snarl. "Would anyone care to stop me?"

Annah shook her head. Nina saluted. Sophia nodded upstairs.

Rebecca wanted to know one thing. She pointed to Nina.

"Aren't you going to arrest her?"

Nina picked a slim blue passport out of her pocket and waved it with a shrug.

"Diplomatic." Her smile filled the room. "Also, one small point: I never shot anyone." Nina pulled the sides of her mouth into a faux frown. "I'm just an innocent bystander."

"Then at least get her out of my house."

Nina shrugged and got up with a stretch. Rebecca ground her teeth and walked over, catching her arm, moving closer to the person responsible for bringing such terrible things to her sanctuary. She could smell her perfume, could see her perfect barely there make-up and flawlessly styled hair.

Rebecca whispered harshly.

"You tell quite a tale. Not really a bedtime story. Nazis and holocaust."

Nina unpeeled her hand and freed herself.

"Who said I was telling a story. As I mentioned, to tell the good guys from the bad guys you need to read the whole book, not just two pages." She lay a noisy kiss on her cheek. "You haven't even managed the first paragraph, Rebecca." Nina glanced across at Annah and leant closer so Rebecca could feel her warm breath on her ear. "She's not even a pawn. She's the felt disk on the bottom of a pawn; designed only to allow the real pieces to move." Nina stepped back, an arrogant smile on her lips. "Knowledge is my gift to you."

And then she was gone.

Rebecca looked at her reflection in the gilded mirror that hung opposite. She wiped a red stain from her cheek then walked out and slammed the door.

Chapter 42

In the middle of difficulty lies opportunity. Albert Einstein.

Rebecca wasn't sure how long she'd been sitting there. The house remained surprisingly silent. The only thing giving anything away were the headlights of various cars in her drive. Slats of flickering white glowed on the walls. And then they stopped. Her door opened. She looked up at Annah. Annah looked very uncomfortable.

"They've gone."

"Is that meant to make me feel any better?"

"No." Annah shifted. "I'm sorry."

Rebecca looked up into the face of someone she thought she knew.

"I don't want apologies. I want an explanation." It was like looking at a total stranger. "Who are you? Is your name even Annah?"

"Of course." Annah sat down, leaning forearms on thighs and staring at the floor, utterly dishevelled. "I work for a covert protection unit sequestered to the NATO alliance."

Rebecca frowned making Annah explain.

"Like M.I.5. just a private firm. We've been following her for years."

Rebecca snorted with angry distaste.

"Who is she?"

Annah glanced up.

"We don't know for sure. First name Nina. We've codenamed her The Blonde because Pain In The Ass is too long."

Rebecca motioned for her to go on.

"Elliot owned several companies in Gibraltar. The Russian mafia likes to launder cash there. I guess he got swallowed by something larger than him.

"However rich you are, it doesn't buy you safety or favours. Elliot was skimming and signed his own death warrant. We tried to get the evidence before they got to him, but..."

"You didn't manage it."

"No." Annah sighed sadly. "It was obvious that things were coming to a head. We thought you were either involved with his business or another body looking to happen."

"How nice."

"It was my job to protect you."

Rebecca snorted again. Annah looked insulted.

"Are you dead?"

Rebecca held her arm up.

"Not from want of trying."

"If you're still breathing then I did my job."

The silence hung heavy until Rebecca waved her good hand, restarting Annah's story.

"Kent was nothing to do with me. Getting you out of the U.S. was my superiors. When it was obvious you weren't involved, we wanted you home where we could control the situation, where we could protect you properly."

Rebecca didn't get a chance to raise her arm again.

"I know. We didn't do such a good job."

Rebecca looked down at the crusted blood on her sleeve.

"Sense would suggest you slipped into overkill."

"We think he dealt with Elliot and the others. I wasn't taking a chance."

"He killed Elliot?"

Annah nodded. Rebecca frowned.

"She said they had nothing to do with it."

"Because she's so trustworthy?"

If anything, Nina had taken great pleasure in telling the truth.

"True. She lied to my face and then shot someone in front of me. No, wait, that was you."

Annah shifted but stayed quiet.

"Why didn't you just arrest them?"

"Diplomatic passports. And Nina is protected by people with more power than us. She can do what she wants and all we can do is deport her until she acquires a new one - normally from Africa or a small Caribbean island. To be honest, my employer would rather know where she is."

"And how does your employer plan on explaining a diplomatic death?"

Annah looked up.

"How does any coroner explain a heart attack? By signing a death certificate."

"You emptied his brain in my library."

Annah looked away.

"The coroner will decide that."

"One of yours?"

"Does it matter?"

"Convenient. And who polices the police?"

"We have controls."

"How do you know I won't blow this out of the water and put you on the front page of a tabloid?"

Annah straightened.

"No editor would be allowed to publish this. We're not a branch of the Transport Police checking your travel card. We're affiliated to the British Government and if we need to stop a paper, we do."

Rebecca looked directly at the woman in front of her. Annah looked exhausted. There was a lot of that going around.

"I trusted you."

"Rebecca, you need to understand that..."

"I want you to go."

Annah didn't move.

"I know that you might...."

Rebecca didn't raise her voice a lot, but at times it was warranted.

"You don't know a bloody thing. Am I safe from that woman?"

"We're escorting her out of the country, so I'd say she won't be back."

"And am I safe from you?"

Annah blinked and straightened her shoulders from that blow.

"I wouldn't do anything to hurt you?"

"Except lie through your teeth. Nazis, money laundering, offshore companies, the mafia? Who am I meant to believe?"

Annah tried to take a step forward. Rebecca's eyes narrowed into fierce slits. Annah stayed put.

"I was protecting you."

"And now you don't have to."

Annah went to say something but changed her mind. Her shoulders sagged and gaze dropped. With one nod Annah walked to the door and looked back only once.

"I never lied about my feelings for you. That was all true and it still is."

Rebecca needed to have another shower.

"Goodbye, Annah."

The door clicked gently and she was alone. A dull fuzz suffused her mind - something to feel grateful for. But through the haze of shadows one thing surfaced. Rebecca turned to the side table where the USB key was - and now wasn't. In its place was a small square sticky note with a happy face and the letter, 'N'. Rebecca reached over, grabbed the note and scrunched it as hard as her hand would allow. She threw it into the bin.

Rebecca shut the bathroom door and locked it.

Chapter 43

The word pain derives from the Latin poena meaning a penalty, a fine or punishment.

Her favourite place in the city wasn't doing its usual job of leeching out stress. Jamming her hands deep in her pockets, Rebecca faced the gusting wind. It was biting. It stung. She closed her eyes tightly and sighed. There was still a hallowed stillness. It wasn't enough, though. It didn't trick her mind into concentrating on that pain and forgetting the other. She kicked a branch, turned on her heels and headed out of the park, back to the office.

She could feel Joy's eyes tracking her movements as she walked by. It had been an odd few months since the crash. Physically, things were getting back to normal. Her cast was off; physiotherapy was hard but progressing quickly; she was free of pain medication and, despite Joy's pointed looks, back at work full time - and more, sometimes. Emotionally? She'd been shredded. It wasn't an easy task to find the strips and glue them back together again.

She hung her coat and scarf up and stood by the window, looking out over the city. The wind blew dots of rain and then stripes and then slashes as the sky cried bleakness.

A knock and the door opened. There was a bare rustle of papers.

"I've got your letters and memos. I've filtered your urgent e-mails. Sophia called to say she'll pop in later."

"Great. Thank you."

Grey buildings. Grey sky. Grey clouds. Grey days.

"Annah left a message."

And grey news.

"Leave it on my desk."

Rebecca knew Joy wanted to say more but also that she wouldn't. The door opened and closed.

She sorted through her letters and binned most as junk, unimportant, boring, or just unnecessary. Twenty minutes was all it took to answer the urgent e-mails. Her memos took even less. She glanced at the slip of paper with Annah's message on. With one finger on the centre she slipped it along the wood, opened the drawer, and watched it float on top of the others. A little pile of attempts. She sighed and closed the drawer.

Some things are better left unsaid and unseen.

The secret to living an oblivious life was to keep busy. It had been a heading in the fashion magazine she'd digested while spending her forth sleepless night in the library. Despite the article being from a distinctly comic angle, she'd applied it to everything. The house had become spotless, her closet was now ordered in usage and colour. She'd even taken pictures and attached them to the outside of her shoe boxes.

Whilst keeping busy, Rebecca was never more than twenty feet from a phone. Some part of her wanted the attempted calls and messages. And messages there were. Annah was persistent. She looked at the drawer with those secrets. Even now, months later, she wasn't giving up even if the frequency had significantly lessened.

Rebecca called Joy in, and then went over to the plan on her wall, the one with that single missing square of land on. It had been niggling all this time.

She stared at it then pivoted.

"Send someone to cut off his utilities."

Joy's pen remained paused over the page.

"Rebecca, he's seventy-three."

"Then he'll get cold very quickly and want to move to the fantastic house I offered him four months ago."

Joy stared at her, obviously biting back a comment. Joy cleared her throat and nodded.

"I'll organise it."

However, her assistant didn't move.

"Something else?"

Joy's gaze was clear and unwavering.

"Don't punish others because of one person." Joy paused at the door. "Your lunch is coming."

Rebecca leant back on her desk with a sigh.

"I'm not..."

"Then put it in the bin."

Joy shut the door.

Carefully she sat back in her chair, the leather accommodating softly. She found the remote for the music system and filled the room with the haunting cello of Jacqueline Du Pré. It wasn't long before the door swung open with a bang. No need to look around because only Sophia would dare to do that.

"Do I need to confiscate your letter opener?" Sophia paused. "Wait. What would you do without Joy?"

Rebecca swivelled around in her chair.

"I am not depressed."

"You are a veritable rain cloud of gloom."

Sophia fell into the chair opposite and kicked her shoes off, continuing. "And what did you do to Joy? She said she'd send me an invite to next month's festivities when you're set to torch the local orphanage." Rebecca burst out laughing and pressed her finger down on the intercom. "Joy?"

"Miss Cavendish?"

Sophia, eyes wide at the formality, laughed quietly and wagged her finger. "What shoes do you suggest one wears for razing the local orphanage?"

"Fire retardant ones."

"Thank you."

She lifted her finger and the intercom died. Sophia shook her head.

"Miss Cavendish, what have you done to your assistant?"

Rebecca's smile slipped away and gaze fell to her desk drawer.

"I know. I've turned into a beast."

"Have you spoken to Annah?"

"No."

"Perhaps you should reconsider that?"

"Perhaps. Perhaps not."

"If you value something then don't let it go. You did that with the divorce."

Rebecca frowned.

"I didn't value Martin at the end."

"I'm talking about your holiday home in Roma."

Rebecca waved a hand.

"That was his."

Sophia smiled gently.

"Don't let her go if you like her."

"I do like her, but the trust issue.... I don't know who she is."

Sophia in her usual inimitable style condensed it all down to a pinhead.

"No, you don't know what she does. There's a world of difference. She didn't steal your purse. She protected you from a murderer."

"The end justifies the means?"

"You're alive and eight people are dead. She's on my Christmas card list."

"The man who puts extra pickles into your sandwich at lunchtime is on your Christmas card list."

"He gets a small card. Annah will be getting one with glitter."

Rebecca laughed.

"I'll think about it."

"That's all I ask. But enough seriousness. I'm taking you out to lunch. Get your bag, leave your bad mood here, and let's go have some fun."

Three hours at their favourite restaurant, two bottles of Sauvignon Blanc and a heap of olives, capers and fruit later, things didn't seem so gloomy.

Rebecca drained her glass.

"A taxi for us, I think."

Just then her phone rang. She picked it up and without thinking.

"Rebecca?"

She knew that voice immediately but she did a quick double check on the screen. Annah's name was bright and clear.

"Yes."

She had no idea what else to say. What is there to say after avoiding someone for months?

"I'm not prepared. I expected your voicemail again."

Sophia caught her eye and quirked an eyebrow, clearly realising who it was.

"I can let you speak to my voicemail if you wish?"

She could hear the smile in Annah's tone.

"I've talked more to her than my own sister in the past months."

Rebecca's arm began to ache, even though it hadn't for quite some time. Phantom pains for a phantom woman.

Annah wasted no time.

"I'm sorry about the way things went."

"Me, too." A strange feeling passed over her, as if she needed fresh air. Perhaps it was all the wine catching up with her? The restaurant suddenly felt clawing. "I have to go. Take care, Annah."

Before she could get an answer she'd hung up. Sophia opened her mouth; Rebecca grabbed her bag.

"Please don't. Let's just go."

The cab seemed to fly through traffic. Sophia frowned but rubbed her arm.

"Why did you hang up on her?"

"Sophia." Rebecca pleaded.

There was no let up.

"Tell me and I'll leave you to sink in the quagmire that has become your week."

It was quite simple, really.

"I didn't know what to say to her."

Rebecca turned and watched the buildings stream by. Concrete and glass melted to form an elongated strip going nowhere.

Sophia grasped her hand and whispered.

"This is a rare moment when I shall be serious."

Rebecca looked at her friend.

"So I should pay attention?"

"You certainly should because like solar eclipses, it's an experience you don't catch often." Sophia's expression sobered. "You have a chance."

"I know, but..."

Sophia lay a finger on her lips, silencing the argument.

"And someone up high has seen fit to keep giving you these chances. But eventually, they will stop and you'll lose this possibility. So you need to decide what's important here, Rebecca. Is it the fact she lied to you, or the fact she is the reason you're in this car and still breathing."

There was nothing like a motivational speech from Sophia. It really was quite succinct.

"Stop here." Rebecca said suddenly as she recognised a long series of metal railings.

Her park. The place she could think. She got out.

"I need some air. Call me later."

Sophia shrugged and nodded.

The cab left her in the dusk of the dull grey day.

She walked along the path to her bench. It was just how it always was, quiet and private. The water lulled her crushed senses. It comforted her. She sat down heavily, leaning arms on thighs. What a dreadful year. One thing after the next. She looked down at her phone. Maybe one thing hadn't been so bad.

Rebecca pressed A, hit call, and put the phone to her ear. Annah's ring tone sounded in stereo. She stood up and turned around, and walking towards her was Annah. Annah, who'd turned out to be something else and something the same, all at once. Annah, with those ethereal azure eyes and courageous energy that keep her coming back.

Rebecca smiled and patted her bench.

~ Finis

www.ingramcontent.com/pod-product-compliance
Lightning Source LLC
Chambersburg PA
CBHW021037130626
46552CB00005B/1886